Mike Ripley

is the author of the award-winning Angel series of comedy thrillers set mainly in the East End of London. In *Double Take* he moves up West big time, to London's Wild West frontier around Heathrow airport and with a new multi-cultural cast of characters all determined to make crime pay. It has been said that Mike Ripley 'paints a picture of London Dickens would recognise' and apart from being recognised as one of Britain's funniest crime writers, he is also a respected critic of crime fiction, reviewing for the *Daily Telegraph*, *The Times*, *The Good Book Guide* and the *Birmingham Post* for over twelve years.

First Published in Great Britain in 2002 by
The Do-Not Press Limited
16 The Woodlands
London SE13 6TY
www.thedonotpress.co.uk
email: mr@thedonotpress.co.uk

Casebound edition: ISBN 1 899 344 82 9
B-format paperback: ISBN 1 899344 81 0

British Library Cataloguing in Publication Data. A catalogue
record for this book is available from the British Library.

1   3   5   7   9   10   8   6   4   2

Printed and bound in Great Britain by
The Guernsey Press Co Ltd.

Double Take

The Novel
and
The Script

by
MIKE RIPLEY

Double Take

Double Take

The Novel
by
MIKE RIPLEY

Part I:

The street value of talcum powder

THE REASON THEY didn't pull anybody at the Crackenthorpe Street bust was because Big Benny got an attack of the munchies about six a.m. after a five-hour game of three-card brag and two lines of sampled merchandise. Not that he ever needed that to give him an appetite.

Result was that when the door went in, there was the stuff all packed in cellophane bags and laid out in the hallway, but Big Benny, Ash the Cash and the rest were nowhere to be seen. So, only half a result as far as the Unclean Ones were concerned.

To say they were less than impressed would be putting it mildly. After all, a lot of thought had gone into the raid. Lot of resources, too. Plenty of uniforms and flashing lights in evidence, Drug Squad, CID, sniffer dogs (the little spaniel ones straight off *Pet Rescue*), probably an Armed Response unit or two down the side streets and no doubt a smattering of Customs & Excise in there to make up the numbers. Cast of fucking thousands, it was. Must have cost a fortune. Certainly must have cost more than the coke they scooped now that it's down to £40 a gram on the street (if you're lucky) and cheaper than E to the after-dark brigade.

But they seemed happy enough in their work as they smashed the front door in with a hand-held battering ram, the sort they call 'the Master Key'. On the business end, one of them had stuck a sticker that said 'You've just met the Met' and nobody'd seen one of them since the miners' strike. Maybe they were old stock. All the old stock gets shunted out to the Wild West. Not the West *End*, mind you, but the real West: Southall, Heston and Dodge City itself – Heathrow. Where London ends and the frontier begins in a great, green sweep towards the sunset and eventually, some say, the sea. But most don't go further west than Terminal 3.

It only took a couple of swings of the Master Key to get the door in on the Crackenthorpe Street house. In fact, the ram was probably surplus to requirements as the door would have collapsed if you'd just looked at it funny. Anyway, the hinges bust and the whole thing crashes flat-arsed on to the hallway floor, and one of the leading pigs – though he looked more like a turtle, his neck sticking out between his body armour and his helmet and visor – pokes his head in and there's dead quiet for a minute or two until he says:

—Anyone home?

Just like that, like he was the fucking rent man or something, and he stands there expecting an answer.

Of course this lasts about half a microsecond, then its cut to the old Marx Brothers' movie where they're all trying to get through the doorway at once, all pushing and shoving and treading on the tails of the sniffer dogs. And climbing over the frontline troops is none other than the Chief Defective himself, the one who thought up the whole raid thing in the first place: yours truly, Detective Chief Inspector McEvoy.

—Come on, come on, shouts McEvoy. Upstairs the lot of you. The little shaggers are probably sleeping it off.

The hobnail boots go up the stairs at, like, about a

hundred and twenty beats per minute, leaving McEvoy to survey the loot. And even McEvoy can't miss it 'cos there's all that cholly in the hallway, bagged up ready to be retailed, wholesaled, cut, sniffed, snorted, rocked or nuggeted, fresh off the boat from Holland that morning. Well, if truth were known, it had arrived the night before on a lorry off a ferry into Harwich, tucked snugly inside a hollowed-out roll of newsprint heading for the printing works of one of the posher newspapers down in Docklands. It's amazing, all the stories those papers carry about how 99% of all the bank notes in London have traces of cocaine on them, when they should be testing the very paper they're printed on.

Just how much cholly there was has never been truly revealed. The Unclean Ones kept quiet about it – not surprising in view of what happened later – and Big Benny was hardly likely to put in an insurance claim, was he? Afterwards he would say he was out four hundred grand, but that's probably the street talking. No one does cash-on-delivery for a transaction like that anymore; you go for electronic banking, so it was likely Benny hadn't actually handed over a penny of someone else's hard-earned. But anyhow, there's a lot of gear there and it's been well worth our Boys In Blue getting up early and doing the business before the traffic builds up in Southall. Thoughtful, that.

So Sheriff McEvoy is standing there, counting the bags and trying to manage without taking his shoes and socks off, and talking to his deputy, a new Defective Sergeant he's breaking in, called Jim Driver, who's joined the Met from some country parish like Manchester or Birmingham and they have to give him the job because they can't find any London coppers who aren't related to villains.

—Can't argue with the quality of your information on this one, says Driver, sucking up to his boss. Just like you predicted, sir. Wouldn't like to have a go at next week's lottery numbers, would you, sir?

And McEvoy says:

—I'm a detective, Jim, not a clairvoyant.

Just like that, without a laugh, dead straight.

Then one of the uniformed Plods sticks his head over the top of the stairs and shouts down:

—Upstairs secure, sir!

And McEvoy asks if any of them have given him any hassle, to which the Plod has to reply:

—Upstairs is secure, sir, but there's nobody on it. In it. Up here.

—Nobody? says McEvoy. There's nobody watching over all this gear?

Like he can't believe it; and why should he? Never been heard of before, all that gear just left there in the hallway like somebody's delivered an Ikea bookcase and you don't know where to start.

—There should be at least four, shouts the Sheriff. Big Benny, Ash the Cash, and perm any two of the neighbourhood smackheads.

He names names, to show off the quality of his information received, just in case some of his fellow officers are beginning to think things have gone pear-shaped. His faithful non-Indian companion, Sergeant Driver, gets on the radio to help him out.

—Rear team, rear team, report any activity now.

But the message comes back that there's no sign of life at the back of Crackenthorpe Street. Nobody's come out of the house, nobody's giving it a large proportion of leg down the road.

—They *must* be here, says McEvoy to anybody who'll listen. It doesn't make sense. They take delivery of all this prime gear, sit on it all night, then leave it so that any kid out on the rob on his way to school can have it away? Where the fuck are they?

—Maybe they've just popped out for....

Driver tries to think of something to keep his boss happy, but McEvoy jumps down this throat.

—For what? A spot of breakfast? What kind of dipshits do you think we're dealing with?

The dipshits were having breakfast.

Benny always did have an appetite on him. He wasn't called Big for the size of anything else of his. And the munchies would take him at certain times of day so that nothing else mattered. One of those times was always when he was on the toot and it didn't matter what the substance, just the merest whiff would get his juices going. For a man his size he had a spectacularly low tolerance of all forms of drugs except tobacco and alcohol, which aren't proper drugs anyway. He could put away ten big bottles of Cobra with his lunch like he had hollow legs but two pulls on a generous joint and he'd be flying, and ten minutes later he'd have the roaring munchies.

They'd taken delivery of the coke just before midnight – out of the back of a Transit van painted in the colours of a well-known newsagent wholesaler – and stashed it in the house on Crackenthorpe Street. The house was unoccupied, like most on the street, but nobody had bothered to get the electric turned off, so Benny's crew settled down to a card game to while away the hours until it was daytime and they could start filtering the stuff out to their customers under cover of all the comings and goings of a normal business day. If that sounds doolally, just think about it. A bunch of boys like Big Benny's crew scooting about the parish in the middle of the night are bound to raise a few eyebrows. They walk the street with a toothpick and they get pulled for going equipped for burglary. But in daytime, most of the world is out on the streets of Heston and Southall, strolling along the banks of the Grand Union; going to prayers; doing business; doing business while they're at prayers; moving merchandise; arranging marriages; doing this, that and the other.

So, there was Big Benny with three of his most trusted crew. There was Ash the Cash, of course. Ash was never very far from Benny's side and some said that if he wasn't the brains of the business he was certainly the wallet; the accountant who kept an eye on all the income and expenditure, but mostly income. Ash was the one all the mothers went for because he looked good in a suit and could have passed for a doctor if he'd worn glasses. In fact, he'd got a degree from the London School of Economics – picking up an English wife there along the way – and then inherited a flock of newsagents in the Sutton-Croydon-Purley triangle. He'd put managers in and he terrorised them each once a month; otherwise, he spent all his time in Southall hanging out with Benny. His wife and kids thought he was a travelling rep for wholesale confectionery and rarely left the family home down in posh Warlingham in leafy Surrey. Suited Ash just fine.

Rafik was with them too. Rafik never said much when Benny and Ash were around. As a kid he'd been brought up in a Christian enclave on the coast of Mysore and it must have taught him to know his place. All the kids in the area thought he was really laid back and ultra cool and they related to him, which was good for business as Ash reminded them of a successful uncle and Benny was just too fucking big to be anything other than scary.

And there was Julian, a white kid from over Chiswick way, who never said anything but would just sit there flexing his muscles, which he kept in good shape down at one of the three gyms he was a member of. Some said he would have done what he did for Benny for no pay if it hadn't been for the membership fees down the gym and his occasional drug habit. But then one of the perks of hanging around Big Benny was that there were plenty of free samples.

So the four of them were sitting in the house on Crackenthorpre Street with an incriminating amount of prime cholly in the hallway. After not too long they realise that they've forgotten some of the basic essentials of life. Like, there's no TV in the place, or VCR, though Rafik does offer to nip out and nick a set for them and they know he can as he's done it once before. The telly was still warm when they turned it on and there was still a pirate copy of *Sarafarosh* in the video, which only needed rewinding.

A few other essentials were also missing, like furniture, so the guys parked themselves on the floorboards, pooled their supply of Kingfisher beer and settled down to a game of three-card brag to while away the midnight hours. It wasn't supposed to be a marathon session, they were just following the basic rule of the game, which was that Benny always won. Trouble was, Benny seemed determined to lose so proceedings took a while and even Benny was bored long before he got far enough ahead to rub their noses in it.

It was only a matter of time before one of them suggested sampling the merchandise and if it wasn't Big Benny's idea, they would have made sure he thought it was. And anyway, Benny liked to play the generous host and wouldn't have taken much persuading to chop out a couple of lines each on the back of a playing card, ensuring sweetness and light all round for an hour or so.

Then Benny starts to come down and the munchies set in. There's nothing to eat in the house and Ash hasn't even got his usual emergency supply of Mars bars in his car, which he keeps just in case Benny needs a sugar rush.

Benny starts pacing up and down, stomping round the house like a seasoned-up hyena, slowly coming to the boil, suggesting they use their mobiles to ring for a pizza delivery until somebody points out that it's near six a.m. and the only pizza deliverers around would be those being held hostage for extra pepperoni.

It was Rafik, not so much laid-back as laid out by this time, who casually mentioned that there was an Indian two streets away where he'd had a good curry, cooked fresh, before now.

That was the magic word as far as Benny was concerned – fresh. Benny had an appetite on him and a deep love of curries, but they had to be fresh, cooked while he waited. If a curry turned up and he suspected a reheat job or something vacuum sealed and then microwaved, somebody was in trouble in the kitchen. Somebody was quite likely to have their gonads removed with a rusty Swiss.

—Fresh? They do fresh curries, like cooked to order?

—Yeah, sure. It's called the Star of Bengal, says Rafik, taking a stab at the name.

—But not at this time of the morning, says Ash, who is keeping it together better than the rest of them.

—You know the place? asks Benny. We do any business with them?

—Course we do, says Ash. It's a Bangladeshi family, live above the shop. We keep an eye on things for them. They're on the books.

—They owe us?

—Not that I can recall. Keep themselves to themselves, work hard, send money home. We've pushed a few things their way wholesale and they've paid up. No complaints.

—Well I've got a complaint, says Benny. I think they're missing out on a lucrative breakfast trade and I think we should go round there right now and point out the entrepreneurial folly of their ways.

—You mean go and knock them up?

—Why not? They should be grateful for the custom.

There's no point in arguing with Benny in this mood; Ash knows that, but he does try.

—What about the stuff?

—Who's gonna come calling this time of day? says Benny. It's been years since anyone's seen a milkman round here.

Now there were some fucking famous last words.

Off they trooped, on foot, as their cars were well out of sight two streets away so as not to draw attention to the house where the drop had been made. Face it, a car with all its wheels in that neighbourhood would have been a talking point and, in any case, only Ash could actually focus enough to see to drive properly so it was best overall that they hoofed it.

All that walking sharpened up Benny's appetite even more, as he constantly reminded them and Rafik began to get really jumpy, hoping he'd remembered the restaurant right and praying that the owners were home. He had and they were, and they were mightily upset when Julian started hammering on the back door with both fists. Probably thought he was a skinhead, though nobody's seen one of them in Southall for

ages. Probably *wished* it was a skinhead once they made out
Ash the Cash standing there in his suit, six o'clock in the
morning.

Ash got them to open up, no trouble, and told them that
all they had to do was get the kitchen going for a bit of breakfast and then they could get themselves back to bed. The two
brothers who ran the place, plus one of their sons – all of
them still in stripy pyjamas like something from a chain gang
– shuffled off to turn the gas on or whatever, and Julian went
along with them just to make sure they didn't spit in the food.

Big Benny, Ash and Rafik wandered through into the
restaurant, picked themselves a table and settled down to
read a menu each.

They were still reading when the first police van scorched
round the corner and disappeared into Crackenthorpe Street.

Where, after the storm-troopers had gone in, there was
Detective Chief Inspector McEvoy and his stooge Sergeant
Driver, up to their knees in packets of white stuff, wondering what the bloody hell to do next. And not having too
many bright ideas as, according to their game plan, they
should by now be busy cuffing Big Benny and his boys and
leading them off for a lengthy stretch of R and R at the
most convenient establishment in the Windsor Hotel
Group.

Instead, they've got more cholly than saw in the
Millennium in the whole of South London and not a suspect
in sight.

What's worse, the forensic boys in their white spacesuits
can't find a decent fingerprint anywhere on the stuff itself and
conclude that the absent owners of this quality merchandise
must have been wearing gloves. Which, of course, they had
been when they'd handled it. Dim they might be, but they
weren't fucking stupid.

And to add to the mix, who should put in an appearance
right there and then (now that it was clear that the premises
were safe) but the Officer In Overall Command, or OIC, or

Oik as he was known even among the Great Unclean themselves. This particular Oik being par for the course; one of
those coppers who wore a uniform like it had been welded on
and smiled like he was looking down a gunsight.

—Nobody home? says the Oik, like he can't believe it,
which he can't. No suspects at all?

—Plenty of suspects, sir, says Driver, real helpful like. Just
nobody caught on the premises.

—Do you know how much this operation has cost so far,
Detective Chief Inspector?

Now McEvoy is not going to argue with his superior when
it comes to budgetary policy, is he? He's more concerned with
saving his own arse and getting maximum Brownie points out
of the situation.

—You are absolutely sure about your sources on this one,
McEvoy?

—Pretty solid, sir, says McEvoy. He was right about the
cocaine. This is a useful pull for us, gets a big chunk of merchandise off the streets.

—But no arrests, Chief Inspector, presses the Oik. It's all
very well being tough on crime and tough on the causes of
crime, but we've got to be tough on criminals now and then.
Make a few examples, send them down, confiscate their cars,
freeze their bank accounts. That's the sort of example we
need to make. Without a few collars this lot is just lost property.

—Aw come on, sir, whines McEvoy. Even with the street
price down to under forty quid a gram, you're looking at a
decent haul here in cash money terms. And you know that's
what the newspapers like: big round numbers.

—And the newspapers know we always inflate the street
value of a haul like this. It's only a matter of time before some
smart-arse journalist works out that for the amount we've
spent on this operation, we could have gone on the street and
bought this lot! We need some bodies, Inspector. We need
names and nice fat files for the Crown Prosecution Service.
We need to hear that satisfying clang of a cell door closing on

a villain and that tell-tale clink of of a key being thrown away.

—That's really quite poetic, sir, says Driver.

But the Oik gives him a killer look to show that there's just so much arse-licking even he can take. And then he's back on McEvoy's case:

—Has somebody tipped off Benny, is that it? Is your source playing us off against each other, doing the double?

—That's always possible, says McEvoy, like he doesn't really believe it. But he was pretty solid about the delivery details. Can't think why he'd rat us at the last minute.

—And just who is this source of yours?

Which was the one question McEvoy really didn't want asking.

—A local lad with a bit of form, but strictly ballroom, nothing big.

—Does he have a name?

The Oik thinks he's on to something here, the way McEvoy's giving him the run-around. Well, you don't get to be an Oik for nothing.

—Blind Hugh, sir, says McEvoy swallowing hard.

—I hope that's a code-name, says the Oik without a smile but he notices that good old Sergeant Driver is having a quick snigger. This Blind Pugh person...

—Hugh, sir. Blind Hugh.

—Whatever. We can get this person into court to finger the gang?

—Not likely, sir, says McEvoy.

By this time, Driver's almost having a hernia trying not to laugh out loud.

—And why not?

—He's a touch *budhu*, sir, bit of an *ulluoo*.

—What's that? Some sort of religious thing?

—No sir, it means he's a bit simple.

The Oik thinks about this for a minute, then goes for broke.

—He's not *actually* blind is he?

—No sir, says McEvoy, his pride hurt. It's just a nickname.

—And how did he get this nickname? Asks the Oik, not willing to let it lie.

And dear old Sergeant Driver just can't resist, can he?

—It's what they called Hugh Grant, sir. You know, the actor that had a stonking girlfriend but got caught with a real dog of a tart. It's 'cos he never sees anything worth seeing 'til it's too late.

Meanwhile, back at the restaurant the owners are in the kitchen in their pyjamas – with young Julian standing over them examining the chopping knives, casual like – cooking up a storm for Big Benny.

Ash the Cash, true to his name, has found the roll of twenty-pound notes taped to the back of the till drawer in the cash register. When he trousered it, Rafik said maybe that was a bit mean as the Bangladeshis were, after all, supplying breakfast. Ash gives him a shark-eye stare and says that maybe now they'll learn to use the Barclays bank on the corner. But then he's a shareholder, so he would say that.

Big Benny gets their attention by banging on the table with something flat, brown and the size of a plate.

—What the stonk is this? he asks nobody in particular.

—Looks like nan bread, says Ash. And when Benny hits the table with it again: Yesterday's nan bread.

—I asked for toast, wails Benny. Was that unreasonable of me?

—So maybe they toasted it and overdid it.

Benny holds up the nan, big as his face.

—You find me a toaster to fit this.

—Aw stop moaning, says Ash, one of the few people who can say stuff like that to Benny. Curry and toast for breakfast is a bit spooky anyway.

—It's not spooky, it's multi-cultural. You just don't like curry, that's your problem.

—Not for breakfast do I not.

—Be telling me you're ashamed of your culinary traditions.

—What traditions? I'm from fucking Surrey, I am.

Then two of the Banglas appear with trays and start loading the table with dishes and Benny sits back in his chair and opens his mouth and his nostrils so he can inhale all the spices and suchlike. There was *kofte ka salan* meatballs; a dry *keema* curry; a Goan meat curry (heavy on the aniseed); a hot Madras curry; a plate of pork chops with a *mirchwala* chilli sauce; some butter chicken; and dry *sukhi tarkari* mixed vegetables.

—Where are the eggs? asks Benny. It can't be breakfast if there ain't eggs.

And right on cue, one of the Bangladeshis turns up with a plate of *undey ka salan,* hard-boiled eggs reeking of cinnamon and ginger.

—Ahhh, goes Benny: Spanking!

And he starts to tuck in.

Then he notices Ash sitting next to him but not admiring the food, looking out of the window instead, watching three police cars going by, lights flashing but no sirens.

—What's the matter, Ash? We got a problem here?

—Might have, says Ash.

—So what do we do with all this food?

Mr Senior Policeman, the Oik himself, is coming to terms with there being no bodies to string up by the thumbs and he's thinking of tomorrow's headlines, how it's down to him that £ millions (fill in roughly accurate number) of Class A substances have been taken off the street.

—It is quite a stash, isn't it? he says, almost like he's growing fond of it.

—Too much to claim for personal consumption, you reckon, sir? says Driver, with a twinkle in his eye.

—Personal consumption of Brazil, maybe, says McEvoy.

—Can we be serious, Chief Inspector? Just where do you propose to store all this stuff? Forensics will want a sample but nothing like this quantity. This constitutes a major security hazard.

—I… er… assumed we'd stash it in the evidence room at the local nick, sir, says McEvoy sheepishly. Until we get Home Office clearance for destruction, that is.

—You mean the station house on Dogberry Road? asks the Oik, like his ears are deceiving him.

—Yes, sir. It's very handy, says McEvoy, nodding like a puppy.

—It's also the most decrepit, run-down, falling down, overdue-for-demolition police station in west London. In all London. It should have been condemned years ago. If you tried to serve food there, the Health and Safety people would close you down before you could fry an egg. The security there's a joke, nonexistent. The place is a sieve. We lose more stuff out of the back of that place than they do at Heathrow.

McEvoy thinks: he's been counting the toilet rolls and the paper clips again, but doesn't say this aloud. Instead he goes for chirpy optimism, big time.

—What if we keep it at Dogberry Road just for the one night, sir? I mean, who's to know – unless we tell them?

And that was when he had the Big Idea.

In fact, it was Mr Senior Policeman who sowed the seed of the Big Idea in McEvoy's tiny brain, when he was asking if McEvoy's source, Blind Hugh, had been doing the double. (Which of course he was.) Everything else that happened stemmed from that, though McEvoy wasn't the sort to come out with it upfront. He needed to think it through, refine the details, plan the finer points. It would take him nearly an hour to do it and most of it he did on the hoof, insisting that his trusty Sergeant Jim Driver accompany him on a walkabout of darkest Southall.

The official reason was they had to pay a call on Blind Hugh for form's sake to see how much he'd blabbed, when and to who. McEvoy took the opportunity to give Driver the full guided tour of his stomping ground, acting for all the world like a District Commissioner coming to collect the taxes.

—No, it's not a mosque, McEvoy said to Driver, who had just shown his ignorance. It's a gurdwara, a Sikh temple. They wouldn't open a mosque in an old pub.

—That used to be a pub?

Some detective; the word 'Watneys' still showed through the new paintwork.

—The Marquis of something or other.

—Not the Clive of India, then? says Driver, repartee not being his strong point.

—None of the restaurants round here had licences a few years back, so you used to have to go there and put four or five pints of lager down your neck before you went to eat. We used to call it a 'Take-In'.

—You're into all this '*Jewel in the Crown*' shit, aren't you, Guv?

—There's nothing wrong with that, is there?

—No, Guv, never said there was. Just a bit off-centre that's all, you bein' Irish.

—So Paddies aren't allowed to like curry? And why shouldn't us immigrants stick together?

—I thought the police were the only immigrants round here.

—You're not wrong there, Jim. Here we are.

And where they were was outside a greengrocer's shop, no sign above the door, two big tables outside on the pavement showing off the wares. Driver takes one look and realises he can't identify half the stuff on display and wouldn't know how to cook the other half. McEvoy, on the other hand, doesn't look, he closes his eyes *and smells*, taking in big, deep breaths.

—Just look at this lot, he says with his eyes still wide shut. Cardamoms, curry leaves, chickpeas, coriander, split black chickpeas, red lentils, yellow lentils.

Now he opens his eyes as if to see if he'd guessed something right, and starts running his fingers through the dried beans and stuff, picking up handfuls and letting them pour back through his fist like sand in an egg-timer.

—There are over sixty different pulses used in Indian cooking alone, he says, as if Driver's taking notes. Before I left Ireland I used to think turnips were ex-fucking-zotic. And look at the *mirch*.

Driver doesn't know where to look and says: The what?

—The chillis, man. God's way of telling you your palate's jaded. They've got chillis from all over. You could eat your way round the world just on chillis.

—You'll be travelling alone, says Driver but McEvoy's in full flow now.

—Just look at the colours…the *warmth*. That's a *habanero* from Mexico and that's the *Bird's Eye* from Thailand. It's only a little one, but it's a bit of a devil. And there's the *Scotch Bonnet* from the West Indies, the king stinger hisself, the hottest of the hot. You can feel the heat in them, Jim. They can warm you just by looking at them. Do you know just how fucking cold and damp it can be in the west of Ireland?

Driver just shakes his head as all this passes over him like a cloud.

—Shall we get on, sir?

McEvoy sighs, still looking down at all that fruit and veg, then he picks up a small green chilli and hefts it in his hand like a cricket ball.

—Very well, he says. Let's see if Blind Hugh is minding the store. And let's do this as diplomatically as possible, shall we?

Driver nods and makes to follow him, diplomatic like, but is taken aback when McEvoy starts shouting at the top of his voice.

—Hughie! Blind Hughie! Come on down, you skanky little piece of shite. Show yerself!

This is diplomatic? Driver thinks McEvoy could be heard in Wembley even above the sound of the jets circling overhead, looking for Heathrow.

But the man did get results because Blind Hugh comes out of the back room of the shop like a rat up a drainpipe. He's holding a cardboard box full of golden melons, which the box says came from Brazil, and he's wearing glasses so thick it looks like somebody's jammed two Coke bottles into his face.

—Mr McEvoy, you shouldn't be here, should you? he says, stopping dead in his tracks.

—No, Hughie, I shouldn't. I should be down the nick going head-to-head with Big Benny's solicitor because surely, by now, I'd've had him cautioned, charged, fingerprinted and at least *considering* signing the confession I've already written out for him. But I'm not. I'm here instead.

—And why's that, exactly, Mr McEvoy?

Now that wasn't the cleverest thing Blind Hugh could have said under the circumstances. Difficult to say what would have been for anyone, let alone somebody as *budhu* as Hughie. Even his mother admitted he was a bit slow and that, while he didn't have an ounce of malice in him, he did run with a bad lot who had more than enough to go round. So his mother wasn't surprised when two policemen with attitude turned up first thing in the morning, the shop only just open, looking for trouble. Hugh probably had it coming so there was only one thing for her to do, which was to slide out of the shop – the cops not even noticing she'd been there in the first place – into the back and upstairs into the family living room. There she could have a sit down and put on Zee TV on cable until things sorted themselves out.

—Why was that?

McEvoy's fuming; can hardly get the words out.

—Because somebody, not a million miles away from where I'm standing, gave me some double-duff information. Information prepaid with coin of the realm and a promise to look the other way about a certain somebody's uncle who is making a nice living importing illegal Somali immigrants.

—I gave you the goods, I did, pleads Hugh. Told you the where, the when and the who. You went to the wrong house? It's happened.

—We got the right place, Hughie. We get lost, we ask a policeman. Trouble is, nobody home.

—And that means trouble for you, Hugh, says Driver, joining in.

—Hey, what's *your* problem?

—My problem? You make Mr McEvoy unhappy, he takes it out on me, so I take it out on you. Simple as that.

—Oh I get it, this is Good Cop, Bad Cop – right?

—Wrong, says McEvoy. It's Bad Cop, Bad Cop.

And then McEvoy puts one hand on Blind Hugh's neck so he can't pull away and takes the little green chilli he's been playing with and crushes it against Hughie's forehead. Hugh has no idea what's going on, probably expecting a slap, no more. So it comes as a bit of a surprise when McEvoy jams the crushed chilli up his nose; left nostril first, then the right one, going for the full stereo effect.

And all the time, McEvoy's talking to his stooge, Driver, who is no wiser than Hugh as to what's going on, except that his nose isn't getting the raw chilli treatment.

—Told you about this one, Jim, the *Scotch Bonnet*. Small, but deadly. And the seeds, they're the killer.

It seems that Blind Hugh agrees because tears are flooding out from behind his glasses and he's trying to work out why his brain is on fire and how to jerk his head away from McEvoy's grip without dropping the box of melons he's holding. He's gulping and crying and it's like a sneeze gone off half-cocked but he finally manages to shout:

—*Suerkabacha!*

But he's picked the wrong man for that sort of abuse.

McEvoy rams what's left of the chilli – just a stalk really – right up Hugh's left nostril until it stays there this time, dangling like a napalm bogey.

—Don't you call me a son-of-a-pig, you little tosser, or you'll get another one up your Marmite canal and you'll have to keep the toilet roll in the freezer.

—Didn't know you spoke Hindi, Guv, says Driver, not actually sure what language it was.

—Only the swear words, says McEvoy, all conversational. It's a gift the Irish have.

Blind Hugh is sobbing and sneezing and wheezing and seriously in danger of really going blind by this time, his nose lit up like Rudolph's, but he's still holding the tray of melons, hopping from one foot to the other.

—I gave you what I knew, Mr McEvoy. Big delivery from Holland, sit on overnight and start distributing today. Not my fault if the stuff didn't arrive.

—You're not listening, Hughie. The dope was there all right, tons of it. I'm up to my ankles in white powder, but no bleedin' Benny or his mates. No sign. They get tipped off as well, you think?

—That's plain daft, innit? I wouldn't do the double on you, Mr McEvoy.

—So where was Big Benny when we gave him his wake-up call this morning?

—I dunno, do I? Maybe he popped out for a bit of breakfast or summfing.

—Do I look *baywakoof*, Hughie? Do I look slow? Am I the one standing here with a chilli up my nose? Do you really think Big Benny's gonna leave half a ton of pure driven snow unguarded while he pops out for an Egg McMuffin?

—He gets the munchies real bad, Mr McEvoy...

—Oh, shut it, Hughie. I'm going to hold this against you personally because you know what I've got to do now?

—No, Mr McEvoy, says Hughie crying.

—Of course you don't. I've got to go back and explain to my bosses why I've got half the gross national product of Colombia on my hands but not a single, solitary arrest. That doesn't make me look good. And have you any idea how much paperwork this'll mean? And what do I do with all the stuff? I have to cart it round to Dogberry Road nick, which is in such a state it'll fall down come the next high wind and has a lower security rating than a tart's knickers. Have you any idea of the headaches you're causing me, Hughie? No, you don't but you will, because these might be my problems but I'm putting them down to you.

As he says this, McEvoy pulls what's left of the chilli out of Hugh's nose and drops it, daintily, in among the melons Hugh's holding.

—Don't try and sell that, will you?

McEvoy dusts his hands together in front of Hughie's face, which is like a traffic light on stop now, and gives him a big smile. Driver does likewise and to Hughie, squinting through the tears, it must have looked like an out-take from *Night of the Evil Dead VI*.

As soon as the two laughing policemen turn and march out, Hughie drops the melons like they were on fire rather than his sinuses and dives for the cold drinks cabinet in the corner, where the shop keeps its Coca Cola and Tango and Sprite, and where they used to sell Bacardi Breezers until they got reported for not having a licence.

Hugh rips the door open and grabs a can of 7-Up, not caring that his mother will have heard the door go and will want the money in the till. He shakes it up, pops the ring-pull and directs the cold, squirting liquid right up his nose. He almost suffocates, but it's worth it. It's bliss.

Outside on the High Street, McEvoy and Driver are having a chuckle as they're strolling along like they own the place. Then Driver says:

—Was it wise to mention that the stuff is going down to Dogberry Road in there, Guv?

—Wisest thing I've done since I brushed my teeth this morning, says McEvoy as he pulls out his mobile and starts punching buttons.

Back at the restaurant, Big Benny's finishing off his breakfast, wiping gravy up with nan bread. Ash the Cash has been out on a scouting mission round Crackenthorpe Street and can't wait to get back to give Benny the news.

—I'd say we had a problem. Or at least a predicament of some proportion.

Big Benny loves it when Ash talks like that. He doesn't necessarily understand him, but it always raises a smile.

—How big a proportion would that be, Ash?

—Mega, possibly ballistic. Blue is definitely the colour round the corner and I don't mean Chelsea's playing at home.

—And what about our merchandise?

—We don't have any. It's gone. We're out of business.

—Now, now, Ash, you should ungroove yourself. Look on the bright side. We're free and clear, we have our health and we've had a good breakfast. Well, I have.

—And on the darker side of the moon, we've lost a load of gear we still have to pay for, we'll lose half our dealers to other wholesalers, and somebody grassed us up.

Big Benny thinks about this, or looks as if he's thinking about it, then lays down the law.

—You've raised a few issues there, Ash my man. Issues that need action, so let's have some action. Get on the phone and call the crew together then bring the car round. I want to do a drive-by on the house, keep an eye on my investment. Oh yeah, and get a couple of the boys to bring in Blind Hugh.

—What do you want with Blind Hugh?

And Benny looks at him like that was the second most stupid question in the world after "Fancy a blow job?".

—He's the best snitch in the business, says Benny and leaves it at that.

At Crackenthorpe Street, Driver and McEvoy are acting suspicious, even by police standards. The forensic geezers and the fingerprint bods are still crawling all over the place, but now a whole platoon of uniforms has turned up and they're all squashed into the hallway like sardines, with not a cigarette paper between them and each one hoping it's not them who's the first to fart.

McEvoy explains what he wants the Woodentops to do and it makes about as much sense to them as any police briefing does, which is like zero to the power of twelve. But of course they go along with it.

Two of them go outside and one stands there signalling while the other reverses a police Transit van up to the front door of the house, end-on so that it sticks out, blocking the pavement and half the street. Then the one who's been going 'Back a bit, back a bit, whoa' opens the rear doors and the van goes back a few more inches until its open doors now cover the front door of the house. The driver gets out, and he'll and his mate stand either side of the van like they're on point duty or waiting for some old biddy to come up and ask them the time. From down the street (where one of Big Benny's boys is already in place) it looks like the police Transit has just come flying *out* of the front door of the house and you can't see into the hallway at all now except under the open doors of the van, and even then all you can see is feet in police-issue Doc Martens, size 12 minimum.

From inside the house comes the sound of Driver's voice and you can hear it well down the street.

—Let's get this stuff on board, lads, nice and easy. I don't want any spillage and don't forget to put your rubber gloves on.

Then there's a clump of boots and the van dips on its suspension and rocks a bit with the weight of one or two of the coppers climbing in. Then they climb out and two more climb in and the van goes up and down. And this keeps up for fifteen, maybe twenty minutes.

It's obvious what's happening: they're loading the cholly into the van, taking it away for evidence and eventually destruction under controlled conditions at a Home Office location, which is supposed to be secret but everybody knows is in Maidstone.

Except they're not.

What the plods are doing is a real performance. Two at a time they're climbing into the van, stomping down to the front making as much noise as possible, turning round and jumping out again. Two by two, like animals going into the ark. And from outside all you can see is their legs and boots under the bottom edge of the Transit's doors. And that's it. They're not putting anything in the van at all, just going through the motions, doing it for the exercise. Climb in, turn round, climb out. Even the thickest of the plods got the hang of it after a while.

Inside the house, McEvoy says to Driver:

—Keep this up for another ten minutes, Jim, then take your time getting round to Dogberry Road. Make sure you're noticed. Get some motorbike outriders and put all the sirens on. Put on a bit of a show.

—Are they ready for us, boss?

—They will be by the time you get there. The Superintendent's okay-ed it. We can use the holding cells down there, the ones near the back wall.

—Haven't they got prisoners in them?

—The Duty Sergeant's been told to clear them out. Anybody held overnight down there must think it's their birthday.

Not that Dogberry Road police station was the place you'd choose to have a birthday party.

Unless you were a rat, or a cockroach maybe, though they'd probably be the first to agree the place should be condemned. The locals used to call it The Black Hole Of Calcutta but these days hardly any of the younger lot got the reference, thinking it was a restaurant over in Brick Lane. So they just called it Dogberry and when they took their dogs out of an evening it was so they could do a dogberry too.

Within the Met itself, Dogberry Road was a joke. Even the humblest plod knew that it would take a National Lottery grant to get it upgraded to a slum and that it should have been allowed to fall down on its own years ago. It had been surplus to requirements before the M4 was built, but because of the high proportion of immigrant families moving into the area, somebody high-up somewhere decided it would be a good idea to keep the place on as a 'presence' to show the value of community policing, maybe even encourage recruitment from the ethnic minorities. Trouble was, nobody high enough up was prepared to authorise any money to be spent on the place, so it fell apart gradually until it became – fighting off some pretty strong contenders – the most antiquated, insanitary, insecure nick in the Metropolitan area. In the locker room some wag of a plod had pinned up a sign saying 'The Management Takes No Responsibility For Personal Items Which Are Left Here Entirely At The Owner's Risk'. Somebody nicked the sign. The local schoolkids called it the Lost Property Office: if you took anything in there, it was lost within the hour.

The nick was about the only thing left on Dogberry Road; everything else was a building site and had been for years. Developers had tried to buy the site and put up something useful, like a McDonald's, but every time the Met made a move to close the station and sell it off, the local Neighbourhood Watch had raised hell, saying it would leave them in a no-go area as far as policing went, and just the threat of bad public relations like that was enough to scupper any plans. It had happened when the Indians ran the Neighbourhood Watch, then when the Afghans moved in again, and now that the Somalis were getting established. No one believed they were really serious about protecting and preserving Dogberry Road nick, they just did it to piss off the Met.

That morning, a demolition order or a surprise raid by the Health and Safety people would have been welcomed by the duty Desk Sergeant, an overweight, out-of-condition plod called Foster.

It's not like he's got complicated orders. All he's been told to do is clear the place out and don't take any new prisoners that morning. For most plods that would be a real treat because it basically means do bugger all and that's an order, but Foster even has trouble coping with that, which is probably why he's a desk sergeant. He's already had the builders in from the site next door claiming that somebody nicked their Portaloo during the night; nicked it even though it was parked no more than twenty feet from the nick's front door. (And if truth were known, most of the plod serving at Dogberry Road preferred it to the nick's toilets, which look like they were rejected by the set designer of *Trainspotting*.)

That would normally be enough for Foster to string out

into a full shift's work, as he's not the sort to go looking to break sweat on the best of days. But he's also got to cope with the phone ringing more times than your average 0800 chat-line and the prospect of CID detectives and big uniformed brass descending on his station, so there's paperwork to be done and ashtrays to clean and Christ knows what'll happen if they check the evidence room.

And he's got to get rid of his one prisoner, a white, middle-aged drunk who wouldn't give his name when he was booked in because he couldn't remember it and now Foster doesn't want to know it.

Foster hauls him out of his cell and the punter staggers to the front desk where Foster hands over his tie, his shoelaces and his wallet.

—There you are, sir, you're free to go.

But the punter's not having any of it.

—What do you mean, free? I'm guilty.

—Come back tomorrow with your solicitor if you feel that way, sir. Don't make any rash statements.

—But I demand to plead guilty. I was drunk. Look at me, man. I'm still drunk!

—That's a matter of opinion, sir. Now if you wouldn't mind...

—I demand to plead guilty to being drunk, says the punter.

Then he pulls himself up to his full height and starts to wag a finger in Foster's face.

—But not to being disorderly, he says. Of that, I am totally innocent.

—Of course you are, sir, says Fatty Foster.

And with a sigh like all the troubles of the world have descended on him and him alone he produces, from under the front counter, a trombone. A real brass trombone with two dents in the end of the slide, as if somebody had trodden on it (which indeed they had).

—I believe this is yours, sir, he says, handing it over.

The punter has a sudden rush of memory to the brain.

—Ah yes. I can explain.

—No need to explain, sir, just take it and go.

And the punter, pissed though he still is, doesn't need telling twice. As for Desk Sergeant Foster, he doesn't even want to look at last night's charge sheet. The bloke could have topped somebody with that trombone for all he cares. He's just amazed that the trombone's been behind the counter all night and nobody's nicked it, Dogberry Road being what it is.

Not too far away, on the other side of the building site and round the corner, Big Benny sits in the back of Ash's Mercedes. Ash sits in the front, gently stroking the steering wheel. He always says he prefers his wife's BMW and only drives the Merc to blend in when he's in Southall as that's what all the Afghans drive, but he loves it really. In the back with Benny is Blind Hugh and all he's thinking about is trying not to soil the upholstery. His nose is like a red balloon held on to his face by static and he's still crying and snotting from his close encounter with the chilli.

—And you reckon they're bringing my merchandise round here to Dogberry Road, do you? asks Benny, quite gentle like.

—That's that bogtrotting Mick-Paddy-bastard McEvoy said, Benny. Straight.

Benny pats Hugh's knee, comforting him.

—Now, now, Hughie. We're a multi-cultural society nowadays and we have to learn to live with each other. You've got to learn to be more tolerant even with a… what was it? A *Scotch Bonnet*? Even with a *Scotch Bonnet* up yer nose.

—That stuff burns, Benny, it really burns.

—Of course it does, Hughie. Dear me, these policemen, they move in here and think they own the place. Was he a bit upset, this McEvoy?

—He was *pagal*, Benny. he'd really lost it. He was blaming me 'cos he had to take the stuff to Dogberry Road, what with the security there being shit an' all. Seemed to resent having to look after the stuff. Would rather have had somebody in a cell, asking them questions with a rubber truncheon.

—I'll bet he would.

Benny takes a roll of notes out of his pocket, peels a few leaves off and stuffs them into Blind Hugh's shirt.

—That's all been very interesting, Hughie, now get yourself home. Normally we'd give you a lift, but we've got pressing business. You go and get something for that nose. Treat yourself; go private, don't waste the day down the health centre.

—I will Benny, thanks, thanks, thanks...

He's still saying it when he's out of the Merc and halfway down the street and it's only then that Benny and Ash crack up; now it's them in danger of soiling the seating.

—That nose! He could read in bed by it!

—Read by it? He could divert fucking aircraft with it! Make a note of *Scotch Bonnets*. I want to specify them next time we have a curry. I like the sound of those devils.

Then Benny gets serious.

—Right. Who've we got on the day shift.

Ash doesn't have to look at a list or anything; he's got that kind of a brain.

—Rafik and his brother are watching the house round Crackenthorpe Street. Imran's having the day off in case his wife has the baby. Ashtok Mann and Jo Jo Singh are on standby. Boy Adrian and Slasher Carmichael are trying to off-load those Romanian computers we acquired. The Afghan cousins are up for anything, as usual, and then there's a couple of new boys, Somalis, who have just started freelancing for us.

—What about Baby Face?

—I could ring the school, get him out early; say his grandmother's ill, suchlike.

—Do it. I want a whole stream of visitors to Dogberry Road today. I want lost kids; I want people who want to know the time; I want pregnant women reporting flashers; I want every cat and dog in Southall to go missing. I want the crime statistics boosted. Any excuse. I want people in there with their eyes open who can tell me what's going down.

—You want our people to go *in* to a police station? Like...voluntarily?

—Yeah, make a nice change. Bit of a day out for most of them.

In Dogberry Road, Fat Sergeant Foster thinks he's just about got the place shipshape and most of the overnight vomit washed out of the cells and the crumpled paper suits with all their stains in the bin, when his worst nightmare, the Officer In Overall Command – the Oik himself – turns up to slap the front desk with his leather gloves and ask if DCI McEvoy and DS Driver have arrived yet.

Foster, who didn't know they were coming in the first place, says no because it's easier just to be dead ignorant when brass like the Oik are out and about.

Fortunately, the Oik gets waylaid almost immediately by a female PC with a raincoat over her uniform. She's holding out boxes of freezer bags, the plastic jobs on a roll you buy in the supermarket, and asking the Oik if these will do.

He says yes, yes, getting a bit tetchy, and asks if she's got the flour. She says she sent two civilian staff out for it but they came back with wholemeal and granary, which didn't look right, so she thought about talcum powder and would that do?

—Yes, yes, says the Oik. It's only for show.

Then, almost to himself, he says:

—Show? It's a bloody circus.

And Fat Foster stays behind his desk, really rather relieved that he doesn't know what the fuck is going on.

He's not much wiser when a Transit arrives complete with motorcycle escort and drives round to the back door, which nobody's used in living memory except to put the rubbish out. The Oik tells him to get it open and lend a hand so he goes with the keys (though if a drunk leaned on the door it would give way) and opens up. The Transit backs up and the plods get the back doors open, spread wide so that no one not actually in the doorway can see what's going on.

Foster is there and *he* can't see what's going on, can't see at all, because the Transit is empty and for the next fifteen minutes they all have to go through the pantomime of unloading a non-existent load and pretending to stash it in the Dogberry road cells.

Doesn't make any sort of fucking sense at all.

At Crackenthorpe Road it looks like the police operation is winding down, with just a couple of marked cars and a police minibus parked outside the house now.

The hallway of the house, though, is still stuffed with uniforms and when Driver tells him the transport has arrived, McEvoy climbs up three or four steps on the staircase and turns to address the troops.

—Right. You all know what to do. Nice orderly line, don't stop and don't for Christ's sake drop anything. Column of twos out the door and straight into the van. Heads up, shoulders back, eyes front. 'Bags of swank', as Kipling used to say. Proud to be police. Left right, left right. Come on, you must remember how it goes.

The poor plods shuffle themselves into some sort of a line and start marching out the door, some of them having a bit of trouble sorting left foot from right but trying not to let it show.

McEvoy says to Driver:

—Make sure none of them get lost between here and the van, Jim, then go with them to Slough, but hack it back to Dogberry Road as quick as you can.

Driver has a question, which at least shows he's taking an interest.

—Why are we going to Slough, Guv? Heathrow Central is nearer.

—Heathrow? says McEvoy, utterly gobsmacked at what he's hearing. *Thief*row? You going *budhu* on me? The nick down in Slough is one thousand per cent safer. You take that lot into Heathrow and the van would be pinched before the wheels stopped turning.

—You might not be wrong there, Guv, Driver agrees.

—Trust me on this one, Jim, I'm a policeman. Oh, and Jim…

—Yes, Guv?

—I've counted them all out....

Driver takes the hint. What McEvoy is referring to is the fact that each of the uniforms drawn up neatly in marching order is actually loaded with four or six packages of the dreaded white powder: Big Benny's cholly no less. They've got it inside their uniforms, inside their underwear, clenched into their armpits. For once in their lives, each plod has a walking street value of about twenty-two thousand quid.

Doing what they're told, the uniforms march out of the door and across to the police bus where they climb in and take their seats. When they're all in, Detective Sergeant Driver joins them and makes sure the doors are closed. He slaps the side of the bus and it starts up and pulls away.

Driver waits until they're two streets away and then he calls for order.

—All righty, empty your pockets. And I mean *all* of them or I'll personally have to inspect your knickers and I might enjoy that, but you won't.

And one by one – reluctantly, and it does take some time – the plods produce all the packs of cholly from about their persons and make a neat pile on the floor of the bus.

Back at Dogberry Road, Fat Desk Sergeant Foster is earning his pension.

Business is booming. Two Indian women are both reporting a missing cat: the same cat. This develops into a punch-up between the two as to who actually owns the animal. Havildar Singh, who is known throughout Southall as a 'character' (which means he stands on street corners shouting at buses), turns up to see if somebody's handed in a ceremonial sword he lost in 1987. Two young, clean-shaved Somalis in new Nikes both report stolen BMWs. A distinguished, although unarmed, Afghan gentleman stands there holding a sign which says 'Please get me a translator'. Trouble is, the sign is in Russian so it doesn't cut any ice. Even the drunk he threw out a few hours earlier is back and this time his trombone is seriously the worse for wear, the slide part bent in an arc like it's been wrapped round a lamp post. And there's an Asian kid, maybe eight or nine years old, still in school uniform, who has to empty out a wastepaper bin and turn it upside down to stand on so he can be seen over the front desk.

But before Baby Face can say anything, Fat Foster loses his rag. He's got half the division in the back office and the cells, playing around with talcum powder and plastic bags and giggling like big kids. He's got the Oik prowling around finding fault and now this DCI McEvoy throwing his weight around. There's not a single uniform available to help him and he's got a front desk under siege by every time-waster and weirdo in the parish. He's had enough.

—Right! Ladies and gentlemen, for the last time, there is no Lost Property office here. Neither do we have bus timetables, visa application forms for anywhere or the home telephone number of the Attorney General. So will you all....

Then he notices that the baby-faced kid is crying. He smiles down at him, all fatherly. Well, he has to. There are witnesses.

—What is it, son?

—I've lost my mother, sobs Baby Face.

—Where did you lose her, son?

—If I knew where she fucking was, she wouldn't be lost would she?

Fat Foster doesn't know what to say to this, but before he has to say anything there's a commotion from out back in the cells. There's a loud pop like someone has blown up a paper bag and burst it (which is actually more or less what's happened), followed by a mass cheer and hysterical laughter, such as you'd hear if Tottenham scored at home.

The door to the cells opens and out comes a woman PC, her face and hair covered in white powder, and she's laughing so much she can't talk. She takes one look at all the people the other side of the front desk, sobers up some and reaches down behind Fat Foster's legs for the dustpan and brush, which they keep there to stop anybody nicking it. With a quick 'Sorry, Sarge', she grabs the brush and legs it back into the cell area and as the door opens, there's another loud cheer and laughing.

At the front desk you could hear a pin drop and Fat Foster has to do something to recover the situation, so he pulls a telephone on to the counter and says to Baby Face:

—Is there someone you could ring, son?

—Sure, says Baby Face, picking up the phone and starting to dial.

—Haven't the rest of you got homes to go to? he says to the others and then notices the punter with the bent trombone. And I've told you we're not interested so you can sod off. Now come on, people, let's stop wasting police time, shall we? I want everybody out unless it's really serious.

Then he notices that Baby Face is still dialling, and that must be fourteen or fifteen numbers.

—What time will it be in Bombay now? asks the kid.

Ash the Cash has been cruising the streets with Big Benny in the back. They've done a drive-by, at a discreet distance, of Crackenthorpe Street and seen the uniforms march out, climb in their bus and drive off. They've cruised Dogberry Road and seen their own troops go in and come out and Benny's taken a particular interest in the building site next door to the station where half a dozen builders are going through the motions of clearing the site with a JCB mechanical digger.

Ash's mobile goes off for about the twentieth time and he tells Benny that it's Baby Face ringing to fix a meet.

Benny suggests the Bengali restaurant again as they've been going there for all of five hours now and they should be classed as regulars. Anyway, it's a convenient place for the crew to assemble and Benny has a hankering for chillis all of a sudden.

One of the Bengali brothers is putting out an A-board that says 'Lunch specials' when he sees Ash pull up in the Merc. He starts backing off inside the restaurant, thinking maybe he can get the door locked in time, but is too slow. Round the corner comes Rafik, backed up by Jo Jo Singh and Boy Adrian. Jo Jo's a big Sikh with a turban and the beard and a natty three-piece suit. He also wears a Chelsea scarf around his neck. Boy is shaven-headed, wears T-shirts whatever the weather so he can show off his body-building, and supports QPR but doesn't let on about that. You wouldn't want to see either of them on *Crimewatch,* let alone in your restaurant.

Rafik reads the situation and makes sure that Jo Jo and Boy get to the door before the terrified Bengali can call to his family, put the restaurant on the market or stick his head in the gas oven. Jo Jo heads straight for the kitchen to make sure nobody does anything stupid with a potato peeler, while Boy holds the door open for Benny, who strolls in like he owns the place, which he might well by the end of the day if the chef can't do a curry using *Scotch Bonnets.*

Benny gets the boys to put three tables together, turn the sign in the door so it reads 'CLOSED' and then orders bottles of Murree Beer, which he calls the finest beer ever brewed in Pakistan even though, being a Moslem country, nobody there is allowed to drink it and it's only for export. Boy goes behind the bar to help himself and sees on the bottle that Murree is now brewed under licence in Austria, but he doesn't say anything as he knows it's never clever to spoil Benny's moment.

They find some cushions and a chair so that Baby Face, when he turns up five minutes later, can reach the table.

—We've got some fresh curries coming up. Want some? Big Benny says to him.

Baby Face shakes his head.

—Nah, tell them to do me a cheeseburger in nan bread to go. I've got to get back to school.

—You've got it, son. Now, what's happening down the local pig farm?

—Well, something's going down that's for sure.

Baby Face says it's like show-and-tell time in the classroom and as he talks he empties his pockets, putting a stapler, pens, pencils, a policeman's notebook and a ruler on the table; all stuff he's lifted from the Dogberry Road front desk.

—They're running around like headless chickens, but with lots of laughing and shouting too. Like they were enjoying their work.

—Did you see any packets of white stuff, about this size?

Benny holds his hands apart. Baby Face just looks around the restaurant, being cool.

—Oh, the dope? What is it? Skag, horse or snow? Whatever. Saw one of the Miss Piggies with some all over her snout. She looked happy.

—She was sampling it?

—Don't think so. Not while on duty. Looked to me like she'd had an accident. Needed a brush to sweep it up. She wouldn't be snorting there, man. Too many cops around.

—More cops than usual? Benny asks.

—Difficult to say, in'it, it being a police station.

—You know what I mean. Any extra security?

—At Dogberry Road? They don't know the meaning of the word. The CCTV hasn't worked for six months, everybody knows that. The guys on the building site wander in and out to make their tea, use the phone. Some of the locals use it as a bus shelter if it's raining. Kids in my class used to break in there for a bet. Don't any more; it's too easy.

—And all the action seems to be in the back, eh?

—Yeah, where the cells are, near the toilets. I've been in there and used them before now, when I've been caught short.

—You done well, Baby Face. Here's your lunch.

Jo Jo comes out of the kitchen with a big brown bag and as he passes the bar, he stops by a big fruit bowl and takes a banana, a mango and two passion fruit and adds them to the bag.

—You should eat more fruit, he says, handing the bag to Baby Face.

—So I can grown up big and strong like you?

The others go quiet because nobody ever cheeks Jo Jo Singh, or at least not twice. But Jo Jo looks down, and for somebody nearly seven feet tall that's quite a drop, and says:

—Yes.

Baby Face takes the bag and stares up at him.

—Fair enough. Thanks for the thought.

As he hops off his chair and heads for the door, Big Benny watches him go and shakes his head.

—Remind me to retire before that kid gets the vote, he says to Ash.

Then nothing much is said for a bit as the food starts to arrive and the crew discover that the Bengali brothers in the kitchen have taken Benny's instructions to heart and everything comes with extra chillis. Some of the dishes have left Madras and passed Vindaloo without collecting £200. Boy Adrian is the first to crack, not that he says anything, just goes behind the bar for more Murree beer. Ash asks for some plain rice, and this from a man whose mother thinks rice in a restaurant is a Chinese invention. Even Jo Jo goes quiet when he tries the gravy from one of the meat curries. In fact, all of them except Benny seem to lose the power of speech during the course of the meal.

Eventually Benny wipes his plate clean and sits back in his chair, letting his trousers take the strain.

—That was spanking, he says.

Ash gives him a minute to settle himself then says:

—So you reckon it's do-able?

Benny pretends to think this over.

—'Course it is. Last thing they'd ever expect. Everybody knows Dogberry Road is a joke. Baby Face said as much. Loads of stuff goes missing from there.

—I heard the place was condemned. Not fit for animals.

—That's right, it's a pig house. A house built by the little pigs. And we know what the Big Bad Wolf did, don't we?

—You're gonna huff and puff and blow their house down?

—Something like that.

Well after dark and long after the 2 to 10 shift has knocked off, McEvoy goes through it one more time for the benefit of the Officer In Command, even though he's been home for a kip and a change of uniform, while McEvoy and Driver have been up and on the case since sparrowfart and are both beginning to smell a bit by now.

The station house looks deserted. The only two marked cars on duty at night have been on the go since the pubs shut, answering calls about domestics; street fights; flashers down by the Grand Union Canal; rapists; aliens; alarms going off; car theft; and burglars in the back garden. The phone has hardly stopped.

—This is just what we expected, sir, says McEvoy, trying to comfort the Oik.

—It is, is it?

—Absolutely, sir. We had half Big Benny's extended family in here this morning scouting the place and we made sure they saw what they wanted to see. One of the WPCs put on a bit of a show for them so they went away happy. Big Benny will have heard exactly what he wanted to hear; that his merchandise is stashed overnight in the one place that's easier to open than a King's Cross prozzy's knickers.

—So he won't be able to resist trying to get it?

—Not Benny, sir. Think of his street cred if he pulls it off. Think of his street cred if he just lets things lie. Right now he'll be sitting out there with his boys, watching the comings and goings, getting his crew to make all those phone calls so he can judge what our strength is.

—Which is?

—There are ten of us including you, sir. I've got them lying low in the cells with the lights off.

—Back up?

—Two mobile teams of the heavy mob, but they're at least ten minutes away so Benny's scouts don't spot them.

—And the stuff itself, the real merchandise?

—That's secure down in Slough, sir, Driver chips in, just to earn a few Brownie points with the big chief.

—We're absolutely sure on that?

—Absolutely, says Driver, saw to it myself.

The Oik nods and mutters 'Good, good' and then takes McEvoy on one side.

—This is one hell of a risky set-up, Chief Inspector. We've gone well over budget already for this operation.

—Look sir, we've got the drugs; it's a handsome haul and it's tucked away all safe. We put a little more time and energy into this and we pull Big Benny and his crew as well. Double result.

—And if anything goes wrong? Big Benny has sharp lawyers, you know. They could make a good case for entrapment. In fact, thinking about it, this is not very good public relations, is it? I mean, *encouraging* a known criminal to rob a police station? Maybe we should get the duty press officer on to this.

—The fewer in the loop the better, sir.

This from Driver and the Oik looks at him with new respect.

—Good point, Sergeant.

When it comes, it's just after one o'clock and it comes at force six on the Richter scale.

The moment he heard the engine of the JCB digger on the neighbouring building site start up, McEvoy knew the take was in progress. He pressed the Send button on his mobile, said 'Go', and allowed himself a smile.

But even he was surprised at the impact of the JCB on the back wall of Dogberry Road, which was like an explosion in a cement factory. The digger's bucket only needs one hit at the wall and the whole thing came in like a giant fist had punched it from outside. The air is filled with flying bricks and dust and then the sharp bits hit the stacks of plastic bags and they start bursting and so a faintly scented (lavender and rose) dry mist of fine powder fills the air.

Through all the dust and the flying crap, it's Big Benny – wearing goggles and looking like he's in the Afrika Korps heading for Tobruk – who is first to climb in over the rubble. He sees the pile of plastic packs bulging with white powder and pauses to stroke one, lovingly, before sig-

nalling the JCB digger forward, bucket lowered to scoop up
the goodies.

—Guess who's nicked, Benny! shouts McEvoy but nobody
can hear him over the chaos.

More of Benny's crew pour into the station through the
hole in the wall, though it's difficult to recognise any of them
as they've been clever enough to wear dust masks and
goggles, which of course the plod never thought of. So half a
dozen uniforms burst into the cells area, prepared to pounce
on the unsuspecting villains, but end up coughing and sneezing and stumbling about, and basically the whole thing is a
farce.

The JCB manages to get a decent load of plastic bags in its
bucket and starts reversing out of the station, bringing more
of the wall down in the process. Through the hole in the wall,
and the clouds of fine dust, McEvoy can make out two cars
(no doubt freshly picked from some pub car park) and a van
waiting for the getaway, and a couple of Benny's crew already
legging it towards them. And then he hears why, as the sirens
from his back-up teams are suddenly very close and it looks
as if something's going right at last.

The first police car on the scene does a handbrake stop and
turn at the entrance to the building site, and two uniformed
plods jump out and run round to the boot. They take out a
stinger, their latest secret weapon against joyriders, which is a
flexible mat of metal spikes rolled up like a carpet. This they
throw down so that it rolls out across the entrance to the site,
ready to shred the tyres off anything that tries to drive over it.
A second plod car draws up and the uniforms in it do the
same so there are parallel lines of spikes hemming in the
getaway cars.

The stingers might not have stopped the JCB digger if it
had decided to make a break for it, but then again, with a top
speed of about 25 m.p.h., it shouldn't have been a problem to
catch. But it never came to that. Whoever was driving the JCB
threw a wobbler and started going round in circles, a ghost
trail of lavender-and-rose scented powder streaming from its

bucket, until it trundles too close to the edge of a drainage ditch and slowly topples over on to its side, wheels spinning, the trail of powder now a mini-Hiroshima of a dust cloud.

A cheer goes up from the arriving plod who are now running across the site, batons drawn, ready for a ruck. From above, Dogberry Road police station looks like an ants' nest somebody has trodden on and then sprinkled ant powder on.

When they find him, Big Benny is leaning against a sign saying 'Danger – Men At Work'. He's got his mobile in one hand and a Mars bar in the other.

—Double result, sir, says McEvoy to the senior Oik. We've got the drugs off the street and Big Benny, Ash the Cash, Rafik Jarman, Boy Adrian and two others in custody. Not a bad day's work, if you ask me.

The Oik looks at McEvoy as if to say he hadn't asked him anything, but he's more worried about the white powder all over his uniform and how it just makes it worse when he tries to brush it off.

—There is the small matter of the destruction of a police station, Chief Inspector.

—Oh, come on, sir, the place was falling down anyway. They can't but increase your budget now, can they?

—I suppose not.

The Oik cheers up at this thought. Maybe it's a triple result. Then his face turns to thunder as he sees a smartsuited bloke with a briefcase casually picking his way over the rubble, climbing into what's left of the cells area.

—Who the hell are you?

The suit comes on, carefully picking where to put his feet so that he doesn't spoil his tasselled loafers. As he reaches the Oik he makes a big gesture of shooting his cuff back to check his watch, which is, natch, a Rolex.

—My name is Tim Mawson, Chief Superintendent. I believe you have my client in custody.

—Big Benny, Driver whispers in the Oik's ear.

—That was quick, says the Oik to himself. *Bloody quick.*

—Rumour has it that Big Benny carries Mr Mawson here in the back of his car, bit like a spare tyre. Just in case.

The Oik glares at McEvoy as if to say: that's not helping, but it doesn't throw the solicitor at all.

—Spot of home improvement is it, gentlemen? says Mawson with a smile like glass. Hope you've got planning permission.

—Show him through, says the Oik so tight-lipped his cheekbones hurt.

Driver waves Mawson to follow him to the interview room, one of the few rooms left with four walls. As soon as they are out of earshot, the Oik starts in on McEvoy again.

—I assume you'll be charging them with damage and destruction of police property, Chief Inspector. Have you any idea how much this lot is going to cost to repair? Not to mention the JCB from the building site and the cars they used, which will be stolen no doubt. There'll be another claim there.

—Haven't actually checked the insurance policy today, sir, have you? You know, the home and contents section… ?

—Don't get smart with me, Chief Inspector. Not until we've locked this lot down and thrown away the key.

And then Driver is back with them, though he's only been gone a minute or so.

—Sorry, sir, but that brief – Mawson – wants a word. You as well as Mr McEvoy.

—Time to do a deal? asks McEvoy.

—No deals, Chief Inspector, says the Oik. This operation has cost too much. We throw the book at them, but we try not to look smug.

—Could be tricky that, says McEvoy with a grin like a big kid.

In the interview room, Big Benny and the brief, Mawson, sit one side of a table.

Big Benny's eating a Snickers bar and his black face is covered with white powder, except for the outline of the goggles he'd worn. This makes him look like a fat owl and him sitting there, smiling and blinking, just adds to it.

Mawson doesn't stand up, doesn't even look up, when the cops file into the room. He just keeps making spidery notes on a pad of paper he's taken from his briefcase. McEvoy bets himself that there's nothing else in the briefcase except a supply of Snickers bars for Benny.

—I fail to see why my client is being held at all, Superintendent.

When Mawson says this, the three cops look at each other and McEvoy says:

—Are we in the right room, Jim?

Mawson ignores this.

—My client and some of his friends were simply driving down Dogberry Road when they saw an unidentified youth obviously joyriding on a motorised digger, presumably stolen from the adjoining building site. When they tried, but failed, to prevent a serious accident, they themselves were arrested.

—Rubbish! says the Oik.

—Bollocks! says Driver.

—Total bollocks! says McEvoy.

—Perhaps you have some proof that my client was doing anything other than what he says? Video tape, perhaps, from the security cameras?

The Oik looks at McEvoy.

McEvoy looks at Driver.

Driver knows that only one camera was actually in working order and that had been taken out by the digger straight away. He shakes his head. The Oik doesn't like this, but puts on a brave face.

—Please don't play games, Mr Mawson. Your client has been caught, red-handed, in possession of a huge amount of a Class A....

—Class A *what*, Chief Superintendent?

Still Mawson doesn't look at the cops, but he reaches a finger over towards Benny's face and draws a line across his forehead through the film of white powder. Then he puts his finger to his nose.

—Class A flour? Or is it talcum powder? Rose-scented, if I'm not mistaken. You are charging my client with being in possession of talcum powder? Tell me, Superintendent, what *is* the street value of talcum powder these days?

There's a deathly silence then for maybe half a minute and the three cops all turn away like they've seen a bad traffic accident and they're going to throw up.

—Oh my sweet Lord, says the Oik.

—Oh fuck! says McEvoy.

—It was the Chief Inspector's idea, sir, says Driver. The whole thing...

Part II:

They're drugs, Jim, but not as we know them

ONE YEAR LATER

—THIS MUST BE it, says Driver swinging the car off the road towards the gate.

—Nice place, says Detective Sergeant Moon who is sitting beside him.

Moon sounds impressed but Driver's not sure whether it's because of the scenery – willows weeping into a slow-moving river, swans gliding by in neutral, skylarks tweeting like they're a backing track – or whether it's because the security cameras actually seem to work here, which makes a nice change.

The sign on the gate says TYLER PHARMACEUTICALS and the gates open automatically to allow them through so they can drive up to the front, double-glass doors of a curved, single-storey building. The name of the company is painted on the glass, along with signs telling them that the building is solar-powered, air-conditioned, and protected by laser-guided CCTV cameras and temperature-activated alarms.

—It's the Starship fucking Enterprise, says Moon.

Driver presses a button on the control panel where the door handle should be and there's a beeping sound; he leans in and says:

—Detective Inspector Driver and Detective Sergeant Moon, Metropolitan Police. Here to see Mr Tyler.

—Enter and turn left into Area A, says the machine.

The doors swish open and then close behind them with a hiss when they kiss together.

—See. Told you, says Moon.

To their left a screen on the wall flashes AREA A at them and more doors hiss open as they get near. A real smoothie appears in the electric doorway. No mad scientist this, not even a white coat. Head-to-toe in Paul Smith, if Moon's not very much mistaken; probably as much again spent on the haircut. He holds out a hand to shake or maybe just to show he goes to a manicurist as well.

Driver does the honours.

—Mr Tyler? I'm DI Jim Driver and this is DS Simon Moon. It's good of you to spare us the time.

—Yes, it is actually, says the suit. What's this all about?

—It's about one of your products, Mr Tyler. Is there a private office we could use?

—We don't believe in an office culture, Inspector. We have a sterile laboratory in Area B. That's about as private as you can get. Follow me.

They follow the suit across the entrance lobby they've just come through and more doors hiss; this time they're in an airlock of sorts.

Tyler puts his palm up to an electronic eye on the wall and there's a double hiss as doors swish behind them and then open in front of them.

—You make drugs here, don't you, sir? says Driver.

—Yes, Inspector, but not as you know them.

As they step into a glass corridor and everything they can see behind the glass is pure white or bright stainless steel, Moon nods to himself, content. That had just proved it.

—We develop pharmaceuticals, very advanced ones. Nothing that would interest you people, says Tyler, as if giving the guided tour to a coach party of OAPs from a low-security hospice.

—You seem very security conscious, though, says Moon trying hard not to add 'Captain' or to ask where they keep the dilithium crystals.

—Industrial espionage can be a problem. That and the animal-rights loonies who think we test on animals. We don't, by the way. Well, only on rats and only if we have to. And nobody minds much about rats.

—Because their tails are naked, says Moon.

—I beg your pardon?

—If rats had furry tails, there'd be a campaign to protect them. They'd look more cuddly.

Driver looks at his Sergeant and wonders just where the Met is getting them from these days. Tyler makes a point of looking at his watch. And not just to show he's a Rolex man.

—Is there anything *relevant* you want to ask me, Inspector?

Tyler has decided that ignoring Moon completely is probably the best policy. Driver is half way to agreeing with him.

—It's about Coletoxore, if that's how you pronounce it, says Driver.

Tyler is genuinely puzzled by this but tries not to show it.

—What do you know about Coletoxore, Inspector?

—Very little, that's why we're here.

—But what's the…*context* exactly?

Which just confirmed what Driver had already decided; that here was a man who dealt in cultures and concepts and, no doubt, Third Way strategies, intellectual properties and participatory brand ownerships. With a worse education he could have been a Chief Constable.

—It has come up in the context of police intelligence gathering operations, sir. We have to check it out.

—What, here? I have regular security meetings with the local Crime Prevention people...

—No, not here in Cambridge, sir, down in London.

—In London?

—Southall to be precise. Near Heathrow.

—You mean our shipping company?

—Yes, sir. Angel's Wings, isn't it?

—Has somebody robbed them or something?

—No, sir. Not yet.

Tyler takes them through another airlock into a glass corridor. This is what he calls he calls the sterile laboratory area and it's stuffed with computers; centrifuges; robot arms waving test tubes about; and a conveyor belt, padded with foam rubber, on which vials of clear liquid move about the room for no apparent reason. They can tell it's hi-tech because there are no people about until Tyler presses a button on a panel on the wall and says: 'Roma to Area B3; immediate' like he's an air traffic controller.

—This is where we do the final analysis on Coletoxore and I've asked Dr Patel to join us. She is one of our senior chemists and is responsible for quality control on all the Coletoxore that leaves this facility.

When Dr Patel joins them, the sharp intake of Moon's breath is almost as loud as the hiss of the doors closing behind her.

Moon has never seen an Asian bint so at ease with her body. She's small, only about five-two even with high-heeled shoes; bright red shoes, which go with the red miniskirt she's wearing underneath her open, white lab coat. She's got decent tits too, bouncing bra-less under a Gap scoop-top like two babies in a sack. She's also wearing glasses; small, almost heart-shaped frames, made from that new flexible metal that you can twist and then reshape, which is just as well as she more or less rips them from her face and scrunches them up in one hand while she holds out the other one to shake as she's introduced. Moon gets a whiff of a perfume that could be pure lime zest and suffers another rush of blood to the groin as he grasps her dry, firm hand and thinks: What a pity, what a waste, what he couldn't do to, and for, her if she wasn't an Asian bint.

—If I can help at all....

Roma Patel is polite, cool and relaxed. As there aren't any chairs in the airlock corridor, she leans back against the glass wall, crosses her ankles and folds her arms under her breasts.

—Roma here is our expert on Coletoxore, Tyler says. You can ask her anything you like.

Driver decides to jump in before they clock the fact that Moon is grinning like a loon.

—We need to get some background on Coletoxore, but we need it in layman's terms.

—Don't worry, Inspector, Dr Patel has been specially trained to talk down to laymen, says Tyler.

Roma Patel's eyebrows shoot up, not at what Tyler's said but at the fact that he doesn't realise what he's said.

—What sort of thing do you need to know, Inspector? I presume you are not interested in the chemistry of the drug.

—You're right there, Miss...sorry, Doctor. What we want to know is a bit more down-to-earth, like what's it worth and what would be the black market in it.

—Now wait a minute, Inspector.

Tyler has butted in before Roma can draw breath and inflate her Gap top even further.

—There is no black market in Coletoxore. This isn't something you buy from the black kid on the street corner.

Driver notices that Roma Patel is flashing daggers from her eyes into the back of Tyler's head. Moon is still looking at her tits.

—Coletoxore is a high-value pharmaceutical at the cutting edge of cancer research, says Tyler.

—Experimental, says Roma, getting a word in. It's an experimental treatment.

—So it's a cure for cancer?

—It helps, Inspector. It's a treatment, not a preventative cure.

—A treatment that works?

—We are getting excellent clinical reports from all over the world, says Roma, getting into her flow.

—So there is an international market for it? Driver asks, but it sounds like he knows the answer he wants from her.

—Yes, but it's a specialised one. Hospitals, clinics, hospices. You won't get it on prescription from a family doctor. Nor would you drop it at a rave or buy it from a black kid in the playground. It doesn't give you a high.

There's an edge in her voice as she says this and it's clearly directed at her boss.

—Not even if you mix it with anything? Driver persists.

—I'm afraid not. It is of absolutely no interest to street dealers.

—They're drugs, then, but not as we know them?

This is Moon's contribution and he thinks it's pretty funny but nobody else does, least of all Jim Driver, who doesn't get it and wants to get back on track.

—So who would buy it?

—Any reputable medical institution, says Tyler pompously.

—With four million quid to spare, adds Roma Patel which makes her boss glare daggers at her.

—Dr Patel, here, is an idealist. She thinks we should give it away, without realising that we would also be giving away her generous salary.

Driver ignores this and goes back to Roma.

—So what do you get for your four million quid?

—Ten thousand vials of 10 milligram doses is the usual batch size, she says professionally.

—And what's that in layman's terms? A barrel-full? A tanker load?

—Actually it's an insulated cube, specially strengthened and weighing about three hundred pounds. Why?

Tyler tries to cut back in here; show he's still boss.

—Yes, why, Inspector? Why the interest?

—Because we believe there will be an attempt made to steal a consignment of Coletoxore.

—When? asks Roma.

—We're not sure, but very soon.

—How?

—We don't exactly know.

—Where?

—We don't know that either.

Tyler has been watching this exchange like he watches tennis and he can't resist putting a real twist of sarcasm in his voice.

—I don't suppose you know *who* is going to steal it, either. Do you, Inspector?

Driver picks his moment with relish.

—Oh yes, sir. We know that.

They know that because Blind Hugh is keeping them informed; telling them every time he gets a phone. Not a phone *call*, but an actual phone.

One of the first things Detective Inspector Jim Driver did to celebrate his promotion was to recruit Blind Hugh as his personal snitch, to be paid in cash money, threats and mild violence in roughly equal proportions.

It was an arrangement Blind Hugh had become used to. The only difference was he now had a new boss. Well, he had to have, once Mr McEvoy bit the bullet and was awarded the DCM – the Don't Come Monday medal – after taking the rap for the Dogberry Road fiasco. Driver had organised McEvoy's leaving do (and it's not easy to find licensed premises willing to host CID socials) at the Master Robert, the pub with a motel tacked on the side, out by the A4. The venue proved perfect as Driver was able to book a room overnight for McEvoy, so the rest of them could pour him into it after closing and then leg it so they didn't have to listen to any of his memories or case histories.

The next day, Driver took over McEvoy's desk, his computer password and his snitch, although it was getting on for a year before Blind Hugh came up with anything worth more than a folded £20 note, a slap, or the threat of telling his mother about those Asian Babe porno videos he was supplying wholesale down East to the Bengali pubs around Brick Lane.

What he came up with was a mobile phone, a cheap, bottom-of-the-range plastic cellphone with hardly any features worth having and a memory capacity so low it told the world you were a sad, lonely bastard. It didn't even play any decent tunes when it rang. And it arrived at Blind Hugh's mother's shop in a box of CampoNijar cherry tomatoes from Andalusia, which Hugh reckoned was somewhere near Rotterdam.

The phone was stuffed in between the cartons of tomatoes, in a self-sealing freezer bag to which was stapled a note saying: TAKE TO BIG BENNY. TURN ON AT NOON.

Not naturally being of an inquisitive nature, Hughie did what the note told him and found Big Benny, along with Ash the Cash and Rafik Jarman, in a restaurant with a view of the Grand Union Canal, just off the Norwood Road. He had never been to the restaurant before but something struck him as familiar and then he realised that he remembered the Bengali family who ran it. They had run a place near Crackenthorpe Street until about six months ago, when they had suddenly shut up shop and moved about two miles south to open this one. It was nice to see their regular customers had followed them, though they themselves didn't seem very happy about it.

—Hughie, my man, how they hanging?

Big Benny tucks a napkin into his collar and then karate chops a pile of poppadums, starting in on the garlic pickle and the mint yoghurt.

—I got something for you, Benny, says Blind Hugh, holding out the cellphone in its cellophane bag.

—Is it Christmas? Benny asks Ash the Cash, who is sipping mineral water and looking as cool as usual.

Ash shakes his head.

—Is it Diwali?

This time Rafik Jarman shakes his head.

—Chinese New Year? No, can't be; no fireworks. I'm sure there's some ethnic minority will be offended, but I'm buggered if I can think what it is. So why the present, Hughie? I know it's not my birthday.

—It's a phone, said Hugh.

—I know.

—It's for you.

—I've got one.

—It came in a box of tomatoes.

Benny looked at Ash and then at Rafik and then back at Hughie.

—Okay, you've got my attention.

And Benny waves Hugh to sit down and opens the package, reads the note and switches the phone on and waits for it to ring or the curries to arrive, whichever came first.

When it does go chirp-chirp, it's exactly twelve noon. Big Benny looks at Hugh before reaching for it.

—In a case of tomatoes you said?

He presses the Talk button.

—I'm listening, he says.

And listen he does, for a good five minutes, not saying anything at all. That is actually a policy Ash the Cash agrees with one hundred percent as he's convinced the whole thing is a set-up, especially with Blind Hugh's reputation for doing the double.

When he's finished listening he says:

—Yeah, I'm interested.

Then he presses the End button, puts the phone on the table and pushes it gently towards Ash.

—Ask around, see who retails phones like that, he says, businesslike.

—Who was it? asks Ash.

—Dunno. Man wants to offer us a job. Sounds as if it could be worth a tickle.

But Benny's not going to say any more in front of Blind Hugh.

—You found that in crate of melons, did you?

—No, Benny, tomatoes. Cherry tomatoes, from Holland, says Hugh, pleased that he could remember where Andalusia was.

—What, like with the deliveries?

—Yeah, that's right. New stock dropped off by the whole-saler from the market, this morning.

—You see it delivered?

—Nah, Benny, I'm still in my pit when he calls round. He leaves our order by the back door.

—Well, keep checking your deliveries because my Man Of Mystery on the phone there tells me you'll be getting another little present among the passion fruit over the next few days.

—Tomatoes, Benny. They were cherry tomatoes.

Benny rolls his eyes and Rafik looks for the nod that means he can give Hughie a slap but, when it doesn't come, he taps his own forehead and says:

—*Budhu.*

—Now don't slag the man, says Benny, he's doing a spank-ing job for us. Give him his bus fare home. Just make sure you check *all* your fruit and veg, eh, Hugh?

Driver and Moon left Tyler Pharmaceuticals, pointing their car back south and west using the motorways M25 then M4, coming into Heston heading east then cutting up into Southall. Moon seemed fascinated by the line of jets up in the sky above the car, leaning over the wheel, sneaking a look up through the windscreen.

Driver tells him that there's a jet every ninety seconds over their heads, in a holding pattern for Heathrow. He remem-bers an instance when he was in a car with McEvoy on the M25, the other side of the airport, as planes went over them, taking off from Heathrow almost as frequently. And McEvoy had looked up longingly at one through the windscreen, just like Moon had been doing, and had said almost dreamily:

'Wish I was on that one'. When Driver had innocently asked him: 'Why, where's it going?', McEvoy had simply said: 'I don't know.' But Driver didn't tell any of this to Moon.

Instead, he consulted his A-Z and told Moon to take a left then a right and turn in to a small industrial estate of one-and two-storey brick buildings, nestled around a crescent-shaped access road. In front of each building was a handkerchief of green-brown lawn and on the strip in front of the second building there was a sign propped up against a pile of bricks, which said: ANGEL'S WINGS – INTERNATIONAL TRANSIT.

Driver points a finger.

—This is it.

Super-smooth Mr Tyler has told them that Angel's Wings handles all Tyler Pharmaceuticals' exports, but he didn't notice how the policemen's eyes had lit up when he mentions that Angel's Wings is based in Southall. 'It's so convenient for the airport' he had said, and Driver had just said 'Yes, it is' quite quietly and asked for the address.

At least Tyler is as good as his word when he promises to ring the company, and its boss, to tell them they're coming and to offer all possible co-operation in matters concerning Coletoxore. Although Moon reckons this is just to cover his arse with his insurance company.

The Angel's Wings boss is a handsome Pakistani in his mid-twenties called Naseem, who wears a double-breasted pinstripe and at least four gold rings as well as one small, gold earring. Moon immediately thinks: 'Rich Paki', but recognises that the suit is another Paul Smith. He neither knows nor cares that Naseem would call himself a Kashmiri if anyone had asked him.

Naseem shows them into his office, which is obviously the only private office in the place, the rest being basically a big warehouse. He has put two chairs out in front of a big bare desk, which he sits behind so he can smile at them. On the wall is a framed picture of Margaret Thatcher. There is one bookshelf, which contains A-Zs of every major town and city in the country, and three volumes of the Directory of Asian Businessmen.

Naseem puts his hands on his desk and opens the palms to start the ball.

—Mr Tyler has rung asking me to co-operate fully, Inspector. I understand it's about the shipment of Coletoxore, but I cannot think why the police are interested.

—They are high-value drugs, Mr Naseem, says Driver.

—But not as you know them, Inspector.

Moon almost bites his lip off. The Paki's made a corker without knowing that Driver's name is Jim and even better, Driver still doesn't get it.

—Pharmaceuticals, then, worth four million pounds per consignment.

—That's true, Inspector, and that's why we take extra care with them but we handle lots of valuable cargoes. The point here, surely, is that these are drugs that aren't much use to anyone other than a doctor in a hospital. Are you suggesting that a reputable hospital would buy pharmaceuticals off the street corner from someone like a... a... second-hand car dealer?

—What about abroad, though? Moon jumps in quickly.

Naseem aims his eyes at the Sergeant.

—You mean places like India or Pakistan perhaps? Where everybody is corrupt?

Driver, sensing a complaint to some police/community relations panel somewhere down the line, tries to defuse things pronto.

—My Sergeant didn't mean anything by that, Mr Naseem. [Oh yes he did, thinks Moon.] It's just that your company ships Coletoxore abroad. You don't distribute it in this country.

Naseem looks like he believes him for all of two seconds, but he goes with the flow.

—But someone is planning to steal a consignment in this country, is that it?

—I'm not sure how much Mr Tyler has told you, but yes, that is our information.

—And you are suggesting it must be someone here at Angel's Wings. Therefore, you had better arrest me now.

Talk about a drama queen, thinks Moon, as Naseem leans across his desk and holds his wrists out as if waiting to be cuffed.

—You might as well, Inspector, he says. We are not a big company and I'm involved in everything that goes on, so I must be the guilty one.

—We're not suggesting anything like that, sir, says Driver.

—Nothing's been nicked yet, adds Moon, which for once is the right thing to say.

—But you have information that something will be? Naseem relaxes a bit, like he's not expecting to be crucified just yet.

—The information is relevant to the Southall area and the shipping of Coletoxore through Heathrow. The only distributor is Angel's Wings.

—Fair enough, Inspector. So what you are saying is that we could be the target, not the criminals?

—Exactly. That's why we would like to go through your procedures and security systems.

The young Kashmiri considers this as if he really has an option, then comes to a decision.

—I have been instructed to offer every assistance and I will, but the best person to talk to is my freight manager who is also responsible for any extra security precautions we have to take. I have already asked him to…Here he is.

The door opens and the first thing that comes in is a tin tray with four plastic cups of coffee balanced in brown plastic cup holders. The arm that's holding it is attached to a middle-aged man in a short-sleeved white shirt. He's wearing a dark blue polyester tie, clipped to the shirt front to keep it in place. On the shirt's breast pocket is a metal clip arrangement, which holds two ballpoint pens like miniature handcuffs. He's also wearing a digital watch that Moon guesses cost no more than three quid down Hounslow Sunday market. Whoever this guy is, thinks Moon, he's a conscientious objector in the fashion wars.

—Frank? says Driver and the only sound in the office is the rattle of the plastic cup holders on the tin tray in the older man's hands.

—Hello, Jim.

—I didn't know you worked here, Frank.

—No reason why you should. Came here about three months after the retirement.

Frank? thinks Moon. Retirement? Then the penny drops and fuck him, this must be Frank McEvoy. The former DCI who got turned over in the Dogberry Road circus. The one they used to call 'Kipling' down the canteen. The only serving CID officer never known to try and transfer out of the area.

—I thought you'd moved away. Even heard you'd gone back to Ireland.

—Not likely, snorts McEvoy. The wife did, but I stayed on to sell up the house and things and then drifted into this.

Naseem stands up, takes one of the coffees off McEvoy's tray and waves a hand telling McEvoy to distribute the others. It's a good way of reminding everybody it's his coffee, his office, his firm.

—Former Inspector McEvoy has made lots of helpful suggestions about our security arrangements, says Naseem. And he showed a natural flair for freight management so I put him in charge of that, too.

—That's mostly shipping overseas, isn't it? Driver asks, as if he didn't already know.

—Middle and Far East, India, occasionally Japan. Those are the places we mostly deal with.

—That includes Coletoxore?

McEvoy immediately clams up at that and looks to Naseem.

—It's all right, Frank, says the Kashmiri generously. Tyler Pharmaceuticals have asked us to co-operate two hundred percent with the police.

McEvoy still doesn't say anything, but stares at Moon until Driver twigs what the problem is.

—Oh, sorry, Frank, this is DS Moon. Just started working

out of Norwood Green. You used to call it the posh part of Southall, remember?

—There's nothing wrong with my memory, growls McEvoy but at least he nods towards Moon to acknowledge his presence.

—Didn't imply there was, smooths Driver. In fact, could come in a bit useful.

—Why? What's going down?

McEvoy is on the balls of his feet now, straining forward as if trying to sense something that just might be the old call of the wild.

Driver lays it down for them, savouring every minute he has their undivided. He tells them – though it has to remain highly confidential, of course – that they have received certain information that certain individuals are planning a robbery involving a certain valuable pharmaceutical product, and it is all going to go down in the Southall-Heston-Heathrow area.

—Which individuals? demands Naseem like a bullet.

—Let me guess, says McEvoy slowly.

Somebody was setting up Big Benny, but not for a fall.

Now Big Benny never was the sort of muscle you could just go out and hire like you could recruit a crew from the pool room of the pub for a bit of casual menacing. Benny was his own boss, had been for years, and had even been known to turn down the odd bit of lucrative freelance work for the Triads in Soho and the Yardies down Brixton. Definitely not looking for work and quite happy with his own little empire (he regarded Shepherd's Bush as the final frontier), somebody must have *suggested* the deal to him. Put the word out indirectly, so to speak. Let the word drop that somebody had a buyer for four million quids' worth of cancer-treating drugs, should Big Benny just happen to know where he could lay his hands on them. And when Big Benny had to admit that he was just a touch vague on the actual logistics of getting hold of such a consignment (as he would never admit to not knowing that four million quids' worth of anything was moving through his territory), then the somebody would have mentioned that maybe they'd heard of a plan and perhaps Benny could give his opinion on it. And Benny would have listened and then said something like: 'Well, I wouldn't have done it that way myself, but it could work – with the right crew.' Or similar.

The real hook, though, was the way the pitch was delivered.

Using Blind Hugh was clever because, although he was a known snitch prone to pissing on both sides of the fence, he was also widely recognised to be too thick to have come up with anything like this himself. It was also a truth universally recognised (at least in Southall) that Hughie would tell you the colour of his mother's underwear if you looked at him in a funny way or threatened to use harsh language on him.

Using Blind Hugh to deliver the message via a one-trip, untraceable mobile phone, though, was the masterstroke because Big Benny just loved gadgets and freebies almost as much as he loved curry. To have somebody send him, not just a phone message but the phone itself, was a touch of class and guaranteed to make sure that he listened to that first call.

And the second one Blind Hugh found the next day in a box of pineapples from the Ivory Coast, which he knew must be in India because it had a cartoon of an elephant on the side. And the third (South African seedless grapes) and the fourth (clementines from Spain, which he knew was near Ibiza). Sometimes he would find one every morning, sometimes there would be a day or two gap. Hughie never thought to try and find out how the phones, each in a plastic bag with a Post-It note stapled to it saying 'Big Benny' and a time for switching on, actually got into his wholesale fruit and veg, somewhere between Spitalfields Market and his Mum's Southall shop. Neither did Big Benny, and the serious theory there was that Benny had been told not to even try in that very first call in the restaurant.

Whatever Benny felt about that he never let on, seemingly quite happy to follow his anonymous instructions from the disembodied voice coming out of the cellphone. When a phone arrived, he called it his 'having a One-to-One Day' and put the word out among his boys that if Blind Hugh was looking for him of a morning, they'd better make sure he found him sharpish otherwise something other than a voice could get disembodied.

Ash the Cash and Rafik Jarman were the only two of the crew who saw Benny getting his telephone briefings and they knew to keep it that way. Ash had had his reservations, especially when he'd tried to check out that first mobile. One of his nephews, who hardly looked older than Baby Face but was on an electrical engineering course at Brunel University, told him it was a cheap Korean model, not a brand on sale in the country as far as he knew, and it was worth maybe thirty quid to somebody who could clone a month of free calls on somebody else's account; otherwise, it was just a piece of plastic. The nephew wouldn't give it house room. He had six of his own as it was, and didn't get billed on any of them.

The main doubt nagging at the back of Ash's mind, though, was Benny's increasingly regular 'One-to-Ones' with the voice on the mobile were just that: one-to-ones, with him out of the loop. He got to hear only what Benny wanted to pass on. That he didn't like, but he looked on the bright side. If it all went belly-up, his fingerprints wouldn't be on it.

But when the third mobile arrived and Benny took the call, Ash got involved personally.

Blind Hugh had found the phone first thing and delivered it to Benny by ten a.m. The Post-It note this time said to switch on at two p.m., so Benny took it with him on a little business trip, with Ash driving, over to Brentford. It was as they were heading back up the Great West Road just before two that Benny told him to pull over into a lay-by opposite Osterley Station. Dead on two, the mobile plays a twinkly digital version of 'When the Saints Go Marchin' In' and Benny listens in, saying 'Yeah' and 'Uh-huh' while Ash drums his fingers on the steering wheel of his Merc and looks up at the aircraft overhead in their holding pattern for Heathrow.

Then Benny says 'Say again' into the phone and after a bit: 'You'd better spell that, hang on', and there's chaos in the front of the car while he finds a pen and something to write on, which turns out to be the inside of a wrapper from a KitKat he's just found in his pocket.

Benny writes slowly (that's why he has Ash) then says 'U-huh' again and 'I'll get it checked out', and then the phone goes dead on him and he casually lobs it into the back seat of the Merc without bothering to switch it off.

—That's the goods, Benny says, showing Ash the KitKat wrapper.

There's one word written on it in shaky capitals:

C O L E T O X O R E

—What's that supposed to mean? asks Ash.

—It's drugs, says Benny, like Ash was slow. Well, not proper drugs, more like medicines, but worth a bit. That's why we're going to Hounslow to check it out.

—Hounslow? asks Ash, but he's already started the car.

—Your brother-in-law, he's got a pharmacy in Hounslow, ain't he?

—Yeah, and he's also a son-of-a-pig.

—I'm not asking him out, just want to pick his brains, says Benny starting in on the KitKat.

—If you can find 'em, mutters Ash, pulling out into the traffic.

Yet as it turns out, Ash's brother-in-law does happen to be useful – by not being helpful. That's mainly because he's the sort who takes great pleasure in not being able to help.

Like he knows what Coletoxore *is*, of course he does, he's a qualified pharmacist who keeps up with the latest scientific literature. He knows it's an experimental anti-cancer serum but it's not the sort of thing he dispenses. (Overpriced and useless eyedrops for the elderly and Night Nurse for the local alcoholics to keep in the car in case they're stopped is more his line, thinks Ash.) You'd have to be in a hospital to get Coletoxore, probably a private one, and you'd pay through the nose. Still, if you have cancer, maybe it's worth it. That wouldn't be Ash's problem by any chance would it? And Ash has to restrain himself from giving that smug face a slap by remembering his sister, though what did she ever see in the jerk?

All the time, Big Benny stands there grinning at the fact that there's no love lost in Ash's family, which just goes to show they're no different to anyone else. He doesn't interfere, though he wouldn't be averse to force-feeding the little shit of a chemist a handful of his overpriced Neurofen if the need arose. He just stands there at the counter, finger-flicking the hi-fibre energy bars, but the only one he can find with chocolate on is for diabetics so he doesn't bother.

Back in the car out on Hanworth Road, Ash says:

—So it cures cancer, it's difficult to get and it's expensive. That what you wanted to hear?

—Yeah. Spanking, innit?

Driver is quite pleased with his summary of things to date, but of course McEvoy has a question or three, if only to show his boss that he's on the ball and earning his corn.

—How do you know all this detail if Benny's getting his instructions one-to-one on these mobiles?

—You know Blind Hugh, Frank. He swings both ways like he can't stop himself. You must have trained him well.

—I did, says McEvoy, with a touch of pride.

—So everything he knows, we know. Plus, we've kept an eye on Benny's movements lately; when we've had the spare manpower.

—You can do that on the strength of a word from Blind Hugh? Christ, but the Met must have done some serious recruiting since I was in.

—Not as much as we'd like. The thin blue line is pretty thin, but Big Benny's still a target for us. And we've had corroboration from a second source: Ash the Cash's pharmacist brother-in-law.

—I don't follow, Inspector, said Naseem, to show he was still there.

—There's no reason why you should, sir, says Driver. With the new Drugs Awareness Initiative we're operating, all pharmacists report any requests for unusual drugs or chemical substances that could be used in drug manufacture, to a local police liaison officer. Ash's brother-in-law couldn't wait to drop him in it. That's how we got on to Big Benny's interest in Coletoxore. Benny's based in Southall; Coletoxore is shipped out of Southall; Benny is recruiting a crew for a rob. Too many strands to ignore.

—So this Benny person is going to steal a consignment from here? Naseem says, spelling it out for his own benefit.

—We think he's going to rob it, yes.

—Rob? Steal? What's the difference?

—Steal would be a burglary from here at night, maybe when there's nobody around, says McEvoy quickly, to show he's still on the ball. Robbing it means an in-and-out job, a stick-up, possibly armed. Or a hijack.

—It's going to be a hijack, says Driver.

Following the instructions he got on the fourth mobile he receives, Big Benny starts auditioning for drivers, specifically TADs – Taking Away and Driving joyriders. This meant that the average age was about fifteen, but as none of them had licences they had nothing to lose. Not that Benny wanted them on the job itself, whatever it was; he just needed some cars for a few hours and the kids could steal to order, not worrying about their prints being left all over the place as their prints weren't on file anywhere.

The first two cars Benny ordered were delivered the same night to a disused warehouse off the Ruislip Road, over towards Uxbridge. They were a Ford and a battered Renault estate car, but Benny hadn't been too specific and as long as they had a wheel at each corner, he was happy.

The inside of the warehouse was clear, bar a few rotting boxes of industrial waste and some empty oil drums. The electricity had been cut off months before but that wasn't a problem. Benny, Ash, Rafik and Boy Adrian could see well enough in the headlights of the stolen cars as they stood around, waiting for Benny to finish a cold kebab wrapped in pitta bread so he could tell them why they were there.

Benny just sat there on the bonnet of the Ford not saying anything much worth listening to until Jo Jo Singh arrived carrying a black sports bag in each hand. As he dropped them on the floor, the sound which echoed round the warehouse was like an iron anchor chain being let down.

—Were they where he said? Benny asks, as he unsticks his arse from the car and wanders over to start unzipping the bags.

—Behind the tennis courts near the canal, says Jo Jo and Benny nods to himself like he approves.

None of the others ask what the fuck is in the bags, though they all want to. They wait for Benny to pull on a pair of black leather gloves and unpack one until he's holding a concertina of what looks like thick wire, except it's all metal and there are spikes everywhere. It's like a coil of barbed wire but black and springy, with a weight on one end, and the spikes are bigger, sharks-teeth versions.

—Whoa! goes Rafik. You've got us a stinger! Cool.

—Two, actually, says Benny.

Eight months later, after it was all over, a Health and Safety Officer from Greenford Council, on a routine inspection, found a Ford and a Renault estate car in the deserted warehouse off the Ruislip Road. Both vehicles had been chocked up on bricks and all the wheels removed.

Some time after that, three wheels were fished out of the canal in Southall during dredging operations. All three had their tyres ripped and shredded down to the rims almost as if they'd been chewed off, but nobody could ever remember seeing a shark in the Grand Union before.

McEvoy didn't have an office at Angel's Wings as such, it was just a desk and a chair inside the big swing doors into the warehouse. Because of the height of the ceiling and the air conditioning, he must have needed a coat to work there in winter. Maybe thermal underwear as well.

Apart from a word processor and a clipboard with Proof Of Delivery slips, McEvoy keeps a clean desk. The only personal touch anywhere in sight is an Air India calendar blu-tacked to the wall. Stuck up next to it was a large diagrammatic map with the legend: WORLD CARGO CENTRE LONDON HEATHROW.

—All our shipments to points East go through Cargo Village here at Heathrow.

McEvoy stubs a finger on the map. Jim Driver at least looks as if he's listening, but Moon is wandering a few yards off, snooping around the stacks piled on pallets floor to ceiling. In particular, he's sniffing around the boxes containing CDs and videos, but there's nothing he fancies; most of the vids are Bollywood epics in Hindi and there's nothing on DVD at all.

When he realises that McEvoy and Driver are looking at him with when-you're-ready expressions, he ambles over and stares at the map as well.

—Up here is Heathrow, says McEvoy, slapping the wall above the map. Terminals 1,2,3 and down here in the right-hand corner, Terminal 4. Go round there on the southern perimeter road and you drive by the cargo-centre freight terminal.

He wipes a hand across the whole map.

—All of this is what we call Cargo Village, but there are three distinct sections to it.

McEvoy traces a route with his finger: off the perimeter road and up to the first and biggest solid, black block on the map. It's not identified but McEvoy tells them this is the British Airways import/export terminal; they're a law unto themselves and Angel's Wings don't use them.

Below and to the left is a block that is marked 'Southampton House'. This, McEvoy tells them, is where the freight-forwarding agents hang out, mostly Asians, handling stuff coming in from outside London. Angel's Wings don't use them either. They do the business themselves.

—Mostly here, says McEvoy, fingering the centre of the map.

This section has two parallel blocks of buildings, which are labelled and numbered 557 Lufthansa, 558 Air France, 551 JAL, and so forth. The two blocks are separated by a long, oval central reservation, which is marked as a lorry park. The access road is marked with arrows indicating that it's one-way up the right-hand block, round the curved top of the lorry park and one-way down the left-hand block. Technically, it's two roads, Shoreham Road East and Shoreham Road West, but because of its shape the whole area is called The Horseshoe.

Every airline who is anybody other than British Airways has a freight office on The Horseshoe, sometimes subletting space from the bigger players. Delta, Virgin, Nippon Cargo, Air New Zealand, Emirates, Royal Jordanian – they're all there. Most of the cargo sent abroad by Angel's Wings would come here, be booked in and, if the paperwork was in order, off it went. But. There was a but.

—These guys all carry passengers for a living, so they have a limited amount of cargo space, plus they might not fly on the day you want them to, especially if you're talking long-haul to the Far East.

—So what happens then? asks Driver. You just leave your stuff hanging around waiting for a plane?

—You *could*, McEvoy answers slowly. But security's not up to much.

—What? You pulling my pud? Moon wants to know. This is Heathrow innit? Supposed to be tight as a drum.

—Oh yes, very tight, says McEvoy, like he's talking to a kid. *If you're coming in.* All the expensive security precautions are geared to stop nasty people and nasty things arriving here, not leaving.

—So what are your options? asks Driver, knowing that somebody like McEvoy would have several.

—You use The Hub.

Before they can ask, McEvoy explains that The Hub is

in Dubai and is basically a Middle-East version of Cargo Village. There are three planes a day from London to Dubai, regular, so you've got that many times the chance of getting something at least halfway to India or Pakistan than if you tried to get cargo space on a less frequent, long-haul, direct flight. You consign your delivery to an Emirate flight to The Hub and once it gets there, it's sorted and well-looked-after and put on the next short-haul local plane to the subcontinent. The Hub is like a giant left-luggage office for the Far East and it's pretty secure. There's no petty pilfering there. ('I'll bet' says Moon, pulling his right hand up inside his sleeve and waving the slack around.)

—So, if you're shipping Coletoxore to India, you take from here to The Horseshoe and get it on one of the flights to this Hub place, and from there it gets onward transit as and when? Is that it?

McEvoy nods to show that Driver is with him so far, but the policeman still has a few enquiries which the ex-policeman can help him with.

—That's a bit iffy, isn't it, Frank? I mean you're trusting a very valuable consignment to a warehouse in the desert somewhere, aren't you?

McEvoy shrugs the question off. Says it's worked up to now and as long as the paperwork's in order the cargoes get where they're supposed to. He feels it's a damn sight safer than leaving anything not-nailed-down around Heathrow and three deliveries a day to Dubai is a better hit rate than the Post Office in west London. He'd put having something overnight out in The Hub over any so-called secure facility run by the airlines.

Safer than being locked up in a police station, he thinks, but he doesn't go there.

—So that's your best plan is it, Frank? You load up a van, drive down Southall High Street, out to The Horseshoe and stick it on a plane to this thing called The Hub?

—That's about it.

—You've not exactly broken sweat taking security precautions, says Moon nastily.

—Why should we? The van's doing the run two or three times a day, dropping stuff or off picking up stuff that's come in through Customs. Somebody could rob it any day they wanted to, but most days they wouldn't get much worth a robbing.

—Who would know when a Coletoxore shipment was going out? Driver snapped, to show he wasn't going to miss a trick.

—Tyler Pharmaceuticals, obviously. Us, whoever it's going *to* and the Freight Clerks at Emirates, who would check it in and get it on the next plane. They would fax instructions to Dubai for it to be taken into The Hub and shipped on the first local plane out for Bombay or Calcutta, or wherever.

Driver thinks for a minute. There has to be something else.

—Is that your only option?

—No, says McEvoy, that's just one of the options but the most regular. If you knew when you were shipping and if that coincided with a direct long haulflight, and if you knew for sure there was enough space in the cargo hold, then you'd go and stick it on an Air India plane.

—And you'd do that at The Horseshoe?

—No, their office is here.

McEvoy taps the map again, this time a third block of buildings to the left, west of the The Horseshoe complex, further along the Southern Perimeter Road. McEvoy's fingernail traces the route for them.

—You can't get to it from the Horseshoe. You have to go back out on to the perimeter road as if you're leaving Cargo Village and go past Southampton House and The Horseshoe, then turn right on to the access road. That takes you straight into Peace and Harmony.

Driver looks at Moon and then they both look at McEvoy as if he's lost it.

—Run that by us again, Frank.

—You have to come out of The Horseshoe, which is one-

way traffic, obviously. Then back out by the disused police
station and head towards the exit by British Airways...

—No, no, Frank, not the traffic flow, the place. What you
called it.

—What? Peace and Harmony?

—Yes, Frank, that. Why the fuck do you call it that?

McEvoy shrugs his shoulders. It's no sweat off his forehead.

—I'll show you.

Moon drives with Driver up front next to him and McEvoy in
the back, pointing out the sights as they hit the Perimeter
Road heading west.

Moon can't resist glancing up through the windscreen
every time a plane goes over, coming in low, one landing every
ninety seconds. This is not lost on McEvoy.

—What was it we used to say, Jim? Never go on holiday to
a country where they look up when a big silver bird flies over.

Driver grins, feels guilty, then grins again when he realises
Moon hasn't got it.

McEvoy points out the giant British Airways freight terminal and the twin entrances: one for exports, one for imports.
Then the agents' building, Southampton House, and The
Horseshoe, which you can't really see from the perimeter road
but is over there behind the disused police station and the
building site where they're putting up a multi-storey car park.

For a minute, Moon thinks they've gone right by Cargo
Village; missed it entirely. Then McEvoy tells him to take a
right and he sees a slip road running off and down, which is
signed Sandringham Way. He would have missed it if
McEvoy hadn't called it.

The slip road curves around and down and brings them to
a single row of buildings and a lorry park, which is empty. In
fact, the whole place looks deserted. If people worked there,
they've shut up shop. The small complex is in a natural dip in
the ground and the planes queuing above aren't so noticeable
all of a sudden.

—Peace and Harmony, 'cos it's quiet, right? Driver asks, as they climb out of the car.

—'Cos it's a fucking funeral home, says Moon.

McEvoy shakes his head.

—Uh-uh. Work it out.

The two plods look at each other and shrug their shoulders in stereo.

—The signs, says McEvoy. Look who's represented here.

There aren't many signs, only half a dozen, hanging above half a dozen security doors, all with keypad electronic locks and push bells and video cameras. The signs say: AL ITALIA, AER LINGUS, PIA, AIR INDIA, EL AL and MEA. Still they don't get it.

—Look, says McEvoy, pointing at the hoardings and grouping them. You've got Alitalia and Aer Lingus, Air India, Pakistan International and Middle Eastern Airlines, then El Al. Catholics, Hindus, Muslims and Jews as next-door neighbours and they're not fighting each other! Doesn't happen anywhere else in the world. Peace and Harmony.

Moon just shakes his head.

—If it's so bloody wonderful, where is everybody?

—Either at lunch or prayers or both, says McEvoy, without looking at his watch.

—So, it's a right little United Nations in the middle of a cruel world, says Driver, getting on with business. This is where you'd come if you wanted to send a shipment direct?

—Yeah and I'd probably bring it myself, but it doesn't happen that often.

—The boss doesn't like you driving the company van then?

Moon can't resist but McEvoy ignores him.

—The number of direct flights with space to take something as big as a shipment of Coletoxore is minimal. I keep telling you, it's easier to go via The Hub, but you don't have to take my word for it.

McEvoy leads them across to the Air India door and presses a button on the voice box, giving his name and adding 'Angel's Wings'. There's a buzz and a click, then he pushes the door and they follow him into the small front office.

Behind a counter he can only just see over the top of, is a small, dapper Indian, about sixty, wearing a crisp, short-sleeved, white shirt with a company tie clipped to it with a gold, definitely not company-issue, clip. Moon notices these things.

—Mr Kuli, says McEvoy, shaking his hand. These are policemen. Sergeant Moon and Detective Inspector Driver. We used to work together.

—How is your Superintendent these days, Inspector? the old Indian asks politely. I haven't seen him at the Rotary Club for several months.

Now Driver doesn't know if the old boy is bullshitting or not but he can't take any chances.

—Pressure of work, he says. He's a busy man.

—As are we all, says Kuli. So what can I do for you?

McEvoy explains he's showing the plods the ropes when it comes to shipping something direct and long haul to Bombay. Same-day arrangement. Delivered here and on a plane that day, no hanging about. Kuli asks how big a shipment and McEvoy says one unit, insulated, measuring about one metre cubed. Straight away, Kuli asks how heavy and McEvoy says three hundred pounds. In kilos? About one hundred and forty, maybe fifty. Mr Kuli digests this, then says:

—I am assuming this is legal?

McEvoy and the two cops nod together.

—Export licence and transit dockets all in order?

More nods.

—Nothing corrosive or explosive?

Again, they do the three nodding-dogs routine.

Kuli sucks in his top lip, screws up his eyebrows and turns to the computer keyboard on the counter, pecking at a few keys. Moon notices that the computer has a flat-screen monitor, no more than an inch thick. He's not seen one of those on sale yet, just heard about them. Nice bit of gear.

—I could suggest the night flight on the second Sunday in December, says Kuli.

—December? chokes Driver.

—And I can't guarantee *that* unless you check in with me on the morning of the flight. Even then, something that big... We're never sure how much free cargo space there's going to be on a particular flight until take-off. You'd just have to take your chance unless you've made special arrangements with the airline.

—You mean slipped somebody a chunk of notes, right? says Moon.

—Sergeant! snaps Driver but the damage is done and Mr Kuli looks set on going into major sulk mode.

—I doubt I could get something that big on a specific flight at short notice even if I bribed the cargo handlers, drove the fork-lift truck myself and was related to the pilot. Why not ship it through The Hub? It could be in Dubai by tonight and onward shipped within two, three days.

—Told you so, says McEvoy.

As they leave Peace and Harmony, McEvoy hangs back to shake hands with Mr Kuli while Driver and Moon get the car.

—He called me something, says Moon. As we were coming out, he called me something under his breath. Sounded like *sewerkabotcha*. What's it mean?

—You don't want to know, says Driver.

Next day, Tyler Pharmaceuticals, down in the country near Cambridge, gets a call from Driver's Superintendent. Mark Tyler takes it himself and when it's done he snorts in deep breaths through his nose, holds them till it hurts and then lets them out slow through his mouth. Just like the stress counsellor told him to.

Then he puts a call out on the PA system asking for Dr Roma Patel to join him in Sterile Area B3 immediately. Not for the first time, he curses the dickhead who designed the place without proper offices and then he remembers it was him. So he has to make do with the same airlock where he saw Driver and Moon and when the doors go swish there's

Roma Patel and today, under her open white lab coat, she's wearing white jeans with a gold-coloured rope belt low around her waist and a top that stops an inch short, showing a wide smile of brown skin. Not that Tyler has the time to notice or the inclination to do much about it if he did.

—Dr Patel, we must talk.

—Certainly Mr Tyler. Is there a problem?

—I think there is. The police have been in touch again. They want us to go ahead with our shipment to Bombay next week.

—Mumbai, says Roma.

—What?

—Mumbai. It's what they call Bombay these days, Actually, *they* have always called it that.

—Wherever. That's not the point, he says, with a snap in his voice.

—I'm sorry, says Roma sweetly. What is the point?

—They want us to go ahead *knowing there's a robbery being planned.*

—But if they know, they can stop it.

—And you trust them? Jesus. You know what happens if that shipment doesn't get to Bombay when it's supposed to?

—You don't gets paid, she says right out, eyeballing him.

—None of us get paid! And right now, our cash-flow can't stand the strain. This Bombay shipment would have put us over the clinical tests thresholds the Americans have demanded. Then we'd be home free and into big-time production in the States. Not to mention how long it took me to get the Indians to agree to the right price.

—Right…for us?

Tyler gives her the hard-stare treatment.

—You know what those people are like, always wanting things cheaper, wanting to haggle…

—That's the Third World for you, she says, taking the piss but he doesn't notice.

—Even if they stop this planned robbery, our shipment

could be held up for months to be used in evidence or something. We can't give Bombay any excuse not to pay up.

Roma bites her tongue and promises herself she'll stay out
it. She's lost count of the number of rucks she's had with Tyler,
ethics-wise.

—Where exactly are we on the Bombay shipment?

—All done, ready to roll. It's all sealed and in the cold
store. Just waiting for the documentation to come through
from Angel's Wings. They're aiming for next week still, aren't
they?

—As far as I know. I'll have to talk to Naseem.

As he says the name he sees Roma wince and he takes time
off from his own problems to stick a pin in hers.

—You don't get on with Naseem, do you?

—He's a Kashmiri wide-boy with a funny attitude to
women. He thinks they should stay in their place, he won't
employ any and he sleeps with Margaret Thatcher's memoirs
at his bedside.

—I thought he was a man we could do business with,
taunts Tyler.

—Yeah, well, I'll leave that to you. Can I get back to work
now?

Tyler looks through the glass wall into the lab, where
research techs in spacesuits are carefully cracking open vials
of colourless liquid and pouring the contents into a glass
funnel connected to a centrifuge.

—What are you doing now? he asks.

—This is the latest Batch B, the reject consignment.

—What are you doing with it?

—What you told me. We're doing a ten percent sample test
for the database and then we'll seal up the rest and get Angel's
Wings to deliver it to the chemicals disposal point. It seems
such a waste…

The hairs on the back of Tyler's neck stand up.

—You're not trying out your refining technique are you?

—No I'm not, says Roma firmly. But you know it works in
the lab. There's no reason it can't work on a commercial

scale. This batch is only reject because it's 98.9% pure. I *know* I can wash out at least 1% impurity and it's not a difficult process.

Tyler has heard this whinge many times but still it horrifies him.

—For God's sake, that's the problem, don't you see? Complete purity is essential for our premium price and our clinical trials.

—The doctors out in Bombay, they don't regard it as a trial, they're using it for real.

—Under real conditions, says Tyler. And the results data we make them give us as part of the contract is all the more valuable for that.

—I still think...Roma starts.

—That we should provide free health care for the whole planet. Yeah, yeah, yeah. This is a business.

—But it can't be good business to just dump this entire batch, can it?

Roma pushes her fingers through her hair in frustration and wonders if she tore a few handfuls out, maybe Tyler would take more notice of her.

—With my secondary refinement you can ensure 100% purity and have a saleable product again.

—Which we'd have to explain to the government inspectors. You might as well do a paper on it and fax it to our competitors.

Roma shakes her head and most of her hair falls roughly back into place.

—It just seems a shame to throw it away. Such a waste not to do *something* with it.

And for once Tyler doesn't argue with her.

He just continues to look through the glass at the lab technicians working slowly away, and at the insulated cartons stamped with 'Coletoxore' and the word 'Reject' in letters of equal size.

And he just says 'Yes...'

Quietly. To himself. In his head.

The Superintendent who is going to be Officer in Charge, the top Oik of the operation, is being kept waiting and he doesn't like it. He's already been dragged into the frame on this one by having to phone Tyler Pharmaceuticals and persuade its cheeky brat of a boss to put four million quid's worth of his property in the firing line. And the pisser is he doesn't really know why yet, that's why he's waiting for a briefing from Driver. Add to that, he's had to reschedule a Divisional liaison meeting and cancel the Rotary Club again.

So he's not pleased that Driver is a no-show and he sends Moon to go find him.

Moon leaves the briefing room and almost does it backwards, bowing and scraping as he goes, but not quite. Once outside the door, he stands with his back to the wall and counts to a hundred slowly in his head. He knows where Driver is but he daren't let on. Then he thinks why not start without him, maybe earn a few Brownie points from the top brass? It can't do any harm.

So he goes back in holding his mobile like he's just made a call and says to the Oik:

—DI Driver's been called away, sir, but he won't be long. A possible development in the investigation he says. Would it be OK for me to make a start?

The Oik looks at his watch and snaps yes, yes, get on with it.

Driver has already arranged for a large blow-up map of the area to be blu-tacked to one wall of the briefing room. It's actually two or three large photocopies – the size architects use to do plans – taped together, and it covers Southall and Heston and the roads out to Heathrow. There's a red dot stuck on it where Angel's Wings have their warehouse and from there run two lines in blue highlighter and one in red. The red route goes down through Southall Green, Norwood Green and Heston, alongside Osterley Park and then turns west on the A4. The red line joins with the blue lines on the A30 and from Hatton Cross they merge on to the Southern Perimeter, Road marking the boundary of Heathrow.

The wall of the briefing room has a long, metal pointer chained to it and Moon wonders whether it would be pushing it to use it. He decides to go for it and he stabs the map in the red dot like a fencer going for a target.

—Tyler Pharmaceuticals will release a consignment of their drug, Coletoxore, to the Angel's Wings freight company, here, over the weekend. Their job is to get it to here ...

(Stab, parry, thrust with the pointed stick.)

—... Cargo Village in Heathrow, four miles away.

—What's to stop it being hijacked en route to Angel's Wings? asks the Oik, even though it's obvious that Moon hasn't been expecting questions just yet.

—That delivery will be a joint operation with Cambridgeshire Police, sir. Only they and Mark Tyler himself know the actual details. Once the turnip-heads get near the Met area, though, we'll send out a couple of units to guide them in, make sure they don't get lost.

—Turnip-heads, Sergeant?

The Oik looks dubious at this and Moon's not sure how to play it.

—I mean our fellow officers in the Cambridgeshire force, sir.

The Oik purses his lips.

—We used to call them Carrot Crunchers in my day, he says without a trace of a smile. Norfolk were always the Turnip Heads, just as Devon and Cornwall were The Pasties, as in Cornish Pasties.

—And the Welsh were sheep...

—Yes, thank you, Sergeant. Let's not go there. Why don't you carry on? What's the score with the airlines?

—They're in the dark so far and as any leak is likely to come out of Cargo Village, we're going to keep it that way. A consignment like this is usually routed through Emirates Airlines via Dubai and a thing called The Hub. That's like a left-luggage office for stuff...

—I know what The Hub is, Sergeant.

—I didn't, admits Moon, before he can stop himself.

—That's because you're new to this parish, says the Oik, easing himself back in his chair. You'll soon learn that most of the people who live round here know about The Hub. They've either been there or worked there or know somebody who does. For most of them it's closer than Tower Bridge and probably a damn sight easier to get to. We're policing an international community here, Sergeant, with contacts all over the world. Some of them might look as if they've never been further than the end of their street but believe me, most of them have more Air Miles than you've had microwaved dinners. And where the hell is DI Driver?

Moon doesn't know how to react to this and when the Oik nods at him, prompting him to go on, he can't remember where he was.

—I think you were about to show me the favoured routes, says the Oik wearily.

—Yeah, right, sir. The blue lines are possible routes from Angel's Wings to Cargo Village, but the red one is the favourite.

—Why?

—It gives us the most places for setting up Observation Posts, plus the route goes within a hundred yards of Metford Street where we know Big Benny has a pair of lock-up garages. It's a good bet that he'll use them for the vehicles he'll use in the rob. That's why the main OP will be *here*.

He looks to find it on the map, then does a Zorro flourish until the pointer end rests on a spot near Southall High Street.

—Isn't that a mosque? asks the Oik.

—I believe it is, sir.

Moon doesn't know whether it is or it isn't. Where the hell *was* DI Driver?

—We've got permission from the head man there, sir, and it will only be used as a look-out. The heavy mob will be mobile and will shadow the Angel's Wings van from a safe distance.

—Any ideas as to where they'll hit?

—We doubt very much that it will be in Southall itself, sir. The Coletoxore is too big and too heavy to have it away except with a set of wheels and they'd be up against the traffic.

Moon points to the edge of the map and the Cargo Village section.

—We're pretty sure they'll hit here, in Cargo Village itself, on what they call The Horseshoe. This is where we'll have our rapid response units, undercover in the lorry park on this central reservation. They'll be managed and coordinated with the mobile units by a Command Centre here.

The Oik follows the end of Moon's pointer, screwing his eyes into focus.

—That's the old police station, isn't it?

—Yes, sir. We can slip people and equipment in the night before. You won't be able to tell we're in there from the outside.

The Oik gives him a killer look.

—And nobody's going to suspect there are policemen in a police station?

—Not that one, sir, says Moon, knowing it sounds thin.

—Just exactly *where* is DI Driver?

For once, Jim Driver was actually wanting to be where he was supposed to be, in the briefing with Moon and the Oik back at headquarters in Ealing.

Instead, he's sitting in an unmarked Ford in the car park of Heston Service Area, thinking about how he's going to have to invest in a new pine-scented air freshener in the shape of a fir tree to hang from the rear-view mirror. And wondering if he can claim it on expenses from the Snitch Fund petty cash as it's all down to Blind Hugh.

He wouldn't have suggested meeting in the car if he'd known about Blind Hugh's irritable bowel syndrome, and what beggared belief was the fact that Hughie didn't see any connection between that and the fact that he was constantly nibbling on a long, thin, raw, green chilli.

Driver had noticed the chilli-eating habit a couple of months before. Without seeming to know he was doing it,

Hughie's hand would flit to his pocket and emerge with a chilli, which he'd put in the corner of his mouth like a toothpick and then start to munch with small, slicing movements of his teeth. When Driver had mentioned it, Blind Hugh had been suitably surprised, ripped the chilli from his mouth and looked at it as if to say: Who put that there? And he couldn't explain the habit at all. A year ago, he'd never tasted chilli to his knowledge and he certainly wasn't a curry freak; didn't like hot food at all. Used to ask Burger King to take out the onions; thought Marmite was too spicy. But nowadays he found he'd get cravings if he didn't have a chilli or two on hand.

And the irritable bowel syndrome? That was nothing to do with the chilli craving; he always got that when he was nervous. But didn't the chillis make it worse? Hadn't thought about that. Whoops, pardon me Mr Driver, but that really was better out than in.

Driver opens the windows of the Ford – all the windows – and asks why Blind Hugh is so nervous. Nervous enough to demand a crash meeting like this with no notice. It had better be good.

Blind Hugh says he's been down in Brentford and Driver thinks that while that's an unappealing prospect, it doesn't merit a panic attack in the bowel department. Especially not one that reverberates around the car like the muffler's gone on the exhaust. So he hopes Blind Hugh will get on with it and tell him what the fuck is the matter while he can still breathe and before the car's paintwork starts to corrode.

And so Blind Hugh starts off with him getting up that morning and for a minute Driver thinks he's going to find out whether he had Corn Flakes or Frosties, but Hughie does fast-forward it enough to avoid a slap and gets to the bit where he's bringing in the fruit and veg left by the wholesaler as per usual.

He's half expecting to find another mobile phone as he's delivered six to Big Benny by now. In fact, he's quite disappointed if a day goes by without one but he's not disappointed that morning, though it's not as straightforward as usual. For a start, the phone's in a mixed carton of baby cauliflowers and broccoli heads from Murcia (which he reckons is somewhere near Birmingham as he once had a cousin arrested by the West Murcia crime squad), and that's never happened before.

What's also a first is that this phone arrives in a padded jiffy-bag envelope, along with a crisp £20 note and a business card from a mini-cab company in Heston.

At that point, Hugh lets one rip loud enough to be taped and used as a pigeon-scarer over on the runways at Terminal 3. Driver fans the air and lights up a cigarette though he doesn't really want one.

—So what's the problem? he says. What is it that's got your bowels in such a turmoil?

—It was the instructions, Mr Driver, the instructions. Ooops. Pardon me again, Mr Driver.

—Christ almighty, Hughie, put a cork up there will you? I've got better things to do than sit here being farted at.

—Sorry, Mr Driver, but them instructions really spooked me all the way to Brentford and back. I thought the mini-cab driver was going to put me out.

—I wouldn't have blamed him, Hughie, you're giving off more pollution than a diesel engine.

—I can't help it, Mr Driver, it's me nerves.

—I've got nerves too, Hughie, and you're getting on them. Gawd! Give us a break here....

—Sorry. Beg pardon.

—That one was in F minor. You have to get that seen to.

—The doctor says it's the stress.

—Yeah, right. So what's so stressful about taking another mobile to Big Benny? What's Big Benny doing over in Brentford anyway?

—That's my point, Mr Driver, that's why I've got all this stress and all this gas building up inside me. This morning the phone's not for Big Benny. It's for somebody else.

—Who?

Blind Hugh's face contorts and he says 'Pardon' even before the echoes have died away.

—It was for Mortlake Eddy.

—Oh, fuck, says Driver.

—Thought you'd want to know.

On the back of the card from the mini-cab company are Blind Hugh's instructions, which just say: MORTLAKE EDDY, THE WATERMAN, TIBERIUS WAY, 11.45 a.m.

The £20 note is for the cab fare; even Hughie can work that out. He knows who Mortlake Eddy is and he can feel his stomach start to bubble even as he reads the name. It's a fair bet that The Waterman is a pub and that Tiberius Way must be in Brentford because that's where Mortlake Eddy and his crew operate. The mini-cab driver, when he turns up at Hughie's Mum's shop, says he knows it so no worries. Not that he'd go there after dark as it's on the cab company's blacklist since the last time he had to hose down the upholstery. The cabbie notices that Hugh's chewing on a chilli, holding one between his teeth like an old man would use a matchstick as a toothpick. He says that Hugh must have a stomach like iron and Hugh says he wishes he had.

The Waterman is a grotty 1930s pub, which stands alone as the rest of the street has long since fallen down, and which would have had a nice view over the river if it had been built the other way round. The cabby says that if the pub wasn't there you could see across the Thames to Kew and into the Royal Botanic Gardens, but Hugh isn't listening. To the best of his knowledge he's never been south of the river and he doesn't intend to start now. In fact, he's not that keen on getting out of the mini-cab but he has to when his irritable bowel syndrome kicks in and the cabby says 'Was that you? You're ill, mate'.

The mini-cab won't wait for him, which means he has to spend a few minutes getting his bearings so he can leg it roughly in the direction of Brentford station if need be, before he goes into the pub. And if his bowels were about to betray him on the way there, they were screaming quisling, willing to tell anyone that Anne Frank was in the attic, when he looked around The Waterman.

Not that the pub was anything out of the rut, being a bog-standard Sixties remix of fake beams and horse brasses, which hadn't had a lick of paint since. It had all the traditional lagers on draught, just like every other pub in London, and two taps of Guinness: one cold, one bollock-freezing. Blind Hugh goes for a pint of Foster's as it's quicker and a woman older than his mother tops it with lemonade without even asking him, probably just to make him feel at home.

It's just after half-eleven in the morning and the pub is empty except for four guys hovering over the pool table, leaning on cues, pulling on Becks straight from the bottle. One's black, one's Asian and the other two are white. Blind Hugh knows them all by sight. Two of them he went to school with.

Including Eddy.

Eddy has his hair cut short, regulation Number One, and died a screaming blond so you could pick him out in a line-up in a cellar, and he wears a clean white T-shirt to show off the fact that he works out regular. He's lining up a shot on the pool table when he catches Hughie's eye, just to let him know he's clocked him. Blind Hugh knows better than to approach him until he's finished his shot. He's just praying that his bowels don't burst into a bass riff and put Eddy off his stroke.

The shot taken, Eddy straightens up.

—Hughie, my son, he says loudly. What brings you to this neck of the woods?

—Got a package for you, Eddy, says Hugh, holding out the jiffy bag with the phone in it.

This is the moment of maximum danger for Hugh and he knows it. Mortlake Eddy has a reputation for not taking too kindly to people who have been known to deal with the police and, whilst Blind Hugh has never knowingly got in Eddy's face or done the double on him, there is a principle involved here. In fact, on most things, Mortlake Eddy's attitude is far

less liberal than Big Benny's and in general, his crew is unsubtle and even a touch crude in comparison with the Southall
homeboys.

Eddy looks in the jiffy bag and then looks at Hugh and
says he's got one. A phone that is, and if he was looking, why
would he look at such cheap rubbish instead of a decent one
with call-back and memory and voice mail? And just how
many of them has Hugh got to unload on some unsuspecting
sucker, not that (he hopes) Hugh sees such a sucker in front of
him right now this minute.

So Hugh has to go into grovel mode and say that Eddy's
got the wrong end of the stick and he's not trying to sell him
the phone, he's just delivering a message. And the message is
the phone. Or rather, the message will be on the phone in
about five minutes' time and all Eddy has to do is turn the
thing on and wait and it'll ring.

And when Eddy asks how Hugh knows this, Hugh says
there's a card in there with his instructions on, which is to say
he's only doing what he's been told and doing it pronto,
coming straight down to Brentford as soon as he'd found the
phone amongst the baby cauliflowers and broccoli heads.

Up to that point, Mortlake Eddy's been laughing along
like a good 'un, dead friendly. But now that Hugh's brought
baby cauliflowers and broccoli heads into the conversation,
he's in danger of turning ugly. It's a good job Hugh's left his
lager on the bar because there would have been no way he
could have drunk it with the thick end of a pool cue across his
throat like that.

There's less than four minutes to go now to the appointed
time when the mobile will ring, if Mortlake Eddy decides to
turn it on, that is. But that's plenty of time for Blind Hugh to
tell Eddy all about the phones he's been receiving in various
batches of fruit and veg for over a week now, all marked up for
Big Benny's attention over in Southall. Not that he knows
what's ever said on them, although Benny's been in a good
mood since he started his One-to-Ones, as he calls them. Hugh
just delivers them. And that's what he's doing right now.

Mortlake Eddy takes the cue away from his throat. It's such a daft story he believes it because he knows Hugh couldn't make up anything like that. Plus the fact that Hugh's started to give off a pretty ripe smell, which is another good reason for standing back from him and looking at the phone and the card and the jiffy bag one more time.

As if by magic, when he does press the On button, the phone chirps into life immediately, playing the first six bars of *When I'm Calling You Oo-Oo-Ooo*, though it's not a tune Eddy's familiar with.

—Who the fuck is this? he shouts into the phone.

Whatever the answer he gets, though, he keeps listening. And then he starts talking too and gradually gets his buttocks comfortable on the edge of the pool table, getting himself settled, hearing stuff he likes the sound of.

But of course Blind Hugh can only report one side of the conversation, and even then only the bits he can remember as he's still got three of Mortlake Eddy's crew giving him the evil eye and likely to make him swallow a pool cue if they're given the nod. From the corner of his eye he sees the kindly old lady behind the bar take his lager top and pour it away down the sink, which isn't a good sign. So he concentrates on keeping his sphincter muscles in check and listens.

—Yeah, yeah, I got that part, Eddy says, phone to his ear looking at Hughie.

—I understand you've been sending lots of messages to an associate of mine over in Little India.

—Yeah.

—Uh-huh.

—I wouldn't say competitors exactly.

—Yeah.

—I'm interested. You're paying for the call.

—Yeah, I know it.

—What's that when it's at home?

—Nice. Very tasty.

—'Course I remember it. Had a good laugh about it.

—You're kidding.

—You reckon?

—Yeah, well, it's do-able.

—So when do we have a meet?

—Not sure I'm comfortable with that. I like to put faces to voices.

—Okay, okay, keep your rag on. I can do that.

—Fair enough. I'll do a drive-by today, see if it squares up, then I'll let you know. How do I let you know?

—If you insist. It's your phone bill.

—I don't mind using Blind Hughie here at all. I think he knows how the land lies.

(And here Hughie nods vigorously, not a clue as to what he's agreeing to.)

—He knows Benny's the forgiving type and he knows I'm not. So it's best that he doesn't mention he's been to see me. We agreed on this?

(Blind Hugh nods slowly in agreement whether Eddy's talking to him or not.)

—Right then. Be hearing from you.

Driver can't believe that that was that. Mortlake Eddy switching off the phone and tossing it casually on to the pool table and telling Hugh to piss off out of it. That was it?

Blind Hugh's adamant that's the way it happened and he wasn't going to hang around, was he? Not with Eddy joking with his crew like that.

Joking? Driver's ears prick up. About what?

And when Blind Hugh tells him, he starts the car and poor Hughie is told to piss off out of it for the second time in an hour. (Which is by no means a record.)

Driver hammers the car back to headquarters, all the windows open to get rid of the smell, Blind Hugh's irritable bowels having excelled themselves when he saw Driver's reaction to what Eddy had said.

And Driver's bowels might be coming out in sympathy as he power-walks his way down the corridors to the briefing

room, hoping that the Oik is still there and that Moon hasn't
bored him to death.

—Ah, Inspector Driver. Nice of you to join us.

The Oik is awake after all.

—I'm sorry, sir, but there's been a development.

—A positive one I hope?

—I really don't think so, sir. It's our mystery voice who
keeps sending Big Benny mobile phones.

—Oh yes, our very own Deep Throat. So what's new?
Another phone?

—Yes. Another phone this morning, but not to Benny.
This one was addressed to Mortlake Eddy.

Moon is about to ask who the bloody hell Mortlake Eddy
is but decides not to when he sees the colour the Oik is going
in the face.

—Big Benny and Mortlake Eddy working together?
That'd be a first, says the Oik, but not sounding as if he's sure
of his facts.

—Not together, sir. From what my informant managed to
overhear, Eddy's been told about Big Benny's part in all this,
but not the other way round.

—So our man with mobile phones is – what? Playing one
off against the other? Putting the job out to tender, subcon-
tracting for the lowest bid?

—I think somebody's planning to do the double, says
Driver.

—What, double-cross Benny? Where's the harm in that?
Moon says with a laugh, not understanding why they're
getting all tight-arsed about it.

—No, Sergeant, says the Oik patiently, reaching for a chair.
We're talking about doing a double, not a double-cross. Big
Benny gets to do his hijack and we nick him. Then Mortlake
Eddy re-steals the loot. In this case, the pharmaceuticals.

Moon is having trouble following this and he gets no help
from Driver, who looks like he's agreeing with every word the
Oik says. In fact, he seems glad the Oik's the one saying them
so he doesn't have to.

—Re-steal? Who from? Moon tries.

—From us, says the Oik. Are you sure about this, Jim? Do you have anything to back it up, anything at all?

—Only what Mortlake Eddy was heard to say to his crew after he'd had his One-to-One with our mobile phone man.

—Which was what?

—He said: 'Anybody know where we can pick up a JCB digger for Monday?'

The Oik goes ashen and has to sit down.

—He said *what*? asks Moon, still out of the loop.

—He asked his crew if they could lay their hands on a JCB digger, Driver repeats, with an edge in his voice.

—And this means something?

The Oik groans loudly.

—Oh, my sainted bollocks. It means they're going to do it again, aren't they?

Part III:

Cargo Village People

HASAN SHARIF IS the sort of guy who is faze-proof, laid-back, unflappable. But not cool. He wouldn't know cool if it bit him. Respectable, businesslike, responsible, conscientious. These are better words to describe Hasan, or so he thinks. His teenage sons prefer boring, gruesome, naff and dead, but then they've gone off to form the first Lebanese rap band rather than go to college, and haven't talked to their dad for two years. On the upside, neither has his wife, who has moved out to become the kids' manager.

If only they could see him now. His office at Emirates Airlines is the nerve-centre of intelligence gathering on major criminal activity and the police are there, seeking his advice. Or, to be more accurate, watching his video tapes.

Being the sort of bloke he is, Hasan is one of the few – the very few – who keep their closed-circuit security camera tapes for a month without wiping them. He makes sure they're on Long Play so he gets six hours' worth out of a three-hour tape, four tapes per day, allow 31 days per month so that's 124 tapes, all labelled, dated and ticked with a tick in red ink if Hasan was on duty at the time. He sometimes wondered if he should at least fast-forward through the tapes made when he was not there but, apart from the fact that there were not enough hours in the day to do that, his responsibilities had to end somewhere. The *Not on my shift* line from *Apollo 13* had made a great impression on him. That was all he could do, but he would do it well.

—Where are we now? asks McEvoy, as Hasan inserts another tape into the VCR.

—Yesterday morning. Eleven forty-three or thereabouts.

McEvoy knows there's no 'thereabouts' about it with Hasan, and the timer on the tape shows 11:43.

—There, says Hasan pointing at the screen. The Ford convertible.

The car they're looking at is a soft-top Escort GTI, about five years old. A bit of a girlie car for this area, known as a Tartcart if driven by a woman under fifty. They get to see it in shot for no more than seven seconds and it would have been less had it not been slowing as it went round the bend at the top of The Horseshoe, outside the Emirates offices.

Moon tries not to look too interested, pretends there's something more interesting to look at out in the lorry park on the central reservation of The Horseshoe.

—Do you normally ring Mr McEvoy when you see the same car twice, Mr Sherrif?

—Five times in three days and actually two different cars, says Hasan. I have the other tapes here.

—And actually, Sergeant, it's Mr Sharif, says McEvoy.

—But Mr McEvoy's just a customer of yours. Isn't that right? Moon persists, looking to get a rise out of one of them.

—A customer, yes, but I know he used to be a policeman and he telephoned me. It was as we were talking that I mentioned this car and he said he thought you might be interested.

—Again, please, Hasan, says McEvoy.

Hasan rewinds the tape and McEvoy moves in to take control of the Pause button. He gets a blurry, monochrome image and prods the Frame Advance until the camera gets the car squarely in focus. Or as much in focus as CCTV cameras ever can be. Every copper in the Met knew full well that you could get a better picture from a crashed Mars probe than you could from the CCTV at Brent Cross shopping centre.

—There you are, McEvoy says to Moon, and he stands back so that Moon can get a clear view of the TV screen.

—Yeah, I think I can get an index number off those plates, says Moon, dead casual. See if the car's stolen.

Hasan stands impassive, looks at his fingernails, checks they're clean. Keeps quiet, sensing that the policeman and the ex-policeman have got their own agenda here.

—I don't believe it, says McEvoy, like he genuinely can't. You're worried about the car being nicked?

—It's a start, says Moon defensively. We track the car and find the owners.

—But look, for Christ's sake, McEvoy says, his voice rising. That's Rafik Jarman driving, with Ash the Cash sitting next to him. It's odds-on easy money that the blob in the back is Big Benny.

Moon leans in and makes a play of squinting at the screen.

—You sure?

—Well, I could I.D. them from this.

—I think I'll run the number plate through the PNC just to be sure. Then we'll take it from there.

—And all you'll find is that the Ford is owned by one of Rafik's aunties and he's test-driving it for her after an oil change or something.

—So what do we charge them with, driving away with aunty's permission?

Moon straightens up, wanting to see how McEvoy reacts when he says:

—Didn't you charge them with that when you were in the Job? from what I hear, you tried to charge 'em with most everything else.

McEvoy takes it well enough, which in this case means he

grinds his teeth and doesn't push his fist into Moon's, spoiling that fat, smug grin.

—Did the car stop, Mr Sheriff? Moon asks calmly, like nothing's happened.

—Sharif, says McEvoy but it's under his breath.

—No, not on any occasion, says Hasan correctly.

—Did the occupants attempt to get out? and Moon says it so politely he must be being rude.

—That would have been difficult as the car did not stop, Sergeant.

You can see Moon thinking that he doesn't get paid enough to take stick from a lippy wop, but he reckons he's still got the upper hand.

—So you just happened to be watching out for suspicious vehicles, is that it?

Hasan sighs, which for him is so close to showing disrespect that if he doesn't reign himself in, the next thing he'll be doing is pissing on Moon's mother's grave.

—We notice cars, Sergeant. Most deliveries come to Cargo Village in trucks or vans. Cars are a bit unusual, especially when they appear more than once, driving slowly, obviously checking the place out.

—So they looked suspicious, did they? You don't recognise any of them, do you?

McEvoy shakes his head, not believing Moon's technique and wondering what the modern police force is coming to. He never behaved like this, did he? Picking on witnesses and such like?

—No, I don't know the men in the car, Sergeant, says Hasan, nice and polite.

—But you said they used two different cars, so something must have rung a bell with you.

You'd have thought Moon had just won at Cluedo the way he was leering, thinking he was on to something.

—No, Sergeant, I said there were two different cars meaning two different sets of people. This car went round The Horseshoe three times, at different times, over two days.

The other one went round twice, once. That is to say it went round and then round again.

—Okay, okay, I get that bit. And you just noticed it because it was a car, right? Not a lorry.

—That and the fact that it was being followed by a mechanical digger.

—A what? says Moon, only a microsecond before McEvoy can.

—A motorised digger, a JCB. They were quite clearly in convoy. They came round, turned left at the end by the disused police station, then came round again for another look. It's quite clear. I have it on another tape. Would you like to see?

So Moon and McEvoy stand there and watch another tape, not saying anything in front of Hasan Sharif. Moon wouldn't give him the pleasure of knowing that what's on the tape is the business, whilst McEvoy doesn't want to spook him, because they've both recognised who is on the flickering video.

The car they're using, though it's hard to credit it, is a Volvo. One of the newer models, which doesn't look so much like a box and has a bit of oomf in its acceleration.

The Volvo comes up Shoreham Road East, rounds the bend of The Horseshoe near the Emirates office and then slides out of shot down Shoreham Road West. Then it comes back again and so slowly it's like they're wanting to be filmed by the CCTV. Or maybe somebody's told them that no one ever monitors the cameras, or maybe that the cameras don't work at all and are just there for appearances and to keep the insurance companies happy. On the second tour, the driver of the Volvo even puts the window down so he can get a better look, and Moon and McEvoy have no trouble identifying him.

But it's not just the fact that the Volvo is going so slow it could give kerb-crawling a bad name, it's the fact that the car is clearly riding in convoy with a big, yellow JCB digger. The

Volvo even waits at one point for the JCB to catch up, the driver of the car waving out of his window to tell the digger driver to get a move on.

They watch the tape twice and Moon asks if he can take it away and Hasan of course says yes, anything to oblige. McEvoy is the one who says thanks.

It's not until they're outside, crossing the lorry park in the middle of The Horseshoe, that the ruck starts.

—That was Mortlake Eddy driving that Volvo, wasn't it? McEvoy kicks off.

—Was it? says Moon as if he cared.

—You clocked him as well as I did. What the fuck's going on?

—It's possible there's a new development in our intelligence gathering operation, but I'm not authorised to brief you on it.

Moon is striding away between two parked-up container lorries. Not that there's anybody around but McEvoy realises that they are out of sight of any of the CCTV cameras. He grabs Moon's arm.

—Then *get* authorised if you want my help.

—Your help? Why do I need that? And don't put your hands on me, old man.

McEvoy lets go of Moon's sleeve. It's only fair. McEvoy knows that when he was in the Job he would have had the old extendible baton (the copper's inflexible friend) out and waving if someone had done that to him.

—Look, Moon, I've got a stake in this whether you like it or not. You're asking Angel's Wings to play along, knowing that a crime is likely to be committed. I'm supposed to be responsible for security…

—Yeah right, heavy duty you've drawn there, Frank.

—You got an Off button on that mouth of yours?

—Whassamatter, Frank? You used to dish it out but you can't take it, can you? Bet you miss that.

McEvoy loses it and lunges at Moon, pushing him back up

against the side of one of the container lorries. But Moon is younger and fitter and half-expecting it so he bats away McEvoy's grip and shoots a hand into McEvoy's crutch, grabbing McEvoy's crown jewels and causing serious discomfort in the trouser department.

The lower grasp gives Moon the upper hand and he forces McEvoy backwards on tiptoes until he slams into the side of the container lorry behind him. He's taken a couple of swings, which have bounced off Moon's shoulders, but his eyes are watering so bad he can hardly see. Like all schoolyard fights, it's over dead quick and there's no blood.

—I told you not to touch me, old man, says Moon, putting stress on the 'old'.

McEvoy gets his breath back as best he can. He finds clutching his groin and bending over like he's lost a contact lens is the most comfortable position.

—Yeah, you did, wheezes McEvoy. Don't worry, you won't have to tell me twice.

Moon laughs at that while he's straightening his tie where McEvoy swung on it.

—I'm not worried, old man.

Moon goes into a crouch so he can clock the bent-double McEvoy face to face.

—I *could* make allowances, you know, since you were in the Job. I *could* fill you in and the Brass wouldn't really mind. But I'm not going to. Want to know why, *ex*-Chief Inspector?

—No, but you're gonna tell me.

—Too right I am and somebody should have done it sooner. You're too close to them, old man. That's your trouble.

Moon has his face right up close now, *in* McEvoy's face.

—Them? is all McEvoy can think to say, his groin still on fire.

—Them. The wops and the wogs and the towel-heads who run this place. All your bloody pals – rejects from *Jewel in the Crown*.

McEvoy tries to catch his breath.

—You are sad and sick, he manages to say.

—Least I haven't gone bleedin' native.

—What?

—You heard, or have your ears started to go, old man? You know what they used to call you down Dogberry Road? 'Kipling', that's what, 'cos you don't know there isn't an Empire any more.

—I'm Irish, for Christ's sake.

—Yeah, well, more bloody immigrants.

McEvoy is almost upright by now.

—You're not sick, you just make me sick. Why don't you just fuck off back to Jim Driver and tell him how you spotted Mortlake Eddy on those tapes. That's your style, isn't it?

—I think I'll do just that, Frank. You'll find your own way back, will you? Good. Didn't fancy the smell of curry stinking out the car anyway. See you around, eh?

Moon strides off towards his car as McEvoy is happy just to discover his legs work.

Moon has the key in the lock when McEvoy yells after him like he's just twigged something.

—Oi! Mortlake Eddy and the JCB. You're setting up another Dogberry Road stake-out, aren't you?

—If we are, we won't be using talcum powder this time, Moon shouts back.

As Moon gets in his car, a jet comes in overhead and so he probably doesn't hear McEvoy shout:

—You son of a pig!

Tyler Pharmaceuticals doesn't work Saturdays normally. Mark Tyler dreams of the day when he has to introduce three-shift, seven-day working but then he thinks that if things are going so well, that'd be just the time to take the money and piss off to find a place in the sun, enjoy what was left of life.

Not for him a mission to heal. Bugger that. Leave that to the likes of Roma Patel and her PhD, which might outshine his own poxy degree in chemistry but he was the one with the business nous. He was the one who knew how to chat up the banks; raise the development funding; set up the company; pay himself in share options; focus the research on where the marketplace was going; exploit the high-tech, kinda cool image to attract the best talent – young, enthusiastic and without a clue as to how valuable their work was. Not an inkling as to how rich they were going to make him.

Were going to, though; it hadn't happened yet but it was close. And the India deals were a vital part of the grand master plan.

Tyler knows that in his business it's suicide to go head-to-head with the big multinationals based here or in the States. So he's kept his head relatively down and looked abroad until he finds hospitals and clinics who will not only pay his premium price but, as part of the deal, will keep detailed records of clinical results for him and to hell with patient confidentiality or conflict of interest with a commercial supplier. After all, Tyler only wants results he can use. Positive ones, mounting up to a nice bank account of medical credit that will make Coletoxore and Tyler Pharmaceuticals all that more tasty a target when it comes to selling out to the big boys.

And the hospitals out in India doing all Tyler's legwork for him, saving him millions in clinical trials? Well, they're hooked now, aren't they? These may not be drugs as we know and love them, available on most street corners from your friendly dealer, but the effect is much the same. From the first (free) samples they tried out, they started to get results. No miracle cures, but significant signs that they could punch their weight against the Big C. Naturally, word gets round and more and more punters want the treatment. They've got their jobs to think of – and maybe one or two of them actually like curing people – so they've got to keep on getting supplies, whatever the cost and whatever else they have to do for Tyler.

Tyler the dealer, big time and legal. Only difference: he doesn't have to see his customers. Which suits him better than Hugo Boss.

—You know how much this consignment is worth to me, Mr Naseem?

Naseem looks at Tyler, not sure if he's talking cash money, international reputation, the future of medical science or some sort of heart-breaking sentimental attachment. He decides it's probably not the last one.

—Of course, Mr Tyler, he says. We will take every precaution and as you see, I'm taking delivery personally. No one else knows I'm here today.

—That's something, I suppose. A robbery wouldn't do Angel's Wings' reputation much good, would it?

—They're not generally good for customer confidence, says Naseem.

—No, they're not. That's why *we* are not going to let it happen.

And by 'we', Naseem presumes, he includes Dr Roma Patel who is also on site, bright and early, that Saturday morning.

Considering it's not yet eight o'clock and she was only woken up twenty minutes before by Tyler's charm-school alarm call, basically telling her to get her pretty little PhD arse down to the laboratory or else, she's made an effort. Her hair is brushed back and held in a pony tail by a gold fabric hair band, and when she unzips her leather jacket she's wearing a red silk shirt, tied under her lift-but-don't-separate bra, which provides a six-inch deep zone of naked brown flesh, disappearing into white Levi jeans that she wears without a belt like they've been sprayed on, and which themselves disappear into black leather cowboy boots with three-inch heels and hand-tooled circles of gold ornament.

The cops from the Cambridgeshire branch of Law and Disorder PLC, who are hanging around the front entrance to Tyler Pharmaceuticals, they've certainly noticed her. One of them has a crick in his neck from following that PhD arse as it tick-tocked up the driveway. Once she's out of earshot, one of the uniforms airs the thought that he wouldn't mind strip-searching that particular suspect. His mate says they're there to do some driving, not a drugs bust and anyway, they're not that sort of drugs. And the first one says, who said anything about looking for drugs?

Roma Patel can feel their eyes on her as she approaches the lab doors and flourishes her swipe card in the lock to make them hiss open. She can see Tyler and that preening Kashmiri from Angel's Wings, Naseem, through the glass walls, waiting for her by Area C, the cold-storage facility. Naseem makes a point of looking at his watch as if he's timing her. In her mind, he's cruising for a bruising or at least a severe tongue-lashing.

She goes through two more sets of sliding doors to get to them and when she does, Tyler says:

—Roma, thanks for coming in.

Like she had a choice.

—Sorry this is such an ungodly hour, Naseem says with a fake smile that wouldn't fool a blind nun.

—Depends on your god, says Roma icily.

—Can we recap and bring ourselves up to speed, please?

Tyler sounds like he's chairman of the board – which he is, passing some amendment at the annual general meeting – except there are only the three of them and they're standing in a glass-sided corridor.

—Roma, you go first.

Roma Patel makes no secret of the fact that she doesn't approve of what she's had to do. She sticks to the facts more or less, but her voice goes through two octaves of sarcasm and ends on a B-flat sneer.

Yes, the main consignment of Coletoxore for Bombay is ready and packed in its protective cube. The manifest and export licence are all in order and the batch is marked PQ on the paperwork and on the insulated carrying box. PQ for Passed Quality.

And yes, she's also prepared a consignment from Batch B serum, which averaged 98.9% purity, and she's prepared all the paperwork with an identifying code letter R for Reject, which she's also stencilled on the packing cube. The batch numbers on the cubes are the same so only the R or the PQ distinguish the two consignments on the outside of the containers.

That's her part of the agenda, though she expects they'll also want her to drive the forking truck to help load them into Naseem's Transit van.

Tyler's sure she meant to say *forklift* truck, the small electric one they keep for ferrying stuff around the labs.

—Good, well done that girl. Now, Mr Naseem. Have you done your part?

—To the letter, says Naseem sweetly, and Roma's nose wrinkles like she's found a bad smell.

Of course, it hasn't been easy for him and he has handled the matter personally, despite having the police crawling all over the Angel's Wings' offices all week. But as far as they are concerned, the Coletoxore will be delivered to Emirates Airlines on Monday in plenty of time to be processed and freighted on the 22.00 hours flight to Dubai. The chief shipping clerk there, Hasan Sharif, assures him that onward shipment to Bombay from The Hub will be within twenty-four hours.

Is he sure of this? As sure as he can be of anything. Hasan Sharif and The Hub have never let them down before. The fall-back plan , though, is a bit iffier but that's down to circumstances and not to any shortage of effort on his part.

Kuli Khan, the top man at Air India, couldn't have been more helpful even though he'd already had a run-in with one of the investigating policemen, the one called Moon. (Tyler thinks: Ah, yes, the bright young one.) Funnily enough, that works in Angel's Wings' favour as Kuli Khan is sure something's going on, and while he's not sure what, he's convinced that the police can't handle it.

Naseem tells how, once he'd explained their predicament, Kuli couldn't do enough to help, getting on the phone right away and calling in favours in two languages and four dialects. And he sorts it. Somehow Kuli manages to book enough space for a container of Coletoxore in the cargo hold of Monday's 20.30 long-haul, overnight flight, direct to

Bombay. The booking may not be platinum firm, as things above and beyond Kuli's control can always happen at the last minute, but Naseem would rate it as solid gold.

—Did money change hands? Tyler asks and he's halfway to his wallet as he says it.

—No, says Naseem through his teeth.

He's a bit put out at the suggestion and Roma Patel can't help but smirk at his wounded pride.

—So he's a relative of yours is he, this Kuli Khan?

Naseem is tempted to reply that while Kuli Khan's ancestors may well come from the northern Punjab, all his immediate family hails from Ruislip. But he lets it go.

—No, he's not. He's doing this as a favour.

—In the hope of more of your business, eh? Tyler persists.

—Perhaps.

—It's the Code of the East, Mark, says Roma. You know, the cowboys had the Code of the West, the Asian businessman has the Code of the East. A man's gotta do what a man thinks he's gotta do and all that. Don't ask. Just go with the flow.

—Well, then. Fine.

Tyler risks a smile, then looks out through the glass doors to check that the police escort is still there.

—Then let's get this show on the road, he says. Roma, would you mind winding up the fork-lift so we can start loading?

Roma gives him the look which says I-knew-it but she stomps off nevertheless. This gives Tyler and Naseem the chance to share one of those thought-she'd-never-go moments and means they can get down to business.

—You know what to do, says Tyler, and it's not a question.

Naseem goes through by rote because Tyler's not going to sleep easy if he doesn't show he's memorised things.

—The consignment marked R for Reject is the one we send to The Horseshoe as if it's going to Dubai and The Hub. We follow police instructions all the way, play it however they want us to play it. If anything happens to it en route and there is a chance of any sort of delay, then I take the real PQ consignment direct to Kuli Khan at Air India. He's based on the third-spur development of Cargo Village, so I can avoid The Horseshoe entirely.

Tyler nods, satisfied.

—And if nothing happens?

—Then I call Hasan Sharif at Emirates, leaving it as late as I can, and say there's been a mix-up, get the PQ shipment down to him and swap over.

—Will the real consignment be secure during Monday?

—It seems the police are turning Angel's Wings into some sort of command post. I've never felt so secure.

Tyler nods again and mutters 'good, good'. Very satisfied.

They can see, though they can't hear, through the glass that Roma Patel is manoeuvring an electric fork-lift towards Naseem's Transit. One of Cambridgeshire's finest even opens the rear doors for her, chatting away to her as she carefully places the first metre-cubed block of Coletoxore into the back of the van. Then she reverses expertly about a metre or so, raises the forks slightly and advances to gently push the consignment further back to make room for the second block. By now, two more cops have sauntered over from their cars and are copping a look, chatting her up. She could be loading raw opium for all they seemed to care.

—Can I say something, Mr Tyler? Naseem starts, as if something's been bothering him.

—What?

Tyler's still watching the cops drooling over Roma and he can't, for the life of him, see what they see in her.

—Why make things more complicated than they are? Why not let both consignments go? It's not often we can get on a direct flight at this notice, so why not use both airlines and then one is bound to get through on time, whatever happens.

Tyler suddenly has his attention back on business, full whack.

—My customers expect exactly what they've ordered and that's what they'll get. End of story.

After all, there is no way Tyler wants the doctors out in Bombay to discover that his consignment R for Reject is just as effective as his 100% pure, which attracts the premium price. Plus, though it's no business of Naseem's, cash-flow being what it is Tyler has cut a small corner by insuring only one consignment, and he has no intention of paying two sets of freight charges when he can get away with one.

—If the police want to play silly buggers with my company's future, just make sure they use the reject version.

Naseem doesn't look completely convinced.

—Don't let it prey on your mind, Tyler reassures him. We're just taking precautions. We're not the ones doing anything illegal.

When Naseem has driven off in the Transit, a police car to the front and a police car to the rear, Tyler and Roma Patel use their swipe-card keys to lock up and set the alarms.

—He's a good man, that Naseem, says Tyler. Knows which side his bread is buttered on.

—Doubt it, says Roma. He probably has some women buttering it for him.

—You don't have to like somebody to do business with them, Roma.

—No you don't, she says. But it can help.

Up in Southall, you know it's a Saturday because there are less vans and trucks clogging the High Street and the newsagents all have backache from the weight of the Saturday papers, but those are about the only differences. The planes still circle overhead like vultures, another Friday-night can of Special Brew slips under the surface of the Grand Union Canal and the shops start to open.

Blind Hugh is opening up his Mother's shop as per usual, thinking that with a bit of luck he can have the day to himself. Not that he's got any big plans, but it would be nice not to be at the beck and call of the likes of Big Benny and the much scarier Mortlake Eddy. Surely they'll have other things to do.

Saturdays were for drinking, horse racing and football; nothing else. Weren't they?

Not for Frank McEvoy. He's already up and about and what's worrying for Blind Hugh is that he's up and about in Blind Hugh's Mum's shop. In fact, he's standing behind the door as Hugh comes in from the back carrying a tray of Spanish clementines (which look just like tangerines to him). And the reason he seems to be standing there is solely so that he can give Hugh a heart attack and drop him dead in his tracks from fright.

—Right, you little shagger!

This is the first Hugh hears that he's got a visitor, and it's the last thing he hears for a couple of minutes as McEvoy, standing right behind him, smacks his hands as hard as he can around Hugh's ears. Hughie squeals like a stuck pig and drops the box he's carrying so he can put his hands up to the sides of his head, and when McEvoy's boot connects with his backside, he staggers across the shop, slipping and sliding and squashing clementines underfoot as he goes.

The next thing he knows, the fronts of his thighs have made contact with the main display table of fresh fruit and veg, bringing him up short and giving him a third source of pain. But he hasn't even got the chance to count to three before he feels McEvoy's grip on the back of his neck and suddenly the ground is rushing up to meet his face.

Well, that's what it feels like, but it's not the floor of the shop he has to worry about, it's a display of mixed sweet peppers; red, yellow and green and mercifully soft. As his face sinks into them he's just grateful that they're peppers because the next display section is yams and sweet potatoes and long, thick, white mooli radishes, some as long as his arm; all hard and knobbly. If you had to head-butt an international display of exotic fruits and vegetables, then Hugh reckons that a faceful of sweet peppers is something of a result given the other options.

—Now just what the bloody hell is going on? McEvoy shouts.

He lets Hugh put his head up but he doesn't relax the grip

on the back of his neck, keeping him bent over the display table.

—Mr McEvoy? Haven't seen you for ages. Where've you been?

Even Hughie, spitting out capsicum seeds and shards of green-pepper flesh, realises that this is probably not the brightest of things he could have said. And it seems that McEvoy is of like mind.

—Come on, Hughie, don't go *baywakoof* on me, he shouts, ramming Hugh's head back into the peppers.

—It's honest innit, Mr McEvoy. I don't know what you're talking about.

—Been doin' a bit of business lately? Police business?

—Hey, I didn't know the force was still with you, Mr McEvoy.

That gets him another faceful for his trouble.

—Don't, do not, get cheeky with me, Hughie. I hear you've got a taste for chilli these days. I think that's maybe down to me. Remember when I introduced you to delights of the *Scotch Bonnet,* do you? Well, maybe you need to sample some more of your own produce.

McEvoy's eye has been caught by the next tray of vegetables and, in particular, a mooli about ten inches long, thick as a wrist at its base end and tapering to a pencil point. He can't resist grabbing it and waving in Hugh's face.

—Ever tried mooli, Hugh? Sliced up thin you can't beat it in salads. Puts those bits of radish you get in prawn cocktails in the shade. This is the business and it also comes in useful as a draught excluder and can knock a nail into plaster if you want to hang a picture and you're caught short without a hammer.

Blind Hugh's not taking any of this in, he's just hypnotised by the thin end of the mooli McEvoy is tickling his nose with.

—And the other thing about mooli, McEvoy is saying, is that it can be extremely painful when inserted, no, let's say *pushed* or even *rammed*, up a person's nose. Somebody threatened me with that and I'd tell them anything they wanted to know. Stands to reason. I mean, a person couldn't really *breathe* with one of these up their left nostril. Might have to go to hospital to have it removed.

There's a short, sharp scream at this point, but it doesn't come from Hughie. McEvoy whips his head round to see Blind Hugh's Mum standing in the doorway to the back of the shop, a hand clamped to her own mouth, her eyes on stalks.

McEvoy realises how bad it must look. The floor's covered with squashed clementines and Hugh, with one foot through the crushed box, is bent over double, his head in a pile of green, yellow and red sweet peppers, his arse sticking up in the air. And there's McEvoy right behind him, brandishing a vegetable phallus in a less-than-friendly way.

—Morning Mrs Ramachandra, says McEvoy, relaxing his grip on the mooli so it drops back into the display. Hugh's had a bit of an accident, I'm afraid.

Hugh's Mum takes in the situation, assesses the implications, tries to remember the retail price of clementines.

—Make sure he cleans up after him, she says.

Then she turns on her heels and disappears into the back room. Thirty seconds later and McEvoy can hear the distant hum and buzz of Zee TV.

Hugh stays where he is, doing his ostrich impersonation, even though McEvoy's not holding him any more.

—You heard your mother, Hughie, you can talk while you tidy.

—I don't know what you want me to say, Mr McEvoy.

Hughie stands on one leg while he extracts his other from the box of clementines and starts to flick capsicum seeds off his shirt.

—I want to know what's going on, Hughie. I want to be brought up to speed on things. You do know what I'm talking about, Hughie, and if you know what's good for you, you'll tell me. But then, if you knew what was good for you, you'd have already started cleaning up this mess before your Mum pops back in.

Hughie gets down on his knees and starts scooping up orange pulp and peel, and squashed and popped peppers, dumping all the mess in the box alongside the undamaged clementines. Up in the West End they'd call it a designer salad and charge a packet for it.

—All I do is run errands, Mr McEvoy, you know that. Just like I used to do.

—What you used to do, Hughie, is tell me about your little errands. Remember?

—Course I do, Mr McEvoy.

Hugh looks up and starts to get nervous when he sees that McEvoy has drifted over to the chilli display and is fingering a couple of long, thin *jalapenos*.

—I used to tell you everything, Mr McEvoy, but you always told me not to tell anybody else.

—So what you're saying is that you're being a good boy and playing both ends against the middle as per usual. But somebody doesn't want you to bring anybody else into the loop. That'd be Mr Driver, wouldn't it?

—Yeah, that's right, says Hugh like it's a quiz or something. Used to work with you.

—Work *for* me, Hughie, but now we're working together on something special and that's why I need you to fill in a few gaps. You see, I don't like the idea of showing myself up in front of Jim Driver by admitting I don't know what's going on like I used to. So you're going to fill me in, dot a few 'i's' and cross the odd 't' or two on just what you and Benny and some lowlife called Mortlake Eddy are up to. Or, I might just have to get unpleasant.

This is where McEvoy really starts to fondle the pile of chillis, running them through his fingers, caressing them, selecting one….

And then he stops. Freezes dead in his tracks, a funny look on his face. He rolls up a sleeve and digs into the pile of chillis until he finds something to pull and he pulls it.

—Ah-ha! he shouts like a conjurer in front of an audience who has seen the trick before. What have we here?

What he has there, in his hand, is a plastic bag, one of those self-sealing jobs where you stick that uneaten portion of spaghetti sauce and pop it in the freezer, only to find it nine months later and you're buggered if you can identify what it was.

This freezer bag though contains phones. Two mobiles, each with a sticky label wrapped around the keypad. One label says 'Benny: 2 p.m.' and the other says 'Eddy: 12 noon'. McEvoy reads the labels out loud then turns on Hughie, who is working himself up to a massive attack of irritable bowel syndrome.

—Well look at this, will yer? says McEvoy, all jovial. Telephones among the chillis. That what you call a hot line, is it? One for Big Benny and one – no, let me guess – for Mortlake Eddy. What's the deal, Hughie? You have to ring them at these times do you?

McEvoy pauses and looks at the chillis, then at the bag with the phones in, then back at the chillis, then at Hugh.

—And why the bleedin' hell are you hiding them in among the merchandise?

—I'm not hiding them, Mr McEvoy. That's how they come, in among the fruit and things.

—What, like a special offer down the market? Free phone with every five pounds of parsnips? What do you get if you buy a case of pineapples? A free fax machine?

—I just deliver them, Mr McEvoy, that's all. They turn up at the shop with little notes telling me who they're for and I deliver 'em. That's it, whole story. The time means the time they've got to switch them on. Then somebody rings them.

—Who does? McEvoy snaps then he adds: Is that your stomach making that noise?

Blind Hugh nods sheepishly and tenses every muscle in his lower body.

—I don't know, Mr McEvoy, honest I don't. It's like some sort of Mr Big giving them their orders for the day. I don't get to listen in.

—I'll bet you do, Hughie, 'cos that's what you're good at.

—But Mr Driver said…

—Not to say anything to anybody else except him, right? Well, that's good, Hugh. That's how it should be. But I told you, I'm working with Mr Driver now. Him and his beautiful assistant, Sergeant Moon. So you can tell me what you ear-wigged. It won't go any further.

—But I promised, Hughie whines.

—And I promise not to let on you told me. Now, you trust me don't you, Hughie?

—Well....

—I mean, if I said I was going to see how many different varieties of chilli I could get up your nose before your brain caught fire, then you'd trust me to do it, wouldn't you?

—All I know is it's drugs, Hughie says quickly. But not like normal drugs. These are medical supplies, vaccines of some sort. They ship them out through Cargo Village.

—And Big Benny's going to lift them?

—Rob them, on the move. He's been paying some of the local kids to lift cars for his boys to practise on.

—Where and when, Hughie?

—I don't know, Mr McEvoy, honest. I reckon it's soon and I know Benny's been taking trips down to Heathrow lately.

—And where does Mortlake Eddy fit in all this?

—That I don't know, Mr McEvoy, and I don't want to know either. That geezer scares me. Don't want nothing to do with him. All I know is that Benny's not got to find out that he's been getting a phone too.

—Well, I won't tell him, Hughie.

McEvoy looks at the phones in the bag he's holding.

—So what're you supposed to do with these?

—Deliver them, as soon as.

—You'll be wanting a lift then, won't you? I've got the car outside.

Blind Hugh does his world-famous impersonation of that picture, *The Scream*, as he feels his stomach gases go ballistic at this.

—Oooh, pardon me, Mr McEvoy, but I'm not sure that's a good idea.

McEvoy wrinkles his nose then starts to recoil.
—Yeah. Maybe you're right, he says.

Back at Plod Central the big, blow-up map of the area has now got a plastic overlay so that strategic points can be marked on it in red, blue and green felt-tip pen. The designated route from Angel's Wings' warehouse to Cargo Village, right through the middle of Southall, has been marked in black. The warehouse itself is marked with a blue cross, and there are other blue crosses dotted along the route out to Heathrow. In Cargo Village, there's a blue cross marking the Emirates Airline office and another, bigger one, over the disused police station at the turning into The Horseshoe. On The Horseshoe itself, there's a blue cross inside a blue oblong in the centre of the lorry park.

Driver has made sure he's there on time this time so he can schmooze his Superintendent, the Oik. This is necessary as the Oik has been having very bad feelings about the whole operation ever since he heard that Mortlake Eddy was looking for a JCB digger.

Actually, Mortlake Eddy looking for anything other than a haircut was usually enough to rattle the tea cups in the local CID office. On a scale of one to ten in the unofficial police guide to who they'd like to get alone in a cell without a solicitor for half an hour, Mortlake Eddy would rate a straight ten. Big Benny, on the other hand, had always been a five though he had gone up to about a seven after showing them all up at Dogberry Road.

But you could live with a Big Benny on your patch. You knew he had his limits in the brainpower stakes, even with smart lawyers and wiseguys like Ash the Cash on the payroll. And you knew that certain things did, and certain things didn't, happen on his patch. He didn't like guns, for instance, and some would say (though not to his face) that it was because as targets went, he himself was only just slightly down from the side of a barn. Whatever, none of his crew had been known to use or carry. The story went round that when a young Afghan tearaway who had recently moved into the area was found showing off a Russian Makarov 9mm, an ambulance had to pick him up from a phone box at Southall station. All eight fingers and one thumb had been broken, but they'd left him one thumb so he could dial 999. The gun, if it existed, was never found and the clever money was on the Grand Union Canal. The Afghan suddenly found he'd forgotten how to speak English when asked if he wanted to press charges against anybody for anything.

If he'd ever been asked, Benny would have said knives were okay and in the case of some of the Sikhs, swords with blades up to two feet long. It was a culture thing. But guns attracted attention and the police had to take you seriously. This was London after all, not some frontier town like Manchester or Glasgow.

And Benny was the sort of hoodlum who did at least think about things occasionally. Not like Mortlake Eddy. He never thought at all.

Or not before he acted. That would spoil the fun. Eddy was a loose cannon of the worse kind; one who had made a conscious decision never to make a conscious decision if he could help it. If he had to stop and think about it, he'd blow it. That was the way he'd look at it; if he ever stopped to think about it. And he had a pure vicious streak when he wanted to, and he mostly wanted to when he was awake.

Mortlake Eddy was definitely a tasty target and having him in the equation upped the stakes considerably. That's what worried the Oik, who was not by nature a gambling man. He was the one authorising the resources for an operation in danger of getting out of hand. Against this he was putting the temptation of pulling not one, but two, of the Division's most troublesome crews and getting them off the streets and lodged in a Windsor Hotel for a couple of years.

It would also be a juicy piece of payback for the Dogberry Road fiasco, but the Oik knew that that very thought might blind them, generating more mistakes, more cock-ups. He hadn't got to be an Oik without due consideration of the downside of life. In his book, every silver lining had a cloud and Rome wasn't burned in a day.

That's why he lays down the law before Driver starts the briefing.

—I want belt and braces, fine toothcombs and no stone unturned on this one, Inspector Driver. We must be 110 per cent prepared for any eventuality.

—I hear what you're saying, sir, says Driver.

The Oik isn't impressed with this. He knows that when somebody says they hear what you're saying, it's usually the last thing they're doing. If they were standing in front of you wearing a deaf aid, they would make a point of letting you see it was switched off.

—Very well, Inspector, take me through it and don't cut any corners.

Driver takes a deep breath and starts with the Angel's Wings' warehouse which, according to him, has been turned into a cross between Fort Knox and NASA's Mission Control over the weekend. The only thing this means to the Oik is a massive overtime bill, but he listens quietly and nods wisely as Driver goes into detail.

The consignment of Coletoxore has been delivered with no problems, the Cambridgeshire Carrot Crunchers handing over to the Met's escort as prearranged. Mark Tyler personally supervised the Tyler Pharmaceuticals and the managing director of Angel's Wings, that Naseem chap, drove the van himself. Nobody outside the force and those two even knew the stuff was in London.

—Nobody? asks the Oik, as if surprised.

—No, says Driver, trying to keep his voice steady.

—Not even Frank McEvoy?

Driver relaxes slightly. If the Oik's only concern is keeping the Old Boys' network happy, then he has little to worry about.

—Former Chief Inspector McEvoy will be fully briefed tomorrow morning when he turns up for work at Angel's Wings.

—Does he have a role in the operation?

—Well, sir, that's where we need an executive decision.

The Oik bristles at that. Decisions are difficult enough without being executive ones.

—Under normal circumstances for a consignment like this, Frank would be the one driving the Angel's Wings' van. He's also the company's main contact with the airline. He seems to get on well with all the Cargo Village people.

—You mean the Asians?

—Well, yes, sir. As it happens. I didn't mean anything by that.

The Oik thinks for a minute, sniffing for a downside, working out a pre-emptive strike on the public relations front.

—I'm aware of Frank McEvoy's 'Kipling' tag from when he was on the force. He got on well with the immigrant communities and that was very useful on many an occasion. We're a multi-cultural society now. There are 340 languages spoken in London these days, 120 on one estate up near Shepherd's Bush. We've got to keep an open approach. But I am also aware that some people in the Job thought he was *too* close to the local community, just as some of the community activists thought he was a patronising bastard whom they wouldn't trust as far as they could throw him. He was also a bit heavy-handed at times.

Tell me about it, thinks Driver. But at least McEvoy had been an Equal Opportunities hard man. Didn't matter what colour you were if he thought you were cruising for a bruising.

The Oik makes an executive decision.

—On balance, and only if he agrees to do it, we use McEvoy as the driver. We use him because we don't want to raise any suspicions by doing anything out of the ordinary; we use him because of his local knowledge and contacts; and we use him because as an ex-copper he is fully aware of the risks. That do it?

Driver thinks that could do as a press release or an obituary if anything went wrong, but he keeps that to himself.

—That's the rationale, sir. And of course Frank, can always say no. If he does, though I don't think he will, we'll put in one of our chaps. He'll be wired up with a radio in constant contact with Obs 1, which will be based at Angel's Wings.

—And visual surveillance? How far between the Observation Points? asks the Oik, showing he's on the ball.

—Obs 2 and 3 are mobile units – an unmarked car and an unmarked van – one in front, one behind the consignment. A mobile response team should be no more than half a mile away at any one time.

—You've taken the traffic into consideration?

Good question. Shows he's still awake.

—We've factored it in and, of course, it affects the villains as well. We've put Obs 4 here, which is roughly halfway between Angel's Wings and the A30.

The Oik squints at where Driver is leaving a fingerprint on the plastic overlay near a blue cross on the map.

—That *is* a mosque. Isn't it?

—Yes, sir. Perfect cover for us. It's slap bang in the middle of the designated route and this red cross here across the road, that's a pair of lock-up garages we know Big Benny uses.

—What's to stop him shooting out of the lock-up and ramming Frank McEvoy's van right there?

—I can't see it, sir, it's just too crowded there on the High Street; not enough escape options. We've got Obs 5 and Obs 6 as mobile units on the edge of the A30. We could easily call them in if anything happens in central Southall. But the more you look at the route, sir, the more you come to the conclusion that the hit will be here in Cargo Village, possibly on The Horseshoe itself.

The Oik decides to play devil's advocate – or defence lawyer, as it's sometimes known.

—Surely that's the last place to pull a job. Heathrow has more armed policemen per head of population than anywhere outside Mississippi, hasn't it? You must be running a bit of a risk there.

—Not as much as you'd think, sir. The vast majority of security measures, and the armed teams, are concentrated on the Terminal buildings and the passengers, or on the aircraft themselves. And to be honest, the focus is very much on planes and people *coming in*, not going out. Cargo Village is essentially the tradesman's entrance to Heathrow. There are trucks and vans coming in all the time but there's nowhere much to go except to the freight agents or the airline offices. You can't get near the planes from there unless you go through the handlers and then you'd come up against the serious security checks.

—So what you're saying is that Tyler's drugs are going to be lifted on their way to check-in? If they were a piece of luggage, for instance.

—Something like that, sir. And remember, the general assumption is that anything worth nicking at Thiefrow, or any international airport for that matter, is stuff that is travelling *in* to the country, not out of it. We're just as guilty of that way of thinking, sir. We're far more concerned with villains and naughty substances and guns and illegal immigrants coming in. We don't really give two tosses for what's going out.

—I wouldn't put it quite so graphically, Inspector, but I get your point. So if it's to be on The Horseshoe, what arrangements will you put in hand?

Driver goes back to the map, pointing out the blue crosses dotted around The Horseshoe.

—Obs 7 will be here in the Emirates office on the western side of the 'shoe. That's the downward side in the one-way system. It's also the limit of our area of activity.

—You mean that if the consignment gets there in one piece, we pack up and go home?

—More or less, sir. The Coletoxore will be rushed through and on to a plane to Dubai. That's the last possible point someone could rob it and get away. Once it's through the Emirates freight office, a plane is the only way out.

—So that's where they'll hit?

—That's my favourite, sir. We'll have Obs 8, which is a twelve-man response team, concealed in a container lorry here on The Horseshoe itself in the lorry park, and the mobile response teams will be half a mile or so behind on the Perimeter Road.

—You hope.

—Well, that's the plan. We will also have Obs 9 established here in the disused station. Our people are moving in tonight with the communications gear. There will be no movement in the open by uniformed officers after dawn tomorrow.

—That could be a long wait for our boys in the back of the lorry.

—Yes, sir. I'm hoping they'll be in a right filthy temper by the time they're needed.

—*If* they're needed.

The Oik rubs his eyelids with finger and thumb but it does nothing for the slow-burn headache that is coming.

—Have you cleared this with Heathrow security and the Emirates?

—Yes, sir, both at top level. Heathrow are happy to leave everything to us as long as it doesn't affect the Terminal buildings or the runways and the aircraft. I've talked to the Head of Security for the Emirates and he'll be briefing their main man to co-operate fully. It's a guy called Hasan Sharif and DS Moon has already dealt with him. We got the video tapes of Big Benny and Mortlake Eddy from his cameras.

—But he's not been told anything yet?

—No, sir. By the time he's briefed, we'll have our chaps on observation with him.

—You suspect him of being a leak? Hardly likely is it, him coming forward with those tapes?

—I agree it's not, sir, but somebody is pulling strings somewhere. Big Benny knows about Coletoxore, he's done a drive-by of The Horseshoe and the Emirates freight office, and latest street intelligence is that he's lifting cars and vans so he can practise his ram-raiding technique.

—And what's Mortlake Eddy doing?

—We're not sure, sir. We've got all his regular haunts covered, but we've never been able to get anybody on the inside of Eddy's crew. I checked, though, and three JCB diggers have been reported stolen from builders' yards or motorway repair depots within the Division since Friday night.

—Three? Jesus!

—I'm told that's actually slightly below average for this time of year, sir.

Driver goes all sheepish for once.

—There's quite a flourishing trade in them, I'm told. They get nicked from one local council and sold to another on the other side of London.

—What about the one on the video that chap Sharif supplied? The one Mortlake Eddy seemed to be playing with?

Thought I'd forgotten that, didn't you? thinks the Oik.

—Yes, we did check that one, sir. We got an index number for it off the tape. Turns out it belongs to British Airways, just round the corner in Cargo Village. It was nicked and returned before anyone noticed it was missing.

—The cheeky little shaggers!

The Oik's moral outrage doesn't last long. He's too busy spotting another problem.

—Why was Eddy there in the first place?

—I'm sorry, sir? Driver is thrown for a minute.

—I mean, we're not expecting Mortlake Eddy's crew to do the actual hijack, are we? He's hardly going to chase after a van in a JCB digger, is he? So what's he doing checking out the scene of the crime to come?

—Ah, with you, sir. No, I think it's going to go down just like we've catered for. Big Benny is being set up to do the hit; a stop, smash-and-grab raid on the Angel's Wings van right here on The Horseshoe. We nick him and his crew in the act and we reactivate the old station house as a temporary holding point for villains, the walking wounded and the evidence. Once we've cleared up a bit and things have died down and we've moved the prisoners back here, that's when Mortlake Eddy and his crew come trundling up with their

JCB digger for a touch of smash-and-grab themselves. Their target is the Cargo Village police station, after they think we've gone off with a result. And personally, I don't think they'll need a JCB to get into that nick; a decent hammer would do. It's in a worse state than Dogberry Road was.

The Oik winces at that particular memory.

—So what was Eddy doing on that tape?

—I reckon he was just checking things out, sir. he doesn't know Cargo Village like Benny does. Most of Benny's crew are related to somebody who works there. Eddy's not in that loop. So he's checking things out for himself, seeing if what his phantom phone caller has told him has cred.

—Ah, yes, the phantom mobile-phone man.

The Oik starts kneading his right temple, which has started to throb.

—Are we *anywhere* with our mysterious Mr Big?

—Frankly no, sir. We've not had the chance to intercept one because that would give the game away. They're cheap imports and they're being used as one-trip disposables. If we knew their numbers or the number of the one our Mr Big uses, then the service providers could give us a location within thirty seconds of him using it. Whoever it is, he's got a fair few of them, but we've had no reports of any major thefts. That doesn't in itself mean much, though. Four million of them were sold last Christmas alone. There must be a million more just hanging about, on the move, looking for a buyer. Somebody somewhere's probably got a dozen gross sitting in a cupboard they've forgotten about.

—So apart from knowing he's got access to more mobile phones than British Telecom...

—We don't know much, that's for sure, Driver says with a twinkle and a grin, playing it like the Oik is one of the boys after all.

—We know he knows what Coletoxore is, says the Oik, who is *not* smiling. And presumably he knows how to sell it on after he's got Benny or Eddy to steal it for him.

Driver has to think on his feet on this one. Then he notices that the Oik is massaging both temples and decides that honesty is the best policy.

—We haven't exactly thought that one through, sir.

—It's not a street drug, Jim, not as we know them.

Driver forgets his promise to strangle the next person who said that to him.

—It's the sort of thing that's only bought by hospitals or clinics or health authorities, maybe governments. We're talking four million quids' worth here. That's a fairly specialised market.

—Perhaps we haven't considered the big picture as much as we should.

Driver knows he's on thin ice here and he hopes that phrases like 'the big picture' will go down well with the senior management. It's worked in the past.

—I don't think you've considered it at all.

But it hasn't worked now. So Driver wings it, bullshitting in fifth gear.

—There are some obvious lines of enquiry, sir. It could be one of Tyler Pharmaceuticals' existing customers wanting a batch on the cheap. We don't know that Benny or Eddy are expecting full retail value, do we? They may be working to a flat fee – or think they are. It could be a competitor of Tyler's, a bit of the old industrial espionage. A big American drugs company, for instance.

—With an intimate knowledge of Southall High Street?

—So they hire local talent, sir. Or it could be Tyler himself. Setting it up to defraud his own insurance company.

—Not likely, Jim. I've had Tyler checked out, not just locally but in the City. He needs this shipment to go through for more reasons than one. That way he stands to make megabucks when he sells the company. He's playing the long game, not looking for a short fix. Still, I take back what I said. You do seem to have given it *some* thought.

—The time frame's been against us, sir. We've had to take the pragmatic approach and consider the question of crime prevention as our prime ….directive.

Driver hadn't meant to say 'prime directive' but he'd run out of ideas. But he realises the Oik is saying the words silently over to himself, filing them away for future use.

—Okay, Jim, as long as we're singing from the same hymn sheet, I'm happy.

Driver resists the temptation to ask whether the hymn sheet would be needed at a thanksgiving mass or a funeral.

—Timing?

—The Emirates flight to Dubai is scheduled for 22.00 hours. Normal course of events would be to get the shipment checked in to the Emirates eight hours before, say two o'clock in the afternoon. We can have the paperwork faxed over anytime in the morning and anyway, our lads will be using the Emirates office as an Obs post so they can see it through. To the outside everything will seem normal. The Angel's Wings van makes that run two or three times a week. Mondays especially, so anyone on the lookout will see exactly what they expect to see.

—So, if things go to your plan…

(Driver flinches at the 'your'.)

—… Benny hits and gets pulled about two, two-thirty tomorrow afternoon.

—Yes, sir.

—We then make a big display of housing the pharmaceuticals in a police station that couldn't hold a teddy bears' picnic?

—Basically yes, sir.

—For how long?

—Pardon, sir?

—How long do we sit there waiting for Mortlake Eddy to do the double take?

—I'm sure it'll happen within a few hours. He'll know we can't afford to leave the stuff there too long.

—And he'd be damned right, Jim. Do you want to read a headline that says 'Police Stop Mercy Drugs Mission'? Because I don't.

—Neither do I, sir, says Driver, it being the only thing he can say.

—Good, because I'm imposing a guillotine on you. If nothing happens by eight o'clock you let Emirates take the consignment. Check with them that they can work to that schedule and give them more slack if they really need it. If Mortlake Eddy hasn't shown by then, we scrub. We take Big Benny and we throw the book at him and call it a result. But the bottom line is that those drugs are on a plane out of here tomorrow night. Got that?

—I understand, sir. I'll make it so.

Part IV:

Double Take

FRANK MCEVOY, FORMERLY Detective Chief Inspector of this parish, drives into work first thing Monday morning as per usual, except for his breakfast. As it's going to be a long day, he's treated himself to a good Irish fry-up: bacon; egg; fried soda bread; potato-and-cabbage cake; and two flat mushrooms found in the back of his fridge, now about half the size they were when he bought them. A bit of a change from his usual cornflakes mixed with plain yoghurt, but he deserved a treat.

Apart from that, everything dismally normal. He had the car radio tuned to local radio for the traffic reports and was, as usual, wondering why he bothered. The radio's so-called eye-in-the-sky traffic spotter was wearing an eye patch again when it came to anything beyond the Westway and Wormwood Scrubs. As far as the traffic plane was concerned, anything west of Acton was Dorset and that probably put Southall somewhere in Cornwall.

So, no change there. Usual stuff on the news as well. Government this, spokesman that, survey on the other, layoffs in British Telecom, jobs created in Kentucky Fried Chickens, footballer banned from driving, stock market quiet, weather averagely seasonal. No wars worth talking about, nothing happening anywhere else.

Nothing unusual. Except for the four unmarked police cars watching the entrance to the industrial estate. By the time he's got to Angel's Wings' front door, McEvoy has clocked all four of them and could tell, from a pile of cigarette butts and crumpled packets lying like a mini-volcano in the gutter, where the night shift had been stationed before shift change at six a.m.

It puts a spring in his step, knowing he hasn't lost it.

Naseem's already inside. Now that is unusual, beating McEvoy into work on a Monday. And he's not wearing a suit, so Giorgio or Hugo are getting the day off. In fact, McEvoy can't actually remember ever seeing him without a tie before. But there he is, dumbed-down in jeans and trainers (not even a decent counterfeit brand, just cheap) and a short-sleeved sports shirt with wide, lime-green stripes. The Asian Businessmen's League wouldn't give him houseroom dressed like that.

They'd probably dock him a mark or two for allowing his place of business to be disrupted by half a dozen plain-clothes police – four men and two women – complete with half a ton of radio and telephone equipment.

—Frank…., Naseem starts but McEvoy's ahead of him.

—So today's the day, is it?

One of the detectives, who looks just about old enough to drink legally, gives him the once-over.

—You're Chief Inspector McEvoy, aren't you?

—I used to be. You one of Jim Driver's boys?

The schoolboy in the suit nods keenly.

—DC Sugar. I'll be running things from here. You'll be driving the van, I'm told.

—Will I now? says McEvoy, feigning surprise.

—Only if you volunteer, says Detective Constable Sugar quickly.

—Volunteer? Now there's a word you don't often hear in the Metropolitan Police. Not unless things have changed since I was in the Job.

Sugar doesn't know whether he's being wound up or not and he looks to Naseem for back-up.

—There's no pressure, Frank, says Naseem, like he's deciding whose turn it is to go get the Egg McMuffins. I've told the police that under normal circumstances you would drive a consignment like this one; see to it personally. If we're to keep up appearances, then it should be you in the Transit on your normal route. But, of course, it has to be your choice. It could be dangerous.

—We'll have you in constant contact and be right behind you in case of any trouble, says DC Sugar keenly.

—I've heard that before, says McEvoy. Fuck, I've *said* that before now, but only to unsuspecting civilians. Still, I suppose I'm one of them now.

—So you'll do it? asks Naseem, as if he could care about the answer.

—Absolutely. Looking forward to meeting Big Benny again.

Young Detective Sugar frowns at that.

—You know this character Benny?

—From way back when, says McEvoy. Hasn't Jim Driver...sorry, Inspector Driver...said anything about me?

—Not... exactly. Sergeant Moon has, though.

It's McEvoy's turn to give the young copper the once-over.

—You believe everything Detective Sergeant Moon tells you?

—About half, says Sugar, deadpan.

—You'll go far. Where is he, by the way?

—DS Moon is at Obs Point 4 in Southall High Street. It's roughly the halfway point on the route you'll be taking. We'll be in constant contact with him from here and he'll be able to hear you in the van at all times. So if there's any trouble, just yell and he'll get to you with back-up right away. Once you've passed Obs 4 he'll join the mobile units on your tail. They should never be more than half a mile behind you.

McEvoy wrinkles his nose and clears his throat almost as if he's going to hawk and spit right there on the carpet.

—DS Moon watching my back. Now there's a thought, he says.

Big Benny's on his second breakfast, a pair of those high-energy fruit-and-fibre bars that taste like the sweepings of a hamster's cage glued together with honey. His mother had served up his favourite that morning – half-inch rashers of belly pork, grilled crisp, with beans in molasses sauce – but he knew that was only because she sensed he was going on a job and she was after a new microwave. He'd had to promise to see what he could do. Maybe he'd tell one of the boys to keep an eye out. Might even consider buying the old bat one from the profits if the day went well.

The gang's all there except Ash the Cash, in the two lock-up garages that Benny's had knocked through into one by removing most of the breeze-block partition wall. Now there's space for two cars and room to move around and, when the lease (which is in Ash's wife's name) runs out, they can always slam the blocks back into place. Or not bother, depending whether they felt like it.

Rafik Jarman's there, making sure the others have brought what they were supposed to bring. Jo Jo Singh, for instance, has been lumbered with the two big sports bags holding the stingers, mainly because he's the only one who can carry both of them without breaking sweat and/or complaining. Boy Adrian has a haversack big enough to take a Boy Scout over his shoulder; one that wouldn't look out of place on a marine yomping across Salisbury Plain, except without the hand grenades.

And then there's the Wahid twins, who are Afghans. Benny has used them before, if and when he needed transport on a short-term, no-questions-asked basis. The Wahids, who are still in their teens, are natural-born mechanics and can get in and get started any make or model of car within the times laid down by the insurance companies when assessing risk for their premiums. It was rumoured that they started out on 4-wheel drive Russian Jeeps when they were kids and then graduated to tuning-up Ladas, or even getting them going, which was really impressive. They weren't too hot on the 'driving' bit of 'Taking and Driving Away', mainly because they didn't speak or read English too good, but they certainly had a knack for taking. They carried between them a home-made ignition key for anything up to two hundred different cars, which they'd made themselves on a lathe in the garden shed. Word was they could make you an AK-47 given half a yard of copper piping and a staple gun.

Big Benny couldn't tell the Wahids apart, so he called them One and Two. They had brought a light-blue Escort van and an eight-year-old BMW 3-series saloon to the party. Both have been stolen in Heston since breakfast. The BMW had taken twenty-three seconds to get into and start up, the van had taken seven. They've already put new number plates, not on the stolen list, on both cars, though it's unlikely either have been noticed missing yet.

—So we're ready to rock and roll are we? asks Benny, accidentally spitting a flake of high-fibre oat on to Wahid One's left shoe.

—We're ready, says Rafik. But are we still set?

Big Benny heaves his bulk off the bonnet of the BMW and pats Rafik's cheeks with both hands, giving him the big-smile treatment.

—Looks like it, Rafik my son, because no news is good news. Or in this case, no phone is good news.

—I don't get you, boss.

—Of course you don't. That's why I'm the boss.

—You've heard from Mr Mobile then?

Big Benny shows his teeth again and pats Rafik's cheeks ever so lightly in time with his words.

—No... I... have... not. And that's why I'm in such a good mood. You see, the plan was that I would only get another freebie phone today if there were any *changes* to the plan. No phone this morning, so no changes. No word is a go word.

Benny looks pleased with himself at that and repeats it silently. The Wahid twins try and lip-read him but it still makes no sense to them.

—What if Blind Hugh's running around at this very moment trying to find you with a phone?

—I got Ash to check. Mr Mobile said if there wasn't one there by nine, everything was okay. Ash and Hughie had a good old root through the vegetables first thing. Didn't find nothing. Hope he remembered to pick me up some okra. I promised me mum.

He looks at his watch.

—So we've got about three hours to kill before the stuff leaves Angel's Wings.

—You can be sure of that?

—Well, Mr Mobile's not been wrong yet, whoever he is.

Big Benny doesn't like the idea of working for some disembodied voice but he has to admit that Mr Mobile has style. In fact, the whole project has style. Everybody expects the most tempting targets to be coming *in* to Heathrow, not going out. Everybody's looking for drugs these days, but not this type of drug, and there are added advantages there, like not having to work with dealers or worry about treading on anybody else's turf. Security's crap that side of the airport – Benny's driven round three times himself and nobody's stopped him to ask what he was doing there. It's not like they'll be hitting an armoured car or anything, just one man in a Transit van. And they don't even have to sit on the loot for long; six hours tops. They've got an instant buyer in Mr Mobile and by nine o'clock this evening, they'll have met and done the trade. Four hundred thousand of your English pounds, cash money, no cheques, no Euros; thank you very much.

Benny knows that's only a tenth of the value of the consignment, but he's a realist. He wouldn't know where to start to find a fence for such a deal; that'd be too much hassle. Then again, he's only had minimal expenses so far. The

Wahid twins are on minimum wage, Boy Adrian and Jo Jo will take a fair bung and be happy, Rafik and Ash – as senior management – will be on a sliding scale. Even then, Benny is looking at two hundred large in folding notes in his personal pocket. And all for a few days' work with somebody else paying the phone bill.

Spanking.

—So how do we know when to go? asks Rafik.

Benny dips into his pocket and produces a mobile, a flash Ericsson that doesn't fill his fist.

—We get a call.

—From Mr Mobile? I thought you said he didn't send you a phone this morning.

—He didn't. This is mine. Thought I'd invest in one, so Baby Face took me shopping on Saturday while you lot were poncing off watching Chelsea down the Bridge. Baby Face has got one just like it. He's chilling out over near Angel's Wings. Soon as they hit the road, he'll bell me.

Benny opens up the phone, presses buttons and shows Rafik the display unit.

—Look, it's got speed-dial. Baby Face showed me how to work it. I've got the main numbers in here already. See? That's Ash, that's Baby Face's mobile, that's me mum. Oh, and that's Pizza Express.

Whoever it was told Jim Driver that the old cop shop at Cargo Village was in a worse state than Dogberry Road hadn't been kidding. If rats could write they'd have left a sign saying 'Condemned' just before they moved out in disgust.

To preserve the outward appearance of total desertion, the team manning Obs 9 had taken up position just before dawn, stumbling around inside with only shielded torches to guide them. Driver had issued orders not to turn on any lights, but he needn't have bothered as the electricity had been cut off. He had, though, remembered to bring extra batteries for their radios and mobile phones, and a dozen thermos flasks of weak canteen coffee, sugar, a box of sandwiches and two dozen assorted yoghurts. They turned out to be all the same flavour, Fruits of the Forest, which nobody liked. Just as well as he'd forgotten to bring spoons.

The first couple of hours go without incident, unless you count them discovering that there wasn't a working toilet in the place. After that, they begin to take it easy on the coffee.

Driver settles himself into what had once been an upstairs office, the view from the grimed and cracked window is right down The Horseshoe. The lorry park in the central reservation is filling up slowly, though some of the trucks have been there all night.

Across at a diagonal, he can see the Emirates Airlines office down at the far end of Shoreham Road West. The parking bay outside it is empty, like he's instructed, and there are no outward signs of life. Almost exactly opposite, on the lorry park, there's a space that would do very nicely indeed if the bloody response team got there before some civilian driver pinched it.

Before he can get agitated, one of his detectives – looking out of the next window whilst stirring a Styrofoam cup of coffee with a ballpoint pen – tells him that 'the lads are here'.

A forty-foot articulated lorry comes creeping down Southampton Road and into The Horseshoe and down Shoreham Road East. Driver loses sight of it behind other lorries as it rounds the U-bend and starts to come down Shoreham Road West. The lorry driver, whoever he is, is taking the one-way system and the 20 m.p.h. speed limit like it was God's holy writ. There was a giveaway. Any casual observers would have known straight off he wasn't a professional trucker.

But he does seem to know how to park it, reversing neatly into exactly the spot Driver had mentally earmarked, so he doesn't have to get on the radio and bawl him out.

The driver of the truck jumps down from the cab, locks up and legs it. He's done his bit for the day and has been told to make himself scarce, not to head for the old police station.

Driver relaxes because so far, so good. He's got Obs 9 up

and running, even if it feels like working in an unlit sewer. And he's got his response unit in position in the back of the lorry, slap bang in the middle of The Horseshoe. If Big Benny hits the Angel's Wings van to plan, a dozen very pissed off (by then) coppers, half of them armed, only have to fall out of the back of the truck to pull him.

He's brought a pair of binoculars with him and he scans the scene in detail, working his way up the right-hand road and down the left.

The binoculars stop, then go back an inch and freeze, focusing on the side of the truck that houses Obs 8, the response team.

He'd never asked where Traffic Division had borrowed the articulated lorry from, never noticed the logo painted three-feet high on the side until now.

—Oh fuck me 'til I fart, groans Driver under his breath.

EAT BRITISH PORK says the logo and there's a picture of a pig holding a knife and fork next to it. And the pig is smiling.

Undercover? Or what?

Diagonally across from the old police station, Hasan Sharif has arrived for work to find his Emirates Air office heaving with police persons.

A very nice Detective Constable introduces herself as Kate Tallow and apologises in advance for taking over his office and making his life hell for the rest of the day. Perhaps he'd like to ring the security head of the airline, who will tell him what's going on, and she points to the phone with a smile.

Hasan looks around and counts six detectives – four men, two women – all white. It's a fair bet that they don't have a GCSE in conversational French between them.

So he picks up the phone and dials and speaks, and not one of them even has a clue as to what language he's using.

Less than a mile away as the crow flies – though crows like jumbo jets rarely fly in straight lines over Heathrow – Kuli

Khan is parking his car opposite the Air India freight office.

The Peace and Harmony section of Cargo Village is living up to its name, being totally deserted. There aren't even any trucks overnighting illegally on the car park.

But being a careful man, the first thing Kuli does when he gets into his office is to rewind the closed-circuit video tapes covering the last four hours. By fast-forwarding them, he gets through them in about half an hour, spotting absolutely nothing out of the ordinary except, just after dawn, two foxes fighting over a black dustbin bag they're dragging across Sandringham Road.

Only when he's happy that there have been no comings or goings he should know about does he start making phone calls.

Over in Divisional Headquarters, the Officer In Charge has clocked in early and gone straight to the Operations Room, not even calling in on his secretary for his regular cup of instant and one digestive biscuit. This in itself is enough to start the buzz going that something is up.

A uniformed Inspector called Davis takes it upon himself to do a bit of brown-nosing and reports that everything is set, troops are in place, raring to go, champing at the bit. All nine Obs Points have reported in, all have radio and mobile or land-line phone links up and working. He leaves unsaid the thought that the Oik might as well go and have his morning cuppa because there's sod all he can do here.

But the Oik always carries a sneak question with him wherever he goes. That's how he got to be an Oik.

—What about Obs 10?

—Obs 10, sir? Davis says, faintly scanning the large-scale map, looking for a blue cross he might have missed.

—Mortlake Eddy and his crew, says the Oik, in a voice that indicates that there will be no more clues.

—Ah, yes.

Light dawns in Davis' eyes.

—We've had them tagged for the last three days. They are down here, sir, right on the edge of the map. They're colour-coded green.

He points to a green cross just off the Staines Road as it runs along the top edge of Hounslow Heath.

—This area is light industrial works, sir, some of it in use, some empty. We've had it under surveillance since Friday night. Yesterday, Mortlake Eddy and his lieutenants turned up at one of the disused warehouses with a JCB digger, drove it inside, locked up and went down the pub. We've got three officers in a house that overlooks the warehouse. They're coded S1.

—Why S1? Why green?

—To differentiate the two operations, sir. Hounslow is purely surveillance. Mr Driver said nothing was likely to happen until tonight so it's just a question of keeping tabs on Mortlake Eddy's movements. The nine Obs points are coded blue for Operation Cobra, which will be activated as soon as the consignment leaves Angel's Wings. As I understand it, the whole point is that Operation Kingfisher, against Mortlake Eddy, can't start until Cobra is finished.

—If Mr Driver is right about this being a double take. I'm still not completely convinced that Eddy and Big Benny aren't working this together in cahoots somehow. So, we'd better keep alert. Tell S1 I want half-hourly status reports on that warehouse.

Inspector Davis nods enthusiastically.

—I'll get that actioned, sir. Would you like to see the operational plan for Kingfisher?

—What?

—The proposed distribution of response teams for the follow-up....

—No, what did you call them?

Davis doesn't like the look on the Oik's face.

—Call what, sir?

—The operational code names, says the Oik tartly.

—Cobra and Kingfisher, sir.

—Which are both beers you get in Indian restaurants, says the Oik through clenched teeth. Which bright spark thought that up?

—Inspector Driver, sir, says Davis real fast.

At Angel's Wings, McEvoy has had the kettle on and made a cuppa for DC Sugar and his team. Any minute now he'd be telling them about the good old days and what happened on his first stake-out.

—On my first stake-out we were seven hours and fifty-eight minutes before anything happened, says McEvoy, as if on cue.

—Two minutes to shift change? grins Sugar.

—Exactly. But what was worse, we were above a balti house in Brick Lane and none of us had had a meal break. We just had to sit and suffer with all those smells of cooking seeping up through the floorboards. That got the juices running, I can tell you. I'd have killed for a curry. It was like that subliminal advertising, you know? Where they plant thoughts in your brain.

—That why they called you 'Kipling'? asks Sugar, dead innocent, with a smile. 'Cos you like curry?

—That's what they say, is it? says McEvoy, definitely cooling off rapidly.

—Word is that's why you transferred out here to Little India. For the curry. You're supposed to be a dab hand at cooking them too, but that's just, like, canteen talk.

McEvoy sums him up, reckons the kid doesn't mean any harm.

—Yeah, well, I never did go much on canteen gossip. Hardly ever used the canteen here. Their curries were always crap. Mine are shit-hot. And I mean that.

Sugar laughs and feels he can risk another probe.

—Is it true you went to night school to learn Hindi so you could argue with the waiters in the Indians round here?

—Absolutely, says McEvoy, dead straight. Time and money well spent. Went to a brilliant place once, here in

Southall. It was just called Asian Food – just that, above the door. It was an old Wimpy Bar from the Sixties, all formica tables and hard chairs. Hadn't changed a bit. It was like a time warp except they had a reputation for the freshest curries in town. Got taken there by a lovely feller called Yusuf Khan, used to work for United Breweries out in Bangalore, over here trying to put his beer into pubs and restaurants. Well, anyway, I'd have walked straight by this place – had done – without him. Thought it was a takeaway kebab house or something; didn't realise you could go in and sit down to eat. So we go in and there's, like, no other white face in there and nobody speaks English, so Yusuf does the ordering and asks for the three freshest meat curries. The waiter says one of them is extra hot – far too hot for the white-faced bastard. You should have seen his face when I answered that *this* white-faced bastard had cooked curry for the Devil himself and the Devil had been the first one to beg for water.

—And was it good? asks Sugar.

—Excellent. Best I'd ever tasted. And cheap, too.

—Was it hot?

—Fucking thermonuclear.

All the cops laugh at that.

—So where is this place, then? one of them asks.

—Doesn't exist any more, says McEvoy. Yusuf Khan – the guy who took me there – bought the business the very next day and closed it down. It's a charity shop now.

—Why'd he do that? asks Sugar, genuinely concerned.

—The waiter had been rude to me, calling me a white bastard and thinking I didn't understand. I was Yusuf's guest. You don't forget things like that.

It's Naseem that breaks up the All Our Yesterdays seminar. He's looking at his watch and holding a sheaf of fax paper in his right hand.

—The Emirates' freight confirmation has come through, he says loudly. So we can go any time now, if, that is, we can tear ourselves away from telling stories round the camp fire. I do have a business to run here.

Sugar rolls his eyes and purses his lips in a 'Get him' gesture.

—We'd better start wiring you up, Mr McEvoy.

The first thing Sugar wants is for McEvoy to wear body armour and McEvoy's first reaction is to laugh this off, saying he wasn't expecting the gunfight at the OK Corral. Sugar isn't laughing. He says it's highly unlikely that Big Benny will use shooters – he never has before – but they have to go through the motions for the sake of the Met's insurance policies. McEvoy says it would be a shame if the premiums had to go up because of him, so give it here. It's actually one of the new Kevlar knitwear vests and it fits snugly under his jacket like a body-warmer. If it came in red it would be quite a fashion item.

Next they make him strap on a standard police utility belt which has been adapted to include a holster for a mobile phone. From the phone, they run a wire under the Kevlar vest and fit an ear piece and neck microphone so he can use it hands-free.

—This model's known as the wanker's friend, says Sugar. You can dial the 0800 sex lines and keep your hands free.

McEvoy grins politely though he's heard it before.

—Once you leave here, keep it on Send all the time. Don't worry about the phone bill.

—I won't.

—And you'll have a VHF radio in the van with you. Again, keep that on at all times.

—It'll be good to talk, says McEvoy, thinking the whole thing is overkill.

—I know what you're thinking, says Sugar.

—You do?

—What if, for any reason, you *can't* say anything?

McEvoy realises he means *if you have a gun to your head* or similar.

—Well, don't worry, Sugar reassures him. We've got the

van wired with a short-range transmitter so we can keep track of it at all times.

—Now there's a comfort. Which van?

Sugar blanks him.

—The Transit. I thought you only had the one. Is there another?

—It's okay. I usually use the Transit.

—And the Coletoxore is already on board, says Naseem from behind him. Here's your paperwork. Here are the keys.

—Good luck, says Sugar.

—Oh yes, that too, says Naseem.

The Inspector called Davis at Divisonal HQ takes the call and looks around for the Oik, finding him in his office dunking a digestive in a plastic cup of coffee.

—Just got the word from DC Sugar. The van's moving off, sir. We're contacting all the Obs Points.

—Right then, here we go, says the Oik.

Davis wishes he'd said it with a bit more conviction.

So does the Oik.

Detective Sergeant Moon and two plain-clothes men are at their post in the entrance hall to Southall Mosque. A fourth detective has their car, engine running, on double yellow lines round the corner behind the NatWest bank.

He's the one with the plum job, thinks Moon. All he has to do is sit there. He can have a ciggie when he wants one, nip out and grab a burger, read the paper. Might, if he's lucky, have a run-in with a traffic warden.

Moon and his two have to be on best behaviour, standing behind the doors and trying to keep an eye on the side street across the road, where Big Benny has his lock-up garages. They've got to do this and smile politely as a steady stream of the faithful turn up for their midday prayers, or whatever it was they did inside.

And there are far more of them than Moon had envisaged. He'd thought it would be like a Church of England

church service, with no more than half a dozen little old
ladies, 'specially as it wasn't even a Sunday. Instead, there's
at least seventy and they're all blokes. Some have wandered
in from local shops and businesses; some have shared a
mini-cab up to the door; and three have got out of chauffer-
driven cars, all Mercedes. About a third are in traditional
Afghan dress, except for the Kalashnikov over the shoulder.

Moon, fascinated, is looking into the mosque rather than
out of it, at a sea of the faithful who have dropped to their
knees, foreheads to the floor, when his mobile phone trills on
maximum volume.

Before he can reach into his coat pocket, the sea of prayer
before him rises to its knees and, to a man all of them, the
faithful start to fumble for their own phones, wondering who
would have the nerve to ring them at this particular time.

There's one thing McEvoy hadn't counted on before he sets off.
One of the detectives armed with a camcorder insists on video-
ing the Transit, inside and out, front and back, back doors
open, so he can get a good shot of the only thing in there, an
insulated cube of Coletoxore on its freighting pallet, with a
close-up on the consignment number stamped on the side.

—New policy, says DC Sugar implying 'since your day'.
The Superintendent thought it up himself. Could come in
useful in court later, if there's any argument. The tape'll go to
the Exhibits Officer.

—Fair enough, says McEvoy.

—Can I ask you to check the consignment number against
your manifest?

—Sure.

McEvoy unfolds his Emirates paperwork and reads off:
8788/491R.

—Check, says Sugar and he helps McEvoy close the doors.
Do you normally lock them? he asks.

—Oh yes, says McEvoy. Otherwise, if you stop at traffic
lights the local kids like to sneak a look inside; see if there's

anything light enough for them to have away on their toes.

—Fair enough, but don't be a hero about it. If Big Benny comes knocking on the door you give him the keys, right? Don't play silly buggers. We'll be right behind you.

—Hey, you can send him the spare set of van keys for all I care. I've no intention of getting into a ruck with Benny's boys. Mr Quiet Life, that's me.

—Good. We don't expect anything to happen until you're in Cargo Village, but you never know, so keep sharp.

—Do we have any idea yet *how* they'll try it?

—No. Best scenario is a simple crash, bash, smash and grab once you've stopped at the Emirates. Don't try and drive your way out of trouble, we don't want any high-speed chases ending in tears. Just leg it if you can, and leave the keys in the van.

—So, if in doubt, run away?

—Yup.

—Sounds like a plan, says McEvoy.

As the Transit pulls out of the industrial estate, McEvoy signals left and turns towards Southall, checking in his wing mirrors to make sure that the first of the unmarked police cars has started up and is following.

—We're rolling, he hears Sugar say in his earpiece. So far, so good.

—Absolutely, he says into the neck microphone. First hundred yards was a piece of piss.

As he turns into the side street that will bring him to the Uxbridge Road, he passes a young boy in school uniform, sports bag over his shoulder, standing at a bus stop.

If McEvoy even noticed the kid, he doesn't think it worth mentioning.

—Good lad. Top boy. Cut along to school now, before you get a detention.

Big Benny snaps his phone shut and beams at the assembled crew.

—It's time to earn a crust, boys and girls. The show is on the road. Now if we're going equipped, let's make sure we've got our equipment.

—Where do you want the stingers, boss? growls Jo Jo Singh, hefting a bag in each hand.

—One in each, Jo Jo, says Benny, popping a stick of chewing gum to give his jaws something to do. You go in the back of the van with Wahid One. Rafik, you drive and remember, you're the rear-gunner so don't try and overtake us.

Benny looks in Wahid Two's face. At least he's pretty sure it's Wahid Two.

—You know how to use one of them?

Wahid Two nods enthusiastically, bends one knee and does a sweeping motion with his arms like he was in a bowling ally going for a strike.

—Nice follow-through, says Benny. Right, you take one and get in the back of the Beamer and try not to trap your nuts in it. Boy, you checked your sprays?

Boy Adrian goes into a crouch and unzips the giant ruck-sack between his feet. He produces two large, industrial-strength cans of spray paint with black plastic tops. He shakes them and they can hear the ball bearings inside the cans, which keep the paint moving.

—Two each, boss, all full, all working.

—Environmentally friendly, I hope, grins Benny.

—No fucking way, says Boy.

—Oh dear, never mind, says Benny. You ride up front in the Beamer with me. Everybody got gloves?

Everybody nods.

—Right, what have I forgotten?

—What about Ash? asks Rafik.

—Good thinking. I'll bell him now, tell him we're on the way.

—Where is he anyway? Rafik wants to know.

—He's already there. By now he'll have found a nice little parking space on The Horseshoe for a white Mercedes van with Hanworth & Hounslow Pharmacy written on the side. He's borrowed it from his brother-in-law.

—I thought his brother-in-law was a bit of a div, says Rafik.

—I never said his brother-in-law *knows* he's borrowed it.

—Won't that be a bit obvious? I mean, with the sign and all?

—Relax, Rafik my son. It'll do us as far as the M4 interchange. There's a box van parked under the flyover on the hard shoulder, as if you're going round on to the M25. We do a swap there, five minutes tops after leaving Cargo Village. Any cops'll be coming the other way, out of town.

He looks at his watch and seems satisfied.

—Good. At this rate we can be back in Southall for a late lunch. Spot of curry, maybe.

—Movement, says Moon into his mobile. We've got movement out of the lock-ups.

Rapidly – because he hasn't got long before they turn on to the High Street and get through the traffic lights – Moon reels off descriptions of the BMW and the Escort van and their registration numbers, confirming that Big Benny is driving the Beamer.

—Hold it. The van's not turning, he's waiting. The Beamer's pulling off at the lights but the van's not following.

Then one of Moon's officers nudges him in the arm and points down the road.

—Hang on, we have Angel's Wings in sight. So do they. They're waiting for him at the lights. They've got him. They're all pulling away together. BMW in front, the Angel's Wings van and then the Escort. He's in a sandwich heading down South Road. Tell Obs 2 and Obs 3 to keep close. Obs 4 is moving into the car. We should be mobile in two minutes. We'll try and pick them up between Norwood Green and the Heston Road. Over and out.

Moon switches off his phone and says to his two officers:

—Right, let's split this fucking joint and chase some fucking villains.

It's only then he notices that the entire congregation, or whatever they call it, is standing politely a yard from him, waiting for him to finish his phone call before they can leave.

Moon scans the sea of brown faces and wonders how much they've heard. One of the nearest, a small Afghan with a white, pointed beard, flashes him a big smile.

—Go with God, officer, says the Afghan. And get a fucking move on. Some of us have to get back to work.

Inspector Davis buzzes the Oik on the internal and tells him that Operation Cobra is under way and first contact has been made.

—What about Mortlake Eddy? he asks.

—No movement, sir, Davis reports. Operation Kingfisher not yet active.

—Keep me informed, says the Oik. We can't afford to take our eye off the ball.

In the Emirates office – Obs 7 – detective Kate Tallow has been getting on well with Hasan Sharif, asking him about The Hub out in Dubai, which to her sounds really exotic. She's really impressed to hear that not only has he been there, but somebody from the company pops out there once a week from either Heathrow or Gatwick and for them, it's no big deal. It would be for her, she says, as she's never been further east than the Millennium Dome in Greenwich. Hasan Sharif has to admit he's never been to Greenwich. In fact, in London, he's never been further east than New Bond Street.

Kate Tallow gets the call from Moon, relayed via Obs 1, and announces:

—We've got a live one. Stand by your beds.

Hasan Sharif puts it down to the fact that maybe she was once in the Girl Guides and begins to load new tapes into the VCRs of all his closed-circuit security cameras.

McEvoy spotted the Escort van tailing him a microsecond before DC Sugar relayed the message into his right ear. But it wasn't until he was turning into Norwood Road that he caught sight of the BMW 3-Series up ahead. Benny, if it really was him driving, had cleverly allowed a couple of cars to fill the gaps between them so it didn't look too obvious.

Mind you, the fact that Benny was driving at 29 miles per hour and making all the correct road signals should have been a giveaway. He'd never driven that careful, so law-abiding, since he'd had a Scalextrix. If there had been any real policemen on the street they would have pulled him on suspicion by now.

Back at mission control, the Oik is asking Davis for an update.

—DC Sugar is coordinating contact with our target vehicle; DS Moon is now mobile and hopes to pick it up at Norwood Green; Obs 2 and 3 are approximately a quarter of a mile behind the target and are using phones not radios, just in case anyone's listening in. Obs 5 and 6 are waiting on the Great West Road to pick up the target once it clears Heston. Obs 7, that's DC Tallow, and DI Driver in Obs 9, report all quiet out at Cargo Village.

—No unusual movement out there? asks the Oik, biting his lower lip as he studies the blow-up map.

—Nothing. We done a PNC check on all the vehicles in the lorry park at The Horseshoe and nothing's shown up stolen.

—Nothing at all out of the ordinary?

The Oik is really chewing away at his lip by now.

—No sir, says Davis. Everything's going to plan.

—What worries me, Inspector, is *whose* plan?

—Still in visual contact, front and rear, says McEvoy into his phone for the umpteenth time.

—We're right behind you, says DC Sugar in his ear.

The Angel's Wings Transit goes under the M4 and the phone link cuts out but, all McEvoy has to do is press Redial on the unit on his belt and he can hear Sugar again.

—Sorry about the blackout, he's saying. We should have known about that; factored it into the equation.

Factored it into the equation? Fuck me, thinks McEvoy, this kid'll go far.

—I'm going through Heston, says McEvoy. No sign of them making a move yet.

—Our forward units report all clear on the Great West Road and the A30. Looks like they're giving you a clear run to Heathrow.

—So it'll be Cargo Village, then?

—Looks like. Just like we always planned.

The traffic thickens up on the A4, the Great West Road, though they quickly turn off on to the A30, the Great South West Road, which swings round to Heathrow's Terminal 4. At the Hatton Cross interchange, Benny puts his foot down and starts to pull the BMW ahead so he can turn on to the Southern Perimeter Road and into Cargo Village, out of sight of the Angel's Wings Transit.

—You know who's driving that van, don't you? he says to Boy Adrian, sitting next to him.

—Who?

—Our old friend, Frank McEvoy.

—What, the copper?

—Ex-copper, says Benny with a grin. I knew he worked for Angel's Wings but I didn't think he'd fallen as low as truck driver.

—Yeah, goofs Boy Adrian. Just how low can you get?

—Oh, I dunno, says Benny, as if he's thinking about it carefully. I reckon in Mr McEvoy's case there's still room.

—I'm coming up to the Cargo Village turning, McEvoy says into his phone. The Escort's still behind me but I've lost the BMW up front. I haven't made any of your cars yet.

—Don't worry, Frank, says Sugar. Keep cool.

It's the first time Sugar has called him Frank and if it was meant to reassure him it did exactly the opposite. The little creep was probably reading from the Met's Best Practice Guide for Hostage Situations.

—The Escort's following me in.

—We're with you, Frank. We've got five cars behind you and three units ready and waiting up ahead on The Horseshoe. You're in Cargo Village now, Frank. They can't get out without going through our lads.

Yeah, right.

Because they almost did. Get out, that is.

Almost, but not quite. Actually, not at all in the strict physical sense. It was only later that...

—We've got movement, says one of the cops with Jim Driver in the old police station. It's a civilian on The Horseshoe.

—What? Driver says, diving to the window. Where the fuck did he come from?

—Out of that van, sir.

Driver grabs his radio.

—Obs 7 from Obs 9, you've got a civilian on The Horseshoe coming straight at you.

—This is Obs 7, squawks DC Kate Tallow in his ear. Where? Where's he come from?

—Out of the van.

—What fucking van? shouts Kate Tallow. Sir.

Ash the Cash takes the call from Benny, telling him that the BMW is entering Cargo Village, and he gets out of the van marked Hanworth & Hounslow Pharmacy. By a total fluke, he's parked it behind a container lorry which has EAT BRITISH PORK written big-time on the side, so he's completely hidden from the Emirates office and their security cameras. The pharmacy van is not on any hotlist of stolen vehicles yet, though it will be later today, as the owner thinks it's in the garage having an oil-change and a forty-thousand mile service. Ash has never liked his brother-in-law.

Ash is wearing plain white overalls, and a baseball cap two sizes too big pulled down over his eyes. He's got his head down, studying a clipboard with a piece of paper clipped to it, like he's looking to make a delivery. His own mother wouldn't clock it was him from two yards away. Well, okay, maybe his mother would, but nobody else.

Not that there's another soul around, but somebody should have noticed that he's walking oddly with a bit of a shuffle, maybe eight-tenths of a limp, as he crosses Shoreham Road West as if he's heading for the Air France freight office, or perhaps KLM's. The funny walk is because he's got a sledge hammer down his trousers, or rather the wooden shaft of one slotted down the right leg of his overalls. He's nursing the seven-pound head with his right arm curled into his chest.

Once he's in the loading-bay area between Air France and KLM, he's under the overhang of the western block's roof, the edge of which had the security cameras. So now he's *behind* the cameras, all pointing down The Horseshoe. He drops his clipboard and pulls the sledge out of his overalls; gently, to avoid splinters. Then he runs sideways, like a crab, keeping his back to the wall, until he's outside the Emirates office but still underneath the lip of the roof, from which hang three video cameras, all pointing different ways but none of them down or back.

He gives the hammer the full swing, with a style that could have got him into an eighties' Russian Olympic squad, if he'd been on steroids.

Whammo!

The red indicator light on the first camera stops flashing.

—We've lost visuals, DC Kate Tallow is yelling into her radio. We're a camera down!

Her losing her bottle right here, right now, that's all he needs, thinks Driver.

—Two cameras! she shouts.

—Calm down, Constable, Driver shouts back.

He suddenly realises something he should have known from the off, that the freight offices don't have windows on to The Horseshoe. They've got steel doors and electronic locks and no windows, for security reasons: stop anybody breaking in. Trouble is that while they're nice and snug and safe – and blind – inside, it means they have to rely on CCTV to see what's happening outside, which is where the crime is actually about to go down.

—Don't panic, yells Driver into the radio.

—He's going for the third one, says the detective standing at Driver's shoulder.

—Who is it?

—Can't tell from here, says the copper. Could be anybody. He's made bloody sure he won't be on the video tapes.

—Fuck! Then Driver goes back to his radio. Stay where you are, Kate. Do not – repeat – not fucking – repeat – fucking move. Wait for instructions.

The detective behind Driver has binoculars to his eyes.

—There goes the third camera, he says calmly. Mashed that one to pieces.

—Can we get an ID on the guy?

—Not from here, sir. Maybe we should have brought a camera.

Driver just looks at him.

—I'm coming up to The Horseshoe, McEvoy's saying into his neck mike, which he can feel is sliding around in his sweat.

—We're right behind you, Frank, says Sugar in his ear. Stay cool.

Easy for you to say, sunshine.

—The Beamer's up ahead of me. It's turning into the one-way system, Shoreham Road East, the right leg of The Horseshoe.

—Just as we thought, Frank. All going to plan.

Just as we thought? Of course they were turning right, there was nowhere else to go. They were driving into a bottle-neck. And he was following them.

—Where's the Escort? Sugar asks him and McEvoy checks his wing mirror.

—Right up my exhaust pipe. Any closer and you can have them for indecent assault.

Big Benny pops the last bite of a Mars bar into his mouth and lets the wrapper fall to the floor between his thighs as he accelerates down Shoreham Road West. On his left, the lorry park; to his right, the offices and signs flash by: United, JAL, Nippon Cargo, Air Jamaica, Air Lanka, Air Canada. And then he's coming up to the bend that gives The Horseshoe its name.

—Get ready, he says to Boy Adrian and Wahid Two. You'll only have a few seconds.

He risks a look over his shoulder at Wahid Two in the back, unzipping the sports bag.

—Don't get your dunda caught in that, will you?

Wahid Two grins.

McEvoy's fingers have gone white now, he's gripping the steering wheel so hard. He's dropped into second gear to swing the Transit round the bend at the top of The Horseshoe and he can't be doing much more than 25 m.p.h. but it feels like he's screaming.

The BMW's gone – round the corner, out of sight – but he knows it must be just up ahead, waiting. And suddenly, as the Transit takes the bend, the Escort behind him drops out of his wing mirror.

—I'm at the top of The 'Shoe, he shouts into his phone, and hopes that the radio on the seat beside him picks it up as well. Can't see either of them but it's got to happen now if it's going to.

—We're right behind you, Frank, crackles DC Sugar in his ear.

McEvoy catches sight of the Emirates Airline sign as he rounds the bend. Under it, but coming towards him, is a figure in white overalls clutching a sledgehammer to his chest.

Another figure flits into his left eye; a young Asian guy in a crouch, throwing something underarm like he's on a bowling green. Something which scutters out across the width of the road with a metallic clatter, and he knows straight away that the Transit hasn't a snowflake in hell's chance of getting over that yard-wide strip of metal barbs with its Dunlops intact.

He registers that the BMW is parked the other side of the thrown-down stinger and a stocky, muscular guy, wearing a T-shirt with no sleeves and a ski-mask, has got out and is standing in the road like a gunfighter, holding a large, metal canister in each hand.

Without knowing why he does it, McEvoy floors the accelerator and grits his teeth as the tyres explode beneath him.

—Turning into The Horseshoe now! yells Moon into his radio, loving every minute of it. No sign of our Transit but the Escort van's up ahead.

So it is. Stopped in the middle of the road, its back doors open wide, empty. Deserted.

—Repeat, please, message unreadable, Sugar answers him.

—Go, go, go! Moon is shouting at his driver and slapping the dashboard as if to push the car into going faster.

Naturally, he doesn't see Jo Jo Singh lean out from behind one of the parked lorries and whip the second stinger out across the road in front of them.

Front and back tyres go as the car's speed carries them over the stinger, but only as far the parked Escort. By the time they hit it, though, they're only doing about two miles an hour and that on the rims of the wheels, sparks and shreds of torn rubber flying out behind them.

—Aw fucking, shite-ing hell! yells Moon above the scream of grinding metal.

—Repeat, please.

Driver is at the window upstairs in the disused nick at the other end of The Horseshoe.

From where he is, he can see the parked BMW on the left leg of The Horseshoe and, beyond it, the top of the Angel's Wings van. But until he sees Moon's car go careering into the back of the Escort on the right-hand leg, he's not a hundred percent sure what's happening.

Now he is.

He starts jumping up and down; so hard the cops hiding in the room downstairs are covered in plaster dust and cobwebs from the ceiling above.

He has his mobile to one ear and his radio to the other and he's shouting into both:

—Go, go, go! All units, go!

It's all gone dark for Frank McEvoy.

He's not unconscious or anything, it's just that as the Angel's Wings Transit sheds its front-tyre rubber he can't stop himself stomping on the brake and whipping the wheel over. The Transit shudders to a halt, skidding to the right and ending up across Shoreham Road East, well short of the BMW that's blocking the road ahead. As this is happening, he clouts the side of his head on the door arch but that doesn't knock him out. The world goes black because Boy Adrian is spraying the Transit's windscreen with black paint, which quickly and effectively curtains off the outside world.

And then the world sounds as if it's exploding as Ash the Cash slams the sledgehammer into the back door of the Transit and, on the second whack, the lock pops and the doors open.

And McEvoy thinks: they needn't have done that. He'd have given them the keys if only they'd asked.

DC Kate Tallow pushes Hasan Sharif aside with a quick 'Excuse me, sir' and leads her team out of the Emirates Airlines office, flicking out an extendible baton as she jumps down the steps into the loading bay.

DS Moon falls out of his wrecked car, sees the back-up cars screeching to a halt and, from his knees in the middle of Shoreham Road West, points into the lorry park.

—Through there, he yells. A big fucker in a turban. Get him!

DI Driver still has a radio in one hand and a mobile phone in the other as he pounds down Shoreham Road East with his team.

—Repeat, please, says the radio. You're cracking up.

The doors of the EAT BRITISH PORK truck burst open and twelve uniformed coppers – the first six in full riot gear – get their first fresh air for seven hours and they're looking for a ruck.

Back at Angel's Wings, DC Sugar grabs the mobile with the open line to the one on McEvoy's belt.

—Frank? What's happening? What's going on?

There's a gap before McEvoy responds.

—You seen *Saving Private Ryan*? comes back McEvoy.

—Yeah? says Sugar, gobsmacked at the question.

—Well, it's like a quieter version of that.

DC Sugar looks at Naseem, who is listening in at his shoulder, trying to look concerned. Naseem shrugs his shoulders, shakes his head.

—Tell Naseem to get the insurance policy on the Transit, says McEvoy over the air, as if he's in the room with them. He's gonna need a claim form.

Big Benny never even actually got to see the Coletoxore in the back of the Angel's Wings Transit. He went down under the combined weight of three of the uniforms from the Pork truck before he got to the van. Afterwards, he said it was because he was laughing so much at the sight of all those blue uniforms coming out of a pig truck that he didn't have the sense to turn round and leg it out of there.

Ash the Cash and Wahid Two got the doors of the Transit open and their hands on the goods when Kate Tallow's team hit them. In Ash's case, literally, as DC Tallow's baton dead-legged him on his left thigh first blow.

Boy Adrian, seeing the way the wind was blowing and having more sense than most credited him with, sprayed the two cops who got on his case with black paint and then turned and ran down the road, right by the Beamer, keeping on going. Right into Jim Driver's boys, one of whom stopped him in his tracks by bending over so that Boy ran his stomach on to his head. Both of them ended up sitting in the road, one winded, one semi-concussed.

Wahid One was caught in the lorry park without anyone putting a finger on him until it was handcuffs time. He ran round the cab of a parked lorry just in time to meet the last two uniforms piling out of the Pork truck. He turned on his heels and ran back the way he'd come, but looking over his shoulder all the time. Or for about three seconds, until he ran smack into Jo Jo Singh. His head bounced twice as he hit the floor but before he blacked out he thought he heard Jo Jo saying 'Sorry'.

It took five of them to get Jo Jo down and the cuffs on.

DS Moon gets lucky. He's looking down at the rips in his suit trousers where he's fallen out of the car and he's mouthing-off something gruesome. And then he's swearing at the fact that the car's fucked good and proper, its nearside wing embedded in the rear offside of the Escort van, and no doubt he'll have to account for that to somebody. And then he notices that the Escort is moving, just slightly, on its suspension.

So he walks quietly up to the passenger side – not that he has to be quiet with all the racket coming from the other half of Shoreham Road – and looks in. And there's Rafik Jarman, lying across both seats, trying to keep his head down.

Moon raps on the window with his knuckles and makes the wind-down sign. A bit sheepishly, Rafik winds the window down.

—You're nicked, son, says Moon with relish.

He's always wanted to say that.

Hasan Sharif watches all this chaos from the door of the Emirates office, standing there with his suit-coat buttoned, hands behind his back. Could be at a cricket match if it wasn't so exciting.

He sees the police pounce on a man in white overalls and he can't help but wince when he sees that nice lady detective whack him with her stick thing. There's a younger man with him, a young Afghan maybe, in a purple shell suit, and he goes down too. Then there's the muscular white boy who looks like he puts in time down the gym, who sprays paint in the face of the police before running. And he sees a load of uniformed policemen rugby-tackling a large, overweight, black man. Then a big Sikh, wearing a red turban and what looks very much like a Chelsea scarf, is dragged out of the lorry park, two policemen to each leg, one on each arm. In the distance he can hear sirens: two, three, five, then too many to pick out.

He sees Frank McEvoy climb unsteadily from the Transit (which now has tinted windows), indicate to a policeman that he was unhurt and then lean against the side of the van as if getting his breath.

McEvoy looks up and catches Hasan's eye and he nods once.

Hasan goes back into the office and picks up his phone. He gets through to Angel's Wings on the first ring.

—Naseem? I think your consignment is going to be delayed, he says.

It's round-up time. Police cars and vans, with lights flashing and sirens howling, are piling in to Cargo Village like rats up a drainpipe.

Jim Driver is striding proud, walking tall, shouting that everybody and everything is to be taken to the station on The Horseshoe. Makes a point of saying loudly that the station is being re-opened for the duration in Big Benny's honour.

When he comes face to face with Benny, he can't resist it.

—Hello there, Benny, nice of you to drop by. We're going to have a little chat later, me and you.

—I want... says Benny.

—Let me guess, Driver cuts in. You want that dodgy lawyer of yours. What's his name? Mawson, isn't it?

Benny looks hurt.

—I want my lunch actually, he says. My lawyer's already on his way.

At Divisional HQ, the Oik is being filled in by DI Davis.

—Looks like a clean sweep, sir. Big Benny, Ash the Cash, Boy Adrian, Jo Jo Singh and two we've not come across before.

—Jim Driver's happy then? asks the Oik.

—Er… don't know about that, sir. Haven't heard from DI Driver yet. First reports have come from DS Moon.

—He's keen, says the Oik dryly.

—Seems to have taken one of the villains down himself. Quite a struggle, by all accounts.

—Let's not start giving ourselves medals. What's happening with Mortlake Eddy down in Hounslow?

—Nothing, sir. No movement at all, says Davis.

—Yet, says the Oik.

McEvoy is trying to examine the bruise on his forehead in the Transit's wing mirror, without getting paint on his clothes, when Driver gets round to finding him.

—You okay, Frank? Knock on the head?

—My own fault, says McEvoy. Put it down to bad driving, though I've never had to drive over one of them before.

McEvoy looks down at the stinger coiled around the front wheels of the Transit.

—Where d'you think they got that, Jim?

—Dunno, Frank, but they had two. There's another one wrapped round DS Moon's car over there.

—Probably buy them on the Internet these days, says McEvoy.

—Wouldn't surprise me.

Driver shuffles his feet, like he doesn't know what to say next.

—Got to thank you for all your help, Frank. We'll need a statement from you.

McEvoy jerks a thumb at the Transit and then points a finger at the Emirates office.

—I'm supposed to be delivering this...there. It's booked on a flight this evening.

—I know, I know, but we've got the paperwork to go through, as you should bloody well know.

McEvoy draws himself up and puts the eye on Driver.

—You're not doing paperwork, Jim, give me some credit. You're setting up Mortlake Eddy. You're going to stash this stuff in that clapped-out nick down there and wait for him to come and get it, aren't you? When he thinks you've packed up and gone home.

—You been talking to Blind Hugh? Driver snaps.

—Didn't have to. Your DS, Moon, gave it away. But as it happens, I was down near Hounslow Heath yesterday, you know, out for a Sunday stroll, when who should I see taking driving lessons on a JCB digger but Mortlake Eddy. You're setting up this nick here just like we did Dogberry Road, aren't you, Jim? You're going for the double, aren't you?

Driver takes a moment, looks at his boots, then looks back at McEvoy.

—Well, you never managed it, did you, Frank?

DI Sugar's Obs 1 team takes about half an hour to pack up its operation at Angel's Wings and twenty minutes of that is putting empty coffee cups and crushed cans of Coke and cigarette butts into a dustbin liner.

—We'll be out your hair, Mr Naseem. You can get back to work now. Glad to see the back of us, I should think, says Sugar.

—Any news of Frank McEvoy and my van? asks Naseem.

—Well, he's all right as far as we know. Not too sure about the van. I heard somebody calling for a tow truck.

—Can I talk to McEvoy before you take the phone away?

—Sorry, says Sugar. His radio's been turned off and we

can't raise the phone. I should think the battery's probably gone by now. Hasn't he got his own mobile?

—No, says Naseem. Since he left the police he hates the things. Wouldn't have one given.

—Don't know how I'd manage without one, says Sugar. Anyway, I'm sure he'll be in touch. There'll be paperwork and things to do. I'll put the word out, get him to check in with you. We've still got the intercept on your land line. If you're not here and he rings, can we tell him where to get you?

—Don't worry about it, Inspector. I expect you've enough on your plate. Goodness knows, there's plenty I can be getting on with now.

They tow the Angel's Wings Transit, Moon's car and the Escort off the road and into the lorry park; wind up the stingers for evidence; sweep up some broken glass; bag some spray-paint cans and a sledgehammer; and find two policemen's helmets rolled under the British Pork truck.

They bring in a generator from Heathrow services and rig power to the old police house. they even have two Portaloos delivered. With the lights on and cars coming and going, it looks to be back in business.

To the side of it, there's a small area guarded by an ancient set of iron gates and even though the lock on the gates hasn't worked for years, that's where they stash the container cube of Coletoxore. They even accept Hasan Sharif's offer to drive it in there on an Emirates' fork-lift truck.

You can see the cube from just about anywhere on The Horseshoe. It's just left there. Full view. Plain sight.

Anybody could spot it.

Inspector Davis gets off the radio and on to the internal phone to the Oik.

—Movement down in Hounslow, sir, he says keenly. Mortlake Eddy's just turned up at the warehouse we've got staked out off the Staines Road. Three of his boys have joined him in there in the last five minutes.

—Still in there?

—Yes, sir. No sign of them coming out as yet.

—Regular reports, Inspector, regular reports.

—Yes, sir. Just thought you'd want to know before your meeting.

—Meeting? What meeting?

—With a Mr Tyler and a Dr Patel, says Davis, but wishing he hadn't started this. They've just arrived to see you.

Naseem backs up Angel's Wings' other van – a small, high-back white Renault – right into the warehouse. Then he gets on the firm's fork-lift and starts to move pallets around, glad that he's got the place to himself again as he knows he's not that good at it.

He moves a pallet of videos; two of advertising material for a Christmas promotion for a national supermarket chain; one that just says 'Made in Korea'; and one that is only identified by a worrying little label saying 'Best before end 1998'.

Behind that lot is the twin Coletoxore container, serial number 8788/491PQ.

Naseem slides the prongs of the fork-lift in first time, which is a result.

He loads it into the Renault.

McEvoy hasn't gone to Southall Central, where Benny and his boys have been taken. If he's going to give a statement, he's going to do it where he can keep an eye on the consignment he has still to deliver. He's adamant on this and Driver doesn't reckon it's worth arguing about.

They get food sent in and big urns of tea and coffee and the shifts change and officers come and go. If anybody is watching the place from outside, it looks like what it's supposed to look like: a holding operation with a skeleton staff. And unless somebody is watching very closely, they probably don't notice that out of every three policemen who go into the station, only two come out. By late afternoon, Driver has a hardcore team together in the back of the nick where the cells used to be, well out of sight of the front windows.

—When do you think they'll come? McEvoy asks Driver, and he can't resist adding: If they come.

—Soon as it gets dark, says Driver like he was 110 per cent certain.

—So they won't be able to resist it, eh?

Driver doesn't like McEvoy's tone, but he doesn't rise to it.

—We've made a big song and dance about still having the Coletoxore here under minimal guard. All Cargo Village knows by now, so the word'll get around. They'll think we're all down Southall nick taking the rubber truncheon to Big Benny and his boys, then celebration lagers and a curry afterwards. It's too tempting. Eddy won't be able to resist it.

—You're working on the assumption that Eddy has somebody here in Cargo Village? Keeping an eye out for him?

—It's a fair bet, isn't it? Come on, Frank, you know these Cargo Village people better than most. You know what they're like.

—Yeah, McEvoy says quietly.

Inspector Davis shows the visitors into the Superintendent's office himself as this gives him the chance to walk up a flight of stairs behind Dr Patel, who is wearing a pin-stripe, double-breasted suit with a very short skirt, high heels and shiny brown tights with black seams. He follows those seams with his eyes and reckons he could use them as spirit levels.

He can tell the Oik is impressed too, from the way he insists on getting a chair for her, which gives him – privilege of rank – the chance to look down the front of that suit jacket. When the Oik pulls up a chair opposite her and then she crosses her legs and the skirt rides up, Davis concedes that his boss has got the best seat in the house.

—I want to know where my export consignment is, says Tyler, as if anyone remembers him being the room.

—Ah, yes, Mr Tyler, says the Oik. Has Inspector Davis updated you?

Tyler thinks: No, he's been too busy staring at Roma Patel, though for the life of him he can't see what makes all these policemen drool over her.

—Only to say that things are going to plan, he answers. But he didn't say *whose* plan.

Roma Patel decides to try and deflect Tyler's sarcasm by smiling at them. Let's face it, if her skirt rose another millimetre they'd give her the keys to the cells.

—Mark is naturally concerned, Superintendent, she says sweetly. This is a very important shipment for us, scientifically as well as commercially, and our customers are hospitals in a poor country. We're giving them hope as well as medical expertise.

—Of course, we understand your partner's position...

—Dr Patel is not a business partner, says Tyler pompously. She's my chief chemist, responsible for the refining processes involved in Coletoxore.

—Of course, says the Oik smoothly. Well, I can assure you that we have the security of your shipment absolutely top-of-mind. I have personally issued instructions to the Senior Investigating Officer that he must guarantee that your consignment gets on that plane to Dubai tonight.

—Dubai, says Tyler to himself.

—Of course, we may have to cut it fine, leave it to the last minute, skin-of-the-teeth job. That's for operational reasons, which I can't go into at the moment.

—But as of now your shipment is in safe hands out at Heathrow, says Davis, determined not to be shut out, and he looks at Roma when he adds: Our hands.

—Can I get to see it? asks Tyler.

The Oik frowns at this, not expecting it. But Roma Patel smiles at him and lifts her eyebrows as if saying: *I trust you but he's a bit of an old woman.*

—I'm afraid not, Mr Tyler. Your drugs are being held in a secure situation in the Cargo Centre, only a matter of yards,

I'm told, from the Emirates freight office. It is still an operational area for authorised personnel only.

—Is Mr Naseem there, from Angel's Wings?

—I am not aware that he is, says the Oik, looking at Davis for confirmation.

—I can't say I'm happy with the situation, says Tyler.

The Oik looks at his watch.

—I am sure I can put your mind at rest within the next two or three hours, Mr Tyler. If you'd like to give us a number where we can contact you, or you could wait downstairs in our reception area or the canteen...

—We'll wait, says Tyler quickly.

—Good, says the Oik. I'll join you for a cup of tea as soon as I have some news for you. Inspector Davis will show you down.

Davis takes them out and returns after about five minutes to find the Oik sitting where he had been, gazing at the chair Roma Patel had been sitting in.

—Message from Southall, sir, he says. Big Benny's solicitor is raising the roof, demanding to see you.

—See me? says the Oik, kind of distracted.

—Sounds like it. It's that toad Mawson again, same brief as at Dogberry Road.

—Yes, well, we'll let him sweat for a bit.

The Oik gets to his feet, but he's still staring at Roma Patel's empty chair.

—Nice girl, that.

—Yes, sir, says Davis. You ever seen *Basic Instinct,* sir?

—No.

Didn't think you had, thinks Davis.

Dusk is falling and the lights are going on all over Cargo Village.

Driver and McEvoy are in the unlit upstairs office, looking out over The Horseshoe. Nothing's moved much and they've hardly exchanged a word in the last hour.

Then McEvoy says:

—You sure Mortlake Eddy's coming?

Driver looks at his watch.

—There's time, says Driver, but he looks like a man who's just remembered he's left the gas on at home.

—You sure about that, Jim?

—What the fuck is that supposed to mean?

—Don't lose your rag, Jim, just think about it. Mortlake Eddy is still down on Hounslow Heath, right? In the warehouse off the Staines Road?

—Yeah. So?

—How long do you think it'll take to drive a JCB digger from there to here? Can he get here now before you have to get that container on the Emirates flight?

Driver gives him a killer look then clumps down the stairs to where they've got their communications set-up.

In the depths of Southall nick, in Interview Room 2, DS Moon is having another go at Big Benny. He's put three sets of cassettes in the taperecorder so far but he's got nothing more than the sound of his own voice and that of the solicitor, Mawson, saying 'No comment'. That and Benny saying 'Meal break?' on three occasions.

Mawson reaches over and switches off the double-tape machine again.

—Off-the-record, I repeat my request for your Superintendent to be present.

—And on the record, I've said that's not possible at the moment, says Moon through gritted teeth.

—Will it be possible at, say, eight-thirty?

—It might be, says Moon carefully. Why eight-thirty?

—My client may be willing to make an off-the-record statement at eight-thirty, the solicitor says smoothly. But only to a superior.

—*That* shouldn't be hard to find, says Big Benny, with a smile.

Not that far away, Blind Hugh is closing up his mother's shop for the day. He's bringing the outside display trays of fruit inside as he always does when it gets dark, before passing kids start to help themselves.

One by one, he carries the boxes indoors and doesn't even glance at the white Renault van that's parked at the kerb just down from the shop, lights on, engine running.

On his third trip, even he notices something's iffy with the tray of grapefruit. Right in the middle of the box, grapefruits have been pushed aside to make way for six oranges from the next box. The oranges are laid out two, then one, then three in a curve. Eyes, nose, mouth – a smiley face.

Bloody kids.

He picks up the oranges to flip them back into the proper box and finds the plastic freezer bag hidden under them.

This time it's not a phone, it's a Grundig dictaphone machine – about the same size as a mobile – and it's got a label on it, which doesn't say Big Benny or even Mortlake Eddy. This one just says: Hugh.

Hands trembling, he rips open the bag and fumbles the On switch to Play.

—Ever wondered where those phones came from, Hughie? says the voice on the tape. Want to make a few quid tonight?

Inspector Davis has hijacked the Oik on his way to buy Roma Patel a cup of tea, so naturally the Oik's not impressed but he follows him into the operations room.

—Just had DI Driver on, sir, says Davis. He's worried about the deadline you set him. Doesn't think Mortlake Eddy can make it from Hounslow to Cargo Village in time. Not if he's driving a JCB.

—He's cutting it fine, that's for sure. No movement down in Hounslow?

—No, sir. Surveillance reports that Eddy is still in the warehouse with his crew. Hasn't moved all afternoon and no sign of him doing so.

The Oik makes an executive decision, and he just hates doing that.

—I promised Mr Tyler that his shipment would be on tonight's flight. What would we look like if it got out that we missed the plane because we were waiting on a tin-pot Hounslow gangster? Waiting for him to rob a police station, what's more. It could be time to call his bluff.

—Shall we turn them over, sir? We can get back up there in five minutes.

—Do it.

—What do we charge them with?

—Anything you can think of in the next five minutes. Suspicion of stealing a JCB?

—Fair enough, sir, says Davis. There is one other thing, though.

—Good news, I hope, says the Oik, thinking he can get back to Dr Patel now.

—Not sure, sir. It's the intercept we're still running on the phones at Angel's Wings. There's nobody there at the moment and we've taken four calls in the last hour for a Mr Naseem, the owner.

—And?

—Well, one was from a chap at Air India but the other three calls were made from here. From the phone in the reception area where Mr Tyler's waiting.

The cops on surveillance down near Hounslow Heath can hardly wait for their back-up cars to roll to a stop before they're clawing at the sliding door to Eddy's warehouse. It's not locked and it slides back silently on well-oiled bearings.

Inside, the lights are on and there's a big, yellow JCB digger in the middle of the otherwise empty space. Mortlake Eddy and three of his mates are bobbing and weaving around it, kicking a football around, shouting and squealing like kids in a playground.

—Stay where you are, you lot! shouts one of the cops.

The four of them freeze as if they've practised it. Mortlake Eddy is balanced on one leg, his other pulled back like he's taking a Beckham free kick.

—What's up, then? asks Eddy.

—You lot are in trouble, says the cop.

—What for?

—Nicking that, says the cop, pointing at the JCB.

Mortlake Eddy lets his foot drop. He seems more inter-ested in watching the football roll under the digger.

—That's not nicked, he says reasonably. I've hired it for the week.

—Hired it? What the hell for?

—I'm doing a bit of landscape gardening for me mum, says Eddy. Want to see the hire agreement?

Which he promptly pulls out of the inside pocket of his leather jacket and hands over.

With a smile.

—Mortlake Eddy's not coming, says Driver to McEvoy. Happy now?

McEvoy doesn't let his face slip but Driver can smell the smugness coming off him.

—I'll be happier when Tyler's shipment gets checked in and is on its way to The Hub.

—Go for it, then. There's no reason not to, now. Want me to give Hasan Sharif a ring?

—Yeah, you'd better. Make it official. Give him a chitty or something, releasing it from custody. I'll go and get a fork-lift and drive it over there.

—We'll make sure you get there in one piece.

McEvoy looks surprised.

—It's only across the bloody road. What's going to happen between here and there?

—Nothing, says Driver. If I've anything to do with it.

Angel's Wings is dark and deserted; no sign of life and no obvious sign of an alarm system being on. You can never be sure of these things but it looks promising. The front door's locked, of course, but there might just be a loose catch on one of the metal-framed windows round the back of the warehouse.

Blind Hugh is sure there is, 'cos the voice on the dicta-phone machine told him so. Just like it told him that if he fancied a few phones like the ones he's been delivering lately, then this would be the place to find them. And he'd be welcome to them as long as he closed the window after him and didn't break anything. And as long as he didn't touch anything else at all. If anything else was found missing then he'd need one of the phones to call the fire brigade for his mother's shop.

Hugh believes every word on the tape, even the last bit, which says 'Now destroy this tape'. In fact, he really likes that bit because it reminds him of *Mission: Impossible* re-runs.

He has a bit of a job convincing his cousin, Gul, about the job because, in Benny's book, Gul is a bit slow. Plus, he's never heard of *Mission Impossible*. Still, he fancies a mobile phone and Hugh's promised he can take his pick, so he goes along with him.

Somebody has to help Hughie over the fence.

—Come on, I'll give you a lift, says Driver to McEvoy.

They've delivered the Coletoxore to Hasan Sharif at the other end of Shoreham Road East, and he's stamped the paperwork and rushed it through into the Heathrow system. Driver and all his team have walked the length of the road in two lines, flanking McEvoy on a fork-lift truck. McEvoy says it's the first time he's ever had a police escort rather than being in one. And it seems to have done the trick in so much as no helicopter gunships swoop down to steal their load.

—Thanks, I need one, says McEvoy as they walk back down The Horseshoe together. I don't have any wheels here. Literally. God knows what Naseem's going to say about his Transit.

—You haven't told him yet? asks Driver.

—Couldn't get him earlier. We can't get it fixed until your Scenes-of-Crime boys have finished fingerprinting it, anyway. Not that you'll need the forensics. I reckon Big Benny will 'fess up to this one.

—I'll believe that when I hear it for myself. That lawyer of his will try and slime his way out from under. I'd better get over to Southall, see how it's going. Last I heard he was demanding to speak to the Oik in person.

—My, my. Thinks a lot of himself, doesn't he?

—Always did, didn't he? He used....

Driver's phone goes and he stops mid-stride to answer it, turning his head away from McEvoy.

—Yeah? No. No. Just talking about that, actually. Yes I do, he's standing right next to me. Hang on.

Driver holds the phone away from his face and turns back to McEvoy.

—You've no idea where your man Naseem is?

—I think I'm his man, not the other way round, says McEvoy. But no. Haven't seen him since I left Angel's Wings with the Transit. What's up?

—We've still got an intercept on the phone there and we're picking up calls for him. Mark Tyler is one, wanting to know where his drugs are. The other is Kuli Khan of Air India. Mate of yours, isn't he?

—Yeah, I know him. Works over there in Peace and Harmony. So?

—Mr Khan has left a message with our operator. Says it's urgent. Says he can't wait any longer and the flight's gone without him.

—What flight?

—That's what I was going to ask you.

—I don't know. Unless he means the eight o'clock long haul.

—To where?

—Mumbai.

—Where?

—Bombay. It's what they call Bombay nowadays.

They look at each other then Driver puts the phone back to his face.

—I'll get back to you.

Driver whistles to his officers to gather round.

—Get the cars. Frank, you come with me. Show me the way to Peace and Harmony.

As soon as Blind Hugh lands on the floor of Angel's Wings' warehouse, he knows he should have brought a torch. There's nothing for it but to stand there waiting for his eyes to get accustomed to the light.

His cousin, Gul, lands softly beside him, so softly it startles Hugh for a second. Then his cousin amazes him by pulling open the duffel bag he has round his neck and producing a torch. Not only is it a torch, but it's on a headband with a battery to clip on his belt, so he can shine it and keep his hands free.

—Where d'you get that? Hugh asks.

—Nicked it from a sports shop over Isleworth. Marathon runners use 'em when they're training in the winter.

—Oh, right. Good idea. Good man for thinking of it.

—Hey, I've been burglarising before, you know.

Hugh ignores this and makes Gul go first, the beam on his head lighting up pallet after pallet.

—Look, CDs man, says Gul. Wonder if they've got any DVDs.

—Leave it, snaps Hugh. The man said phones only.

—So where they then? There's tons of stuff in here.

—They're in a crate marked Made in Korea.

And they find it surprisingly easily, for a pair of characters who couldn't muster half a brain between them with a mind-meld.

They get it open easily enough too, as the top is only held on with staples, which have been pulled out and pushed halfway back in. And there are phones in there. Lots of them.

—Fuck me, says Hugh. There must a coupla hundred.

—Do they work? asks Gul, as Hugh twists his head so the light shines into the crate.

—Turn 'em on and see.

The phones aren't wrapped in anything, just packed in

shredded newspaper. Gul picks up one in each hand and both seem to work.

—Result, cousin, fucking result. Can I call my girlfriend?

—Not now, you doper. Let's get these out of here. We need something to put them in.

Gul swings the duffel bag off again, almost blinding Hugh as he turns his headlamp. He pulls out a roll of plastic bin liners.

—Thought we might need these.

—Good man, says Hugh, well impressed.

—I've been burglarising before, you know.

Once on the Perimeter Road, Driver puts his foot down hard; two other unmarked cars following do the same.

They flash by the back of Southampton House and then the back wall of the old nick where they've spent most of the day. A couple of minutes more and they're approaching the turn-off to Sandringham Road and Peace and Harmony.

—Right at the lights, says McEvoy, one hand bracing him against the dashboard.

—Fuck the lights, says Driver, swinging the wheel.

When McEvoy opens his eyes, the car is across the opposite carriageway and bouncing down the slip road, angry horns and flashing headlights behind them.

It's not a long slip road, but it dips so that it's not visible from the Perimeter Road after the first twenty or thirty yards.

That's probably why no passing motorist had reported the white Renault van, tilting at an odd angle into the left-hand verge. Its back doors are open, showing it's empty, and once you get closer you can see how the front wheels have dropped due to the fact that there are no tyres left on them. And if you got right in close, you'd see a black, sharp, spikey, metallic rope of some sort wrapped around the front axle. And you might notice that the front windscreen is spray-painted black.

But then if you were that close, you'd have seen Naseem lying there in the middle of the road, bucking like a landed fish, his feet and hands tied together behind his back with nylon washing line, and with wide strips of duct tape across his mouth and his eyes. The headlights from Driver's car show that he has blood on his forehead, but from the way he's jerking his body about he's definitely alive.

He's probably heard the cars coming and thinks he's going to get run over. After all, it's not been his day so far.

Driver stops his car ten feet short of him and yanks the handbrake on with venom. Then he slaps the palms of his hands on the steering wheel with such violence, McEvoy's sure it will break.

—Arseholes! Bastards! Fucking cunts!

—Isn't that an old Ian Dury song? McEvoy asks him.

By the time the Oik gets to see the delightful Dr Roma Patel again, it's after eight o'clock and he's running late if he's got to see Big Benny over at Southall by half past. This doesn't lighten his mood, which is already shit-coloured.

—Mr Tyler, Dr Patel. I'm sorry you've been kept waiting so long but there have been a few developments.

—What's happening? asks Tyler, prepared to be stroppy but catching the Oik's eye and deciding not to chance it.

—You've been trying to get through to a Mr Naseem at Angel's Wings. Eight times now, I believe. Using our phone.

—I'll pay for the calls, says Tyler meekly, and Roma gags on a giggle.

—May I ask why, Mr Tyler?

—We had business to discuss. That's all.

—All? the Oik says it like a High Court judge would. Would this business involve trying to get a second consignment of Coletoxore – *about which we knew nothing* – on to an Air India flight tonight?

Tyler reaches for the knot in his tie. Maybe he'll loosen it, maybe he'll hang himself. Hard to tell.

—It was my insurance policy, he says. Naseem was to arrange a back-up consignment if anything went wrong with the Dubai flight.

—And you thought it best not to tell anyone about this?

—There seemed to be so many leaks. Too many people knew too much as it was....

—Well, because of your action, Mr Tyler, your back-up delivery, as you call it, has been successfully hijacked while my men were guarding the real consignment.

—The real one...? Tyler mutters.

—Whoever did it got clean away with your Coletoxore and we've had to rush Mr Naseem to hospital.

—Oh, no.

Tyler puts his hands to his face. Roma wonders whether she should get him a chair. No, let him fall.

—I'm afraid we'll be requiring a statement from you, Mr Tyler, a very full statement. Right now, here in one of our interview rooms.

—I need to make a phone call, whispers Tyler.

—No you don't. No more calls until we've got a statement. You'll be pleased to know, though, that the consignment we *were* aware of has gone through Heathrow security and is on its way to Dubai.

—Oh, shit.

—No need to thank us, Mr Tyler.

Despite his protests that he's needed at a fresh crime scene, Driver is overruled and told to report to Southall as soon as. If not sooner.

He gets there before the Oik does and finds DC Kate Tallow has pulled a double shift and, even worse, been lumbered with the job of Evidence Officer. She's the only friendly face he's likely to see.

—Hiya, boss, she greets him. Sorry to hear about your bit of bother.

—Yeah, right. What's the score here?

—Big Benny and his brief. They won't say anything until the Super gets here and he's late. Which means Benny's demanding another meal break.

—What about Benny's crew?

Kate shakes her head.

—Absolute zero. Not a word, well-zipped. They're waiting for their solicitor, Mr Mawson.

—Who's still with Benny?

—Yep. They seem happy to sit it out. In fact, I got the impression they were on a timetable. Like they didn't want to say anything *before* eight-thirty for some reason. Watch out. Stand by your beds.

Driver looks to the entrance and sees the Divisional Rover draw up outside and the Oik climb out, uniform immaculate, like he's just stepped out of a dry-cleaners. Driver bets he's had time for a shave, too.

—'Evening, sir.

—Good evening, Jim. Bad news from Heathrow.

—If we'd known in advance, sir…

—I know, I know, but nobody will make allowances for us. I'm only sorry that there's no way we can pin it on the bunch of reprobates we've got in the cells here.

—What do they want, sir?

—I don't know, Jim, but knowing Tim Mawson there will be a deal in there somewhere. Come on, let's get it over with. It's been a long enough day already.

Kate Tallow shows them through into the interview room where Big Benny and Mawson are sitting behind the table, legs stretched out, calm, cool and up for it.

—Thank you for seeing us, Superintendent, eventually, Mawson opens with a sting. My client is anxious to make police bail if you have no objection.

The Oik makes a bad attempt to stifle a grin.

—Just a few minor ones, Mr Mawson, such as charges of robbery with violence…

—*Attempted* robbery. And there was no violence on my client's part, except in self-defence against a total police over-reaction.

—Hah! spits Driver.

—Perhaps you have video tape or photographs of the incident, which would sustain this allegation? says Mawson smoothly.

The Oik prefers to try and override him.

—Stolen vehicles…

—Borrowed. My client did not know they were stolen.

—Illegal possession and use of police property…

—Ah, now *there* my client is willing to help you.

—There's a first, mutters Driver.

—My client believes that certain items of police issue, which I think you call stingers, were indeed stolen. In fact, they were stolen from Dogberry Road police station about six months ago when, I believe, a certain Acting Inspector Driver was station commander. My client is, of course, more than willing to say this in open court.

The Oik grits his teeth.

—Conspiracy to commit….

—Ah yes, now, conspiracy. Now we're getting to it. What you want, Superintendent, what you really, really want, is not my client, is it? You want the man who set this whole thing up. The man with the mobile phones.

The Oik looks at Driver. Driver looks at the Oik.

—And your client knows who it is?

—Oh, no, he has no idea. But he might have a phone number where he can reach him in an emergency. Would you call this an emergency?

—Possibly, says the Oik cautiously. What's the deal.

—My client dials the number he might or might not have. He believes that with the co-operation of the mobile phone service providers, it is possible to pinpoint the locality of someone using a particular number. If they are pre-warned, that is. My client believes this accuracy can be a matter of feet and inches.

—How does he know that? barks Driver.

—He read about it in *Time Out*, snaps Mawson.

—And in return? says the Oik.

—Police bail, a reduction in charges across the board, and a written statement from you that my client has co-operated fully. I have something drafted in my briefcase, but you'll want to get it typed up. I know it will have no legal weight, but every little helps with the Crown Prosecution Service.

Driver looks at the Oik. The Oik looks at Driver.

DC Kate Tallow, from behind them, says:

—I could have the phone companies on line for a search in about fifteen minutes, sir.

—Do it, says the Oik and Driver together.

Mark Tyler is sweating so much his shirt collar is discoloured and he hasn't even started on his statement yet.

DI Davis has put them in an interview room and gone to get cassette tapes. He's not thought anything about leaving them alone like that. It's not as if they've been charged with anything. But Tyler is smart enough to realise he's only got a few minutes to get his head straight.

—We've got to get that reject consignment back from The Hub, he says to Roma, but really he's talking to convince himself.

—So we get out of here, fax them before the plane lands and tell them to send it back, she says.

—No we can't, says Tyler shaking his head. Do you know how much that would cost?

—No, but the insurance would cover it.

—It's not insured, Tyler hisses. The real stuff was, the consignment that got nicked. We can't claim twice.

Roma wants to say 'What's this "we" shit?' but doesn't.

—And anyway, what do we say to Bombay? There's a consignment sitting in Dubai but you can't have it?

—Well they haven't paid for it yet, says Roma reasonably.

—I know that! Tell me about it. But if we piss them off, there goes my clinical trials data. It would be much better if Bombay didn't know about the Dubai shipment. We tell them we did our part and the shipment was en route, but the British police allowed it to be stolen from under their noses.

—And you can use the Bombay hospital angle – vital medical research in the Third World – to pressure the insurance company into coughing up quick.

—Yes, yes, I like it.

Tyler is in danger of cheering up.

—But we have to stop the reject lot being onward shipped from Dubai. How long is it held there?

—Three days on average, maybe less. It would be cheaper to go out there yourself and have it destroyed rather than ship it back.

—Is that possible?

His face has definitely brightened.

—Sure. There's a flight from Gatwick early tomorrow morning.

—There is?

—Yes. I've caught it before now.

—You have?

—Yes. You sent me out there twice last year to set up the distribution chain.

—Then you go.

Roma lets her jaw drop.

—Me? Tomorrow morning?

—Well I can't. I'll probably still be here giving statements. They've no need to keep you here.

—But...

—Come on, Roma, do it for the company. Get out there and get that batch destroyed. Grease a few palms if you have to. You know how to deal with those people out there.

Tyler claps his hands together and starts to pace the room, rehearsing his statement, seeing light at the end of the tunnel, seeing a way out. One part of the problem solved. Now he has to think: where the hell is the real batch of Coletoxore?

He doesn't think to look at Roma, which is just as well.

She's thinking: *What would he do if he knew I already had a stand-by ticket, my passport, the company credit card and a spare pair of knickers in my purse?*

The aircraft levels out at 29,000 feet and the stewardesses start to serve dinner. When they get to a small, distinguished gentleman in a window seat halfway down the starboard side of First Class, one of the attendants – in a glorious red and yellow sari – offers him a half bottle of champagne. Not the standard quarter-bottle and good stuff. Vintage.

—With the Captain's compliments, sir, says the stewardess, who is remarkably pretty. And the Captain would be happy for you to join him at any time on the flight deck.

—Thank you, my dear, thank you, says Kuli Khan. Tell my son I'll see him later.

Kate Tallow volunteers to man the link-up to the mobile servers. She says that once the number answers, it should be located in anything between three and eight seconds. She'll get a call on one of three hotlines they're keeping open. She's also arranged for a tap to be put on the line Big Benny will use, so they can record the conversation.

—It's over to you and your client, Mr Mawson, says the Oik, as a phone is put on the table in front of Benny.

—He said emergencies only, says Benny. And only after eight o'clock tonight.

—Why eight o'clock? asks the Oik.

—Dunno, says Benny.

—That's when he was going to set up the payoff, wasn't it? says Driver. You pull the job and then you ring him to arrange a handover in exchange for a shedful of dosh, right?

—No idea what he had in mind, Mr Driver, says Benny cheerfully. Of course he might have left the country by now....

—Just get on with it, says the Oik.

So Benny dials, punching buttons, knowing that the cops will get the number straight away, but what the hell?

There's a second or two gap, as there always is when you dial a mobile from a land line.

Kate Tallow holds a phone to her ear, her finger poised over the extension line buttons, waiting to hit whichever one lights up.

The Oik runs a finger round the inside of his collar.

A mobile phone rings.

In the room.

—Oh fuck! I'm sorry, sir, I…

Driver's right hand reaches for his inside pocket.

—It's ringing, says Benny.

The Oik is looking at Driver, who fumbles his phone as it rings again. Loudly.

Gingerly, Driver presses the Receive button, holding the phone open in the palm of his hand as if it's going to bite him.

—Hello? says Benny.

Driver doesn't move. He's just heard Benny's voice coming out of his phone as well as in the room, right there, across the table from him.

—Hello? Benny says again.

The middle light on Kate Tallow's phone comes on and she hits the button.

—We've got him, sir, she says.

Driver puts the phone to his ear. Very carefully.

—Hello? he says weakly.

—Hello there, Mr Driver, says Benny with a big grin.

Kate Tallow is glued to her phone.

—He's somewhere in Southall, sir, she announces. Could be really near to here.

Just then, right at that very moment, Blind Hugh and Gul are walking down the High Street, a bulging, black dustbin bag in each hand, when a police patrol car goes by them.

But it's only slowing down because the lights at the junction up ahead are on red.

No need to panic then, thinks Hugh, wondering if Gul has even noticed the car.

No need to risk a bit of stop-and-search though, so he slows his pace, hoping the lights will change and the cops will pull away.

It's debatable whether the cops had even noticed the two of them, or would have noticed them had not all the phones in their bin liners suddenly gone off at the same time.

Gul stands there eyes popping, not believing his ears as roughly fifty phones per bag start ringing.

They don't ring for long, but they make a hell of a noise while they do, a bit like a lorry load of canaries going over a cliff.

The ringing stops, but so now has the police car and two uniforms are climbing out.

Only then does Gul realise that his cousin's bags are on the pavement and his cousin is already across the street, showing a fair proportion of leg.

It's two months before it's showtime at Jim Driver's internal disciplinary hearing.

As expected, he's kept waiting, sitting in full uniform in a drafty corridor of Divisional HQ, for over an hour.

He uses the time to reflect but all he comes up with are the same questions that have rattled round his brain for two months.

What made Tyler double-up on the consignments of Coletoxore? And why? He still wasn't talking.

And what happened to Tyler's chemist lady, that rather tasty piece who shot off to Dubai and never came back?

What made Tyler think he could get cargo space on a long-haul flight at such short notice? It was supposed to be impossible. That Air India guy had said as much. Kuli Khan.

What tipped off the Emirates man, Hasan Sharif? He came up with the videos of Benny and Mortlake Eddy scouting the place. It was like he knew we'd be interested in the tapes, but he told McEvoy first.

Yes, now, McEvoy. There was a link. McEvoy was the link. He was the one who knew Big Benny, knew about the Coletoxore, knew all the Asians down Cargo Village, knew Blind Hugh, knew what a double take was. Even his boss, Naseem, didn't trust him enough to tell him about the second shipment. But he didn't know about Mortlake Eddy. Moon admits he let that slip.

Moon.

If he could think of a way of putting Moon in the frame, he would.

They'd had to release Big Benny and his team on bail and they still hadn't been charged with anything 'pending enquiries'. It would never happen.

What had really got Jim Driver's goat, though, was the morning-after bollocking from the Oik, which had been expected, fair enough. But when the Oik had commenced with *Whose fucking idea was this shambles?* dear old Detective Sergeant Moon had jumped in without drawing breath:

—*Mr Driver's, sir.*

That had hurt.

There was only one way to come back from that. Find out who was behind it all.

The only trouble was that no matter how many times he chewed it over in his mind, he came up with just one, ridiculous, abso-bloody-lutely stupid answer.

They were all in it together.

At roughly the same time, give or take a time zone or two and several thousand air miles, a handsome young Kashmiri stands on the awning-covered terrace of a very posh restaurant in the commercial heart of Bombay, which we now call Mumbai.

The young man wears a never-gone-out-of-fashion crumpled white linen suit and a Panama hat. He holds a length of rope about three feet long and he's demonstrating to a small crowd of children how he can tie knots behind his back, which are as effective as handcuffs one second and then merely loose rope the next as, with a flick and a flourish, he can free himself.

—Stop showing off, Naseem, says a female voice, in English.

—Whatever you say, my dear, he replies, slipping an arm around her white-coated waist. You've got it?

Roma Patel holds up the thin, metal briefcase she's carrying and nods enthusiastically, rubbing her body up against Naseem's chest.

—Where are the others?

—Inside. Come on.

The men inside all stand up to greet her, kiss her hand, call for waiters to bring drinks, generally make a fuss.

Kuli Khan makes the most, treating her like a princess.

Hasan Sharif insists a waiter attends to her every need, calls for *thandai*, milk and saffron sherbet.

Naseem sits next to her, beaming proudly.

But it's Frank McEvoy who asks the question.

—Did you get it?

Roma nods, pats the briefcase.

—Sterling deposit accounts, instant access. I've got chequebooks for everybody. One-point-two million in total. That's £200,000 each.

—So your purification process for the Coletoxore worked, then? says McEvoy with a smile, but the other men scowl at him for doubting her.

—Of course. They got one pure shipment and now they've got two. And they got a bargain price. They would have gone to three million if we'd pushed them.

—It's not just the money, my dear, says Kuli Khan, patting her hand. We have helped to save lives.

—Quite a noble gesture if you think about it, says Naseem.

—It's a fortune out here, says Hasan Sharif. And it means I don't have to go home to my bloody children.

McEvoy makes a play of thinking hard before he smiles at his own secret thought and says:

—It's *more* than enough.

A uniformed Sergeant leans over and taps Driver on the shoulder.

—They're ready for you now, sir, he says.

Driver is miles away, deep in his head. Thinking it through again and again. Always the same answer.

—Inside, sir. The board is waiting.

Driver still doesn't notice the hand on his shoulder.

Suddenly, out loud, he says:

—No way! That doesn't make any fucking sense *at all*.

Double
Take

The Script

by

MIKE RIPLEY

OPENING SHOT *of what appears to be a scene in India or Pakistan. White-dressed Muslims, Sikhs, a temple, perhaps a mosque, all reflected in a dark, still, unmoving river. Suddenly, reflections of a jumbo jet in the water. Then another, a whole queue of them. PAN UP to sign on river bank saying:* **Grand Union Canal, Borough of Southall.** *Follow flight path of landing jets (one every 90 seconds) as they descend. CUT TO sign saying:* **Welcome To Heathrow.**

TITLE CARD:

The street value of talcum powder

CLOSE-UP *on the business end of a Metropolitan Police hand-held battering ram being swung. It displays a sticker saying "You've Just Met the Met". A house door crashes in, revealing armed policemen, menacing in silhouette. The broken door swings back on them in dead silence. It is gently pushed open again. One of the police leans in.*

POLICEMAN
Anyone home… ?

POV *of police: the house is clearly deserted but an area of the hallway is stacked with plastic bags of white powder, about a foot square. Two plain-clothes detectives push themselves forward as the police crowd the hall: McEvoy and Driver.*

McEVOY
Come on, come on! Upstairs, the lot of you. The little shaggers are probably sleeping it off.

Policemen rush past, bounding up the stairs, kicking doors in. DRIVER stops to examine the cache of drugs.

DRIVER
Can't argue with the quality of your information on this one, Boss. Just like you predicted. Wouldn't like to have a go at next week's lottery numbers?

McEVOY
I'm a detective, Jim, not a clairvoyant. It's always down to good information.

An armed policeman comes down the stairs.

POLICEMAN
Upstairs secure, sir.

McEVOY
They give you any hassle?

POLICEMAN
ER… the upper floor's secure, sir, but there's nobody on it – in it – up there.

DRIVER
(Sneaking a look at McEvoy)
Nobody? There's nobody watching over all this gear?

McEVOY
There should be at least four. Big Benny, Ash the Cash, and perm any two smackhead hardcases in the neighbourhood.

DRIVER
(Into radio)
Rear team, report any activity, like *now*.
(The radio crackles)

The back-door boys say they've seen less than
squat.

McEVOY
They *must* be here. My information was they
would be. It doesn't make any sort of sense.
Where the fuck are they?

DRIVER
(Weak)
Perhaps they just popped out for a … …

McEVOY
(Losing it)
For what? You take delivery of half a ton of
prime coke, find a place to stash it, then you pop
out for a bit of breakfast somewhere? What
kind of dipshits do you think we're dealing
with?

CUT TO *inside of cafe, window table. BIG BENNY and
ASH THE CASH are being given plates of food. They have
two other henchmen with them, both obviously stoned out of
their heads. All are oblivious to the large number of police
cars and vans driving by the window.*

BIG BENNY
What the stonk is this?

ASH
Looks like nan bread.

BENNY *hits the table with it.*

ASH
Yesterday's nan bread.

BIG BENNY
I asked for toast. Was that unreasonable of me?

ASH
So maybe they toasted it.

BIG BENNY
(Holding up the large nan)
You find me a toaster to fit this.

ASH
Hey, man, don't down on me. It was you got the
munchies, had to come for bite, so forth, so
fifth.

BIG BENNY
(To Ash, who is Indian)
You just don't like curry, that's your problem.

ASH
(Weary, not noticing the police activity outside)
Not for breakfast do I not.

BIG BENNY
Be telling me your ashamed of your *cooolinary*
traditions next.

ASH
Nothing to do with me, man. This lot are
Bengali. They own all the restaurants. Me, I'm
from fucking Surrey, I am.

BIG BENNY
Still, it was nice of them to open up early for us,
wasn't it?

CUT TO *kitchen where another member of the gang is lounging against a wall, cleaning his fingernails with a knife. Three or four anxious Bengalis prepare a meal. All are dressed in pyjamas and slippers.*

CUT TO *raided house, hallway. Police everywhere, also white-coated forensic officers. McEVOY and DRIVER are joined by a uniformed SENIOR POLICE OFFICER (SPO).*

S.P.O.
You're absolutely sure about your source on this, Chief Inspector?

McEVOY
Pretty solid, sir. He was right about the cocaine.

S.P.O.
Who is he?

McEVOY
A local lad, bit of a gopher, bit of a record, but strictly small-time.

S.P.O.
Does he have a name?

McEVOY
(Glares at DRIVER, who is giggling)
Blind Hugh, sir.

S.P.O.
I hope that's a code name, Chief Inspector. I take it this Blind Pugh person...

DRIVER
Hugh, sir. Blind Hugh.

S.P.O.
… I take it we can't get this person into court to
finger the gang?

McEVOY
Not likely, sir. He's a bit *budhu.*

S.P.O.
What's that? Like a Punjabi?

McEVOY
No, sir. It means he's a bit – simple.

S.P.O.
(Worried)
There's an awful lot of resources gone into this
operation, McEvoy, and I don't like the idea of
there not being a result at the end of the day.

McEVOY
(Indicating pile of drugs)
But *this* is a result, surely? Even with street
prices down to forty quid a gram, you're
looking at a seven-figure retail profit here.

S.P.O.
(Snotty, then fantasising)
But no arrests, Chief Inspector, no bodies. No
examples to be made. We can be tough on crime
and tough on the causes of crime, but people
want to see us being tough on *criminals*. Really
tough. Ruthless… .

DRIVER
Mr McEvoy has a point, sir. This is a pretty
impressive bust.

S.P.O.

But we should be busting people, Inspector, not just front doors of empty houses. *(Thinks)* We are a people business, after all. We have to make arrests so we can come down hard on the guilty ones. Really hard. As hard as…. .

DRIVER
(Shrugs)

Forensics have got nothing so far, sir. Lots of prints around the house but nothing on the stuff itself.

McEVOY

Maybe we could stick it in Lost Property and hope some dork comes to claim it.
(He thinks about this as DRIVER laughs.)

S.P.O.

And just where do you propose we store all this stuff? Forensics will want a sample, but nothing like this quantity.

McEVOY
(Thinking fast)

Er… I assumed we'd stash it at the local nick, sir, just overnight.

DRIVER
(Quietly, to McEvoy)

That's quite a stash.

McEVOY

Too much to claim for personal consumption, you reckon?

DRIVER
What? Personal consumption of Brazil, maybe.

S.P.O.
You mean the Dogberry Road station house?
(McEvoy nods)
It's a bit decrepit, isn't it? Are you sure security's
good enough there?

McEVOY
It'd only be overnight, until we clear it for
destruction with the Home Office, sir. *(Beat)*
And anyway, *(Beat)* who's to know it's there?

CUT TO restaurant. BIG BENNY is coming out of the toilet, shaking his hands. He pauses to dry them on a table cloth, then zips up. ASH is behind the bar, opening the cash register, watched by the frightened owners.

BIG BENNY
They don't call you Ash the Cash for nothing,
do they? You'll not get much, though. Poor
buggers haven't opened for business yet.

ASH removes the entire drawer from the cash register and reaches in, pulling out a roll of notes, flipping it, catching it.

ASH
Seek and ye nearly always find.

BIG BENNY
(Impressed)
Spanking.

BENNY goes back to the table to wake up his spaced-out goons. He notices, for the first time, the growing police presence across the road.

BIG BENNY
Ash, d'yer think we might have a problem here?

They look out the window, police cars reflected in the glass.

CUT TO street scene. McEVOY and DRIVER walking through Southall. McEVOY is pointing things out; nodding and acknowledging passers-by.

McEVOY
No, it's not a mosque, it's a gurdwara – a Sikh temple. They wouldn't open a mosque in an old pub.

DRIVER
This used to be a pub?

McEVOY
Yeah, Marquis of something or other.

DRIVER
(Looking around)
Not the Clive of India, then?

McEVOY
(Ignoring him)
None of the restaurants round here used to have licences, so we used to put four or five beers down our throat in there before we went to eat. We used to say we were going for a take-in before we got the take-away.

DRIVER
You like all this 'Jewel in the Crown' shit, don't you, Guv?

McEVOY
There's nothing wrong with that, is there?

DRIVER
No, Guv, never said there was. Just a bit off-
centre, that's all, you bein' Irish.

McEVOY
So Paddies aren't allowed to like curry? You
think we oppressed minorities shouldn't stick
together?

DRIVER
I thought the police were the oppressed minority
these days.

McEVOY
(As if thinking about it)
You might be right, there, Jim.
*(He indicates a greengrocer's shop with stalls of
fruit outside)*
This is it. Let's see if Blind Hugh's minding the
store.

*As they enter the store, McEVOY surveys the display of fruit
and vegetables with an expert's eye, running his fingers over
things, digging his hand into tubs of dried peas and beans.*

McEVOY
Just look at this lot. Cardamoms, curry leaves,
chickpeas, split black chickpeas, red lentils,
yellow lentils – you know, there are over sixty
different pulses used in Indian cooking? Before I
left Ireland I used to think turnips were ex-
fucking-zotic. And look at the *mirch*.

DRIVER
The what?

McEVOY
The chillis – God's way of telling you your
palate's jaded. They've got chillis from all over.
You could eat your way round the world just on
chillis.

DRIVER
You'll be travelling alone.

McEVOY
(Dreaming)
Just look at them… the colours… the *warmth*.
The *habanero* from Mexico; the *Bird's Eye* from
Thailand – that's only a wee one but a little
devil. And there's the *Scotch Bonnet* from the
West Indies, the king stinger himself, the hottest
of the hot.
(He puts his hands out as if on a fire)
You can feel the heat, Jim. They can warm you
just by looking at them. Do you know just how
fucking cold and damp it can be in the west of
Ireland?

DRIVER shakes his head, more in wonderment than answer.

DRIVER
Shall we get on, sir?

McEVOY
(Sighs)
Very well. Let's do this as diplomatically as we
can.

*McEVOY picks up a small chilli and begins to toss it in his
hand as he steps into the shop.*

McEVOY
(Shouts)

Hughie! Blind Hughie! Come on down!

They enter the shop. BLIND HUGH, a nervous, young Indian with thick-lens glasses is holding a crate of vegetables. McEVOY and DRIVER back him up against a wall and the shop empties of customers.

BLIND HUGH
Mr McEvoy, you shouldn't be here, should yer?

McEVOY
No, Hughie, I shouldn't. I should be down the nick going head-to-head with Big Benny's solicitor because surely, by now, I should've had him cautioned, charged, fingerprinted and at least *considering* signing the confession I'd already written for him. But I'm not. I'm here instead.

BLIND HUGH
And … and… why's that, exactly, Mr McEvoy?

McEVOY
Because somebody… *somebody* not a million miles away from where I'm standing… . gave me some double-duff information. Information prepaid with coin of the realm and a promise to look the other way about a certain somebody's uncle, who has a sideline in importing illegal Somali immigrants.

DRIVER
You've wasted a lot of Mr McEvoy's time this morning, Hughie. He's not happy and he takes it out on me. So, in the natural order of things, I'm going to take it out on you.

BLIND HUGH
What's your problem man? I gave you the
goods, I did. Straight. Told you the where, the
when and the who. You went to the wrong
house or summat? It's happened.

McEVOY
We got the right place, Hughie. We get lost, we
ask a policeman. Trouble is, nobody home.

DRIVER
And that means trouble for you, Hughie.
(He cracks his fingers, tough-guy style)

BLIND HUGH
Hey, come on, I know this. This is Good Cop,
Bad Cop, innit? Seen it hundreds on the telly
and suchlike.

McEVOY
Wrong, Hughie. This is Bad Cop, Bad Cop.

*McEVOY takes the chilli he has been playing with and
crushes it against HUGH's forehead. HUGH looks almost
relieved, as that didn't actually hurt.*

McEVOY
Told you about this one, Jim, the *Scotch Bonnet*.
Small, but deadly. And the seeds, they're the
killer.

*McEVOY pushes the crushed chilli up BLIND HUGH's
nose. He reacts as if electrocuted.*

BLIND HUGH
Suerkabacha!!

McEVOY
(Grinding in the chilli)
Don't you call me a son-of-a-pig, you little
tosser, or you'll get this up your Marmite canal
and you won't sit down for a month.

DRIVER
Didn't know you spoke… .
(pause, unsure)
… Hindi, Guv.

McEVOY
Only the swear words. It's a gift. All the Irish
have it.

BLIND HUGH is gasping, eyes streaming.

BLIND HUGH
(Sobbing)
I gave you what I knew. Benny was taking deliv-
ery last night.
(Sob)
A big consignment, from Holland.
(Gasps)
He was gonna guard it overnight and start dis-
tribution today. What happened? Didn't the
stuff arrive?

McEVOY
Oh, the dope was there all right. Tons of the
bloody stuff. I'm up to my ankles in white
powder. But no bleedin' Benny or his mates; no
sign of them. Did they get tipped off, by any
chance? Are you on the double take by any
chance, Hughie?

BLIND HUGH
That's plain daft, Mr McEvoy, innit? I wouldn't
do the double on you, Mr McEvoy.

DRIVER
So where was Big Benny when we gave him his
wake-up call this morning?

BLIND HUGH
I don't know, do I? He should have been there
with his crew. Maybe they popped out for a bit
of breakfast or summfing.

McEVOY
Do I look *baywakoof*, Hughie? Do I look slow?
Am *I* the one standing here with a chilli up the
nose? Do you really think Big Benny's gonna
leave half a ton of pure driven snow unguarded
while he pops out for an Egg McMuffin?

BLIND HUGH
He gets the munchies real bad, Mr McEvoy...

McEVOY
Oh, stuff it. Look, Hughie, I'm going to hold
this one against you personally because you
know what I've got to do now?

BLIND HUGH
No, Mr McEvoy.

McEVOY

I've now got to explain to my superiors why I've
got half the gross national product of Colombia
on my hands but not a single, solitary arrest. Do
you know how much paperwork this involves?
Of course you don't. Do you know the problems
I'll have just getting the stuff down to Dogberry
Road nick? Of course you don't. Do you know
the security problems I'll have stashing it there
overnight? Christ, the place is falling down. It
should've been condemned years ago. No, of
course you don't know this. These are my problems but, Hughie, I'm putting them down to
you.
(To DRIVER)
Come on, Jim.

*He pulls the chilli out of HUGH's nose, which is red and
throbbing, and puts it into HUGH's hand.*

McEVOY

Don't try selling that, will you?

*McEVOY and DRIVER leave the shop. Behind them,
HUGH dashes to a cold drinks fridge, grabs a can of Coke,
shakes it and squirts it into his face.*

ON THE STREET, the two policeman walk together.

DRIVER

Was it wise to mention Dogberry Road like that,
Guv?

McEVOY

(Pulling out a mobile phone)
Wisest thing I've done since I brushed my teeth
this morning.

*CUT TO BIG BENNY AND ASH in a car, watching from a
distance as the police examine the drug-bust house.*

ASH
I'd say we had problem. Or at least a predicament of some proportion.

BIG BENNY
(Dry)
How big a proportion would that be?

ASH
Mega. Possibly ballistic.

BIG BENNY
You should ungroove yourself, Ash my man.
We're free and clear, we have our health and
we've had a good breakfast.

ASH
But we haven't actually paid for the goods yet.

BIG BENNY
(Reasonable)
There is that.
(Makes himself comfortable)
So I think I'm going to sit here and keep an eye
on our investment, while you get all the crew
together and then go and find Blind Hugh.

ASH
What do you want with Blind Hugh?

BIG BENNY
(As if surprised by the question)
He's the best snitch in the business.

CUT TO drug-bust house. DRIVER is supervising a police van backing up to the front door. With the van doors open, it is impossible from the outside to see what is going on inside the house.

DRIVER
(In the hallway, looking into an empty van)
Close in, close in. Keep it tight.
(Loud)
Now, let's get this stuff on board. Careful, lads,
no spillage.

The policemen act out a pantomime of climbing in and out of the van, thumping and banging. From the outside we see the van bounce on its springs, but back in the interior, despite the comings and goings, the van is empty.

McEVOY
(Coming up behind DRIVER)
Keep this up for another fifteen minutes, Jim,
then take your time getting round to Dogberry
Road. Make sure you're noticed. Get some out-
riders and put the sirens on.

DRIVER
Are they ready for us?

McEVOY
They will be. The Superintendent's okay-ed it to
clear the cells. Anybody held overnight down
there must think it's their birthday.

CUT TO road sign saying DOGBERRY ROAD and a police station, obviously dilapidated, next to a building site. On the building site is a JCB mechanical digger. Inside, police men and women are clearing space, emptying cells, throwing people out. A harassed DESK SERGEANT is signing off pris-oners, rushing through paperwork. The SENIOR POLICE OFFICER (SPO) hovers in the background, concerned. The DESK SERGEANT gives a still-drunk, dishevelled man in a suit his tie, shoelaces and a piece of paper.

DESK SERGEANT
There you are, sir. Come back tomorrow with your solicitor. You're free to go.

MAN
What d'you mean, free? I'm guilty.

DESK SERGEANT
We'll sort that out later, sir. It's best not to rush into these things.

MAN
That's outrageous. I demand to plead guilty. Look at me, man, I'm obviously drunk.

DESK SERGEANT
That's a matter of opinion, sir. Now if you wouldn't mind…

MAN
But I plead guilty to being drunk. *(Pulls himself upright and wags a finger)* But *not* to being dis-orderly. Of that, I am totally innocent.

DESK SERGEANT
Of course you are, sir. By the way —

(He reaches under his desk and produces a trombone)
—I think this is yours...

PAN TO S.P.O. *talking to a policewoman who is holding an armful of plastic freezer bags on rolls (as you buy in a supermarket).*

POLICEWOMAN
I just about cleaned out the local supermarket,
sir. I hope these'll do.

S.P.O.
(Impatient)
Yes, yes, of course they will. Just get them out of
sight. Wait. What about the stuff to go in them?

POLICEWOMAN
We've sent all the civilian staff out to the shops,
sir. We told them to buy flour but the first two
came back with wholemeal and granary, so
we're mixing it with talcum powder. Hope that's
OK, sir?

S.P.O.
Yes, yes. It's only for show.
(To himself)
Show? It's a bloody circus.

CUT TO *interior of a car. ASH is in the driving seat, listening to a cellphone. In the back are BIG BENNY and BLIND HUGH. They are watching the front entrance of Dogberry road police station.*

ASH
(Covering the cellphone)
I've got Rafik watching the house. He says
they're moving the merchandise.

BIG BENNY
Tell him to stay there and keep an eye out.
(To BLIND HUGH)
And you say this is where they're going to stash
it?

BLIND HUGH
(Nose like a red balloon, eyes still streaming)
That's what that Mick-Paddy-bogtrotting-
bastard McEvoy said, Benny. Straight.

BIG BENNY
(Patting his knee, comforting)
Now, now, Hughie, we're a multi-cultural
society these days and we have to learn to live
with each other. Was this before he rammed the
– what was it? A *Scotch Bonnet*? – up yer nose,
or after?

BLIND HUGH
That stuff burns, Benny, it really burns.

BIG BENNY
Of course it does, Hughie. Dear me, these
policemen. What will they think of next? Was he
a bit upset when he did this to you?

BLIND HUGH
He was *pagal*, Benny. He'd really lost it.

BIG BENNY
That's interesting. Hughie. Now you get yourself home.
*(He produces a roll of notes, peels some off and
stuffs them in Hugh's shirt pocket).*

Normally we'd give you a lift, but we've got pressing business. You go and get something for that nose.

BLIND HUGH
(Relieved to be getting out of the car)
I will, Benny, thanks, thanks…
(They wait until he is out of the car.)

ASH
That nose! He could read in bed by the light of it!

BIG BENNY
(Cracking up as well)
Read by it? He could divert fucking aircraft!
Remind me to specify Scotch Bonnets next time
we have a curry. I like the sound of those little
devils. Now, to business. Who've we got on the
day shift?

ASH
(Thinks)
Rafik and his brother are watching the house.
Imran's gone to see if his wife's had the baby yet.
Ashtok Mann and Jo Jo Singh are on standby.
Eddie Adrian and Slasher Carmichael are trying
to off-load those Romanian computers you
bought. There's a couple of new boys, Somalis,
who are freelancing for us. And then there's the
Afghans, who are up for anything.

BIG BENNY
What about Baby Face?

ASH
I could ring the school, get him out early; say his grandmother's ill, suchlike.

BIG BENNY
Do it. Tell him to bring some of his mates. I want to know what's going on inside there. I want lost kids; I want people who want to know the time; I want pregnant women reporting flashers; I want people reporting missing dogs and cats. I want the crime statistics *boosted*. Any excuse. I want people in there with their eyes open.

ASH
You want our people to go *in* to a police station? Like... voluntarily?

BIG BENNY
Yeah. Make a nice change. Bit of a day out for most of them.

ASH shrugs and starts to press buttons on his cellphone.

CUT TO Dogberrry Road police station. In the holding-cells area, police officers are filling plastic bags with flour and talcum powder to duplicate the haul of cocaine. They are not exactly taking this seriously, one of them pretending to sneeze as every bag is filled. At the front desk, the DESK SERGEANT is dealing with a growing queue of 'customers', all there on spurious excuses. Standing in line is the drunk MAN with a trombone. A young Asian kid, BABY FACE, enters and sidles to the front of the queue but cannot be seen over the desk. He finds a wastepaper bin, empties it and stands on it so he can be seen.

DESK SERGEANT
… right, sir, we'll look into it. And no, before
you ask, there's nothing we can do this minute…
(Noticing BABY FACE)
… Just a minute, son. *(To the queue)* Now, once
again, ladies and gentlemen, there is no Lost
Property office here. Neither do we have bus
timetables, visa application forms or the home
telephone number of the Attorney General.
So…
*(He sees tears rolling down BABY FACE's
cheeks)*
… what is it, son?

BABY FACE
(Angelic)
I've lost my mother.

DESK SERGEANT
Where did you lose her, son?

BABY FACE
If I knew where she fucking was, she wouldn't
be lost, would she?

CUT TO *drug-bust house. Outside, one of Big Benny's gang,
RAFIK, is watching a police van leaving, complete with car
and motorcycle escort. He gets on his cellphone.*

RAFIK
Ash? Looks like they're shipping the stuff out.
(Beat)
About a dozen or so uniforms left. Looks like
they're just about to pack up.

CUT TO inside house. McEVOY and DRIVER are organising a line of uniformed police men and women in the hallway, as if in marching order. At the door, DRIVER waves in a police Transit bus with its windows blacked out, up to the kerb.

DRIVER
Transport's here, Guv.

McEVOY
Right. You all know what to do. 'Bags of swank'
as Kipling said. Heads up, eyes front, proud to
be police. Off you go, left, right, left, right.
Come on, you must remember how it goes.

The line of police start to march out into the street and climb into the police bus, watched by RAFIK from across the road.

McEVOY
Go with 'em, Jim, see they don't get lost, then
hack it back to Dogberry Road.

DRIVER
Why are we going to Slough, Guv? Central
Security at Heathrow's nearer.

McEVOY
Heathrow? *Thief*row? You going *budhu* on me
as well? No, the nick down in Slough's far safer.
You take that lot into Heathrow, the van'd be
pinched before the wheels stopped turning.

DRIVER
You might not be wrong, there, Guv.

McEVOY
Trust me on this one, Jim, I'm a policeman. Oh,
and Jim… .

DRIVER
Yes, Guv?

McEVOY
I've counted them all out… .

CUT TO Dogberry Road and growing chaos at the front desk. The DESK SERGEANT hands BABY FACE a telephone.

DESK SERGEANT
Look, kid, is there a relative you can ring?

BABY FACE
Sure there is.
(He takes the phone and starts to dial)

DESK SERGEANT
Now, who's next. Look, I've told *you*, we're not
charging you. Haven't you got a home to go to?
The pubs are open, you know…

He notices that BABY FACE is still dialling – a lot of numbers. Eventually BABY FACE stops and hangs on the phone, smiling angelically.

BABY FACE
What time is it now in Bombay?

The Sergeant's hand-chops off the call. CUT TO police bus. The uniformed cops are climbing in and sitting on the side-bench seats. As the last one climbs in, DRIVER slaps the side of the bus and climbs in himself. The bus pulls away and DRIVER addresses the cops.

DRIVER
All righty, empty your pockets. And I mean all
of them.

Slowly, all the police begin to produce the bags of real cocaine from their uniforms, making a pile on the floor of the bus.

CUT TO Dogberry Road. BABY FACE is now leaning over the front desk, playing with the mouse of the desk computer as the Desk Sergeant shouts through a door into the cells area.

DESK SERGEANT
Well, one of you will have to run him home. I've
got to get this place cleared before Inspector
McEvoy gets back.

From inside the cells area there is a loud sneeze followed by loud laughter. The POLICEWOMAN seen earlier emerges, laughing, holding a handkerchief to her face, wiping away white powder.

POLICEWOMAN
I'll do it, Sarge, where is he?

BABY FACE, still fiddling with the computer mouse, looks up and is horrified.

BABY FACE
That's OK, I'll walk.

BABY FACE climbs down off the desk and leaves. Once on the street, he reaches into an ankle sock, produces a very small mobile phone and begins to dial.

CUT TO street scene. BIG BENNY and ASH are climbing out of their car. RAFIK draws up in another car and joins them. ASH's phone rings and he answers it.

ASH
Yeah, yeah... Top man... Yeah... we're in the
Bengali place, just down the road from the
Temple of the Screaming Light.

BIG BENNY
Shouldn't that be *Serene* Light?

ASH
(To Benny)
No, that closed down last week. This is a new
one.
(Into phone)
Right, see you soon.

BIG BENNY
(To Rafik)
My, my, how things change. Still, you'll like this
place. We've been coming here for – what is it –
(He looks at his watch)
– nearly five hours now.

*We establish that they are outside the restaurant they visited
that morning. One of the staff sees them as he is putting out a
"Lunch special" menu board and he dives back inside but
they barge in. BENNY and RAFIK look around the empty
tables for somewhere to sit. ASH, on another call, keeps
talking as he walks around the bar and up to the till again,
opening it as he did earlier and searching under the cash
drawer.*

ASH
Well, stay there and keep awake. I want to know
if anything moves out of that place. *Out*, got it?

BIG BENNY
(Looking around)
You know, I don't understand how this place
makes anybody a living. Look at it. It's dead.

RAFIK
Maybe the food's crap.

BIG BENNY
Better not be.

ASH
*(Still talking, produces another roll of notes
from the till, flips it, shakes his head.)*
That's right. Any vans, trucks or security
wagons going out? Not coming in?

BIG BENNY
Have a word with the chef, Rafik, my son.
Make sure the curries are *fresh*, unnnerstan? No
reheated rubbish. Fresh today.

RAFIK
Sure, boss. Any requests?

BIG BENNY
(Thinks, smacks lips)
Something with lots of chillis.

CUT TO car interior, McEVOY driving and on car phone.

McEVOY
Don't worry, sir, it'll work. They won't be able
to resist it. I know these people...

CUT TO *restaurant. A waiter is putting cushions on a chair so that BABY FACE can reach the table opposite BIG BENNY. When he is settled, BABY FACE produces a stapler, pens, pencils, a policeman's notebook, paper clips and other stuff he has lifted from Dogberry Road, including a small ball, which he plays with on the table.*

BIG BENNY
You done well, Baby Face. You want to try some
curry?
*(He offers from a wide range of dishes arriving
at the table)*

BABY FACE
Curry makes me fart.

BIG BENNY
Me too. *(Enthusiastic)* Spanking.

BABY FACE
Tell 'em to do me a cheeseburger in a nan bread.
To go. I've gotta get back to school.

BIG BENNY
(He motions RAFIK to do it)
Yeah, right you are. So, what's the form down
the local pig farm, then?

BABY FACE
(Spinning the little ball)
Something's going down, for sure. They're
running around like cockroaches, but lots of
laughing and shouting, too. Like they were
enjoying their work.

BIG BENNY
Did you see any packets about this size?

(He holds his hands apart)

ASH
Packets of white stuff. Powder maybe.

BABY FACE
Oh, the dope? What is it? Skag, horse or snow?
Whatever. Saw one of the female pigs with it all
over her snout. She looked happy.

BENNY and ASH exchange looks. RAFIK returns with a
parcel of food.

RAFIK
Freshly prepared to order. Do you want a Coke
or anything to go with it?

BABY FACE
Got any Cobra beer?

BIG BENNY
Don't push it, little one. Now you hop off back
to school. I'll see you right at the end of the
month.

BABY FACE shrugs, grabs his sandwich and gives the little
ball a final spin, leaving it on the table.

BIG BENNY
What the fuck is that?

BABY FACE
Souvenir.

CUT TO Dogberry Road. McEVOY enters and speaks to the
DESK SERGEANT who is having trouble using the mouse
on his computer. Nothing is registering.

McEVOY
Got the place cleared?

DESK SERGEANT
Eventually. It's been like the Cup Final in here
today.
(He bangs the mouse in frustration)

McEVOY
Lots of visitors? Punters wandering in off the
street?

DESK SERGEANT
(Looking at the underside of the mouse)
Bloody hundreds. Time wasters and rubber-
neckers, the lot of 'em.

McEVOY
Thought you'd be busy. Stuff through the back?

*The DESK SERGEANT nods as McEVOY goes through to
the cells.*

*He unscrews the back panel on the mouse to discover that the
ball has been removed.*

DESK SERGEANT
The little bastard... .

*CUT TO restaurant. The meal is becoming a banquet. There
are still no other customers and the staff are cowering in the
wings.*

ASH
So you reckon it's do-able?

BIG BENNY
'Course it is. Last thing they'd ever expect.
Everybody knows Dogberry Road is a joke.
Loads of stuff goes missing from there.

RAFIK
I heard the place was condemned. Not fit for
animals.

ASH
Just pigs.

BIG BENNY
That's right. It's a pig house. A house built by
the little pigs. And we all know what the Big
Bad Wolf did, don't we?

ASH
(Unsure)
You're gonna huff and puff and blow it down?

BIG BENNY
After a fashion. *(Beat)* Yeah.

CUT TO *interior police station (Night). Plastic bags of white
powder are stacked on the floor of a cell.*

EXTERIOR – *deserted street. On the building site to the
side, a set of headlights come on, followed by the roar of an
engine. From the POV of a security camera, we see it is a JCB
digger, its shovel lowered as a battering ram as it drives
straight for the rear wall of the police station.*

INTERIOR – *the digger crashes through the wall into the
cell, bursting bags of powder. Bricks, dust, powder everywhere, like an explosion.*

Through the dust, BIG BENNY, wearing goggles, climbs off the JCB and goes to stroke one of the plastic bags. He waves the digger forward and the shovel begins to scoop up the pile of 'cocaine' and then reverse out.

EXTERIOR – a flat-backed truck and a car reverse up to the hole in the police station wall. The JCB tips the drugs, bricks and all into the truck. Benny and the gang start to run for the car.

FROM ABOVE we see policemen stream out of neighbouring houses and hear sirens, see the first flashes of blue lights. Cutting off the van and the car on foot, squads of policemen unroll stingers – flexible mats of spikes – which tear open the tyres as the gang tries to escape. The JCB digger goes around in circles in a frantic attempt to escape. Eventually, it trundles across the building site, drives into a hole and tips on its side in front of a "Danger – Men At Work" sign.

FADE TO interior, police station. Police, covered in dust, are milling around congratulating themselves. The uniformed SENIOR POLICE OFFICER (S.P.O.) is conferring with McEVOY and DRIVER.

S.P.O.
And you're sure the real drugs are safe?

DRIVER
Logged into the evidence store down in Slough,
sir. Saw to it myself.

S.P.O.
Well, that's something, I suppose.

McEVOY
(Hurt)
We got a double result, sir. The drugs off the
street and now we've got Big Benny, Ash the
Cash, Rafik Jarman and three others in custody.
Not a bad day's work, if you ask me.

S.P.O.
As it happens, Inspector McEvoy, I *haven't*
asked you about one little aspect of this operation. To whit: destruction of police property.
Namely, an entire police station!

PULL BACK to reveal a rather large hole in the wall.

McEVOY
Oh, come on, sir, the place was falling down by
itself.

S.P.O.
It didn't need any help – who's this?

*A smart-suited TIM MAWSON, clutching a briefcase, climbs
in over the rubble.*

MAWSON
Good evening, gentlemen. *(Looks around)* Spot
of home improvement is it? Hope you've got
planning permission.
(To McEvoy)
Usual place?

McEVOY
You know the way. Follow the yellow brick
road.

They watch him go towards the remaining cells.

DRIVER
Tim Mawson, sir. Big Benny's solicitor.

S.P.O.
That was quick. *Bloody* quick.

McEVOY
Rumour has it Big Benny carries him around in
the back of his car. Like a spare tyre. Just in
case.

S.P.O.
I hope you're going to charge him with damage
to police property, Inspector. Have you any idea
how much this is going to cost to repair?

McEVOY
Haven't checked the insurance policy today, sir,
have you? You know, the home and contents
section… ?

DRIVER tries not to laugh.

S.P.O.
Not to mention damage to that digger from the
building site. And the vehicles they used will
probably be nicked, so that'll be another
claim… .

A uniformed POLICEMAN interrupts them.

POLICEMAN
Sorry, sir, but that brief, Mawson, wants a
word.

S.P.O.
OK, let's throw the book at them and try not to
look smug.

McEVOY
(Smiling)
Could be tricky, that.

CUT TO *cell where Big Benny and TIM MAWSON are
sitting at a table. Benny's face is covered with white powder,
except for the outline of the goggles he wore, making him
look like an owl. He says nothing, just smiles and blinks, as
MAWSON stands and faces the three policemen.*

MAWSON
I fail to see why my client is being held at all,
Superintendent.

McEVOY
(Looking around)
Are we in the right cell, Jim?

MAWSON
My client and his associates were simply driving
by when then saw an unidentified youth obviously joyriding on a motorised digger on the
adjoining building site. When they tried to
prevent a serious accident, they themselves were
arrested.

S.P.O.
Rubbish!

McEVOY
Total bollocks!

MAWSON
Perhaps you have some proof that my client was
doing other than what he says? Video tape,
perhaps?

S.P.O.
(To DRIVER, quiet)
Well?

DRIVER
(Whispers)
Only the one camera and it was the first thing to
get taken out.

S.P.O.
(Sniffing)
Mr … Mawson, is it? … Please don't play
games. Your client has been caught, red-handed,
in possession of a huge amount of Class A… .

MAWSON
Class A what, Superintendent?

*He draws a finger through the powder on Benny's face and
sniffs it.*
Class A flour? No, talcum powder. Rose-
scented, I believe. Or is it lilac? Tell me,
Superintendent, what *is* the street value of
talcum powder these days?

*CLOSE UP on the three policemen in turn as they V/O their
thoughts.*

S.P.O.
(Thinks)
Oh… my… sweet… Lord… .

McEVOY
(Thinks)
Oh... fuck...

DRIVER
(Thinks)
It was Inspector McEvoy's idea, sir, the whole
thing... .

(FADE)

TITLE CARDS:

One Year Later.
They're drugs, Jim, but not as we know them.

OPEN ON *barbed-wire security fence. A video camera moves automatically, threateningly. PAN BACK. It is tracking a swan gliding by on a river and the location (Cambridge?) is idyllic countryside. This is the research station of* TYLER PHARMACEUTICALS. *A car arrives at the main gate and is waved through. In it are* DRIVER *(now promoted) and Detective Sergeant* MOON. *They are there to see the whiz-kid boss,* MARK TYLER, *who meets them in the high-tech entrance lobby.*

DRIVER
Mr Tyler? I'm Detective Inspector Jim Driver and this is Detective Sergeant Simon Moon. It's good of you to spare us the time.

TYLER
(Shaking hands, but aloof)
Yes, it is, actually. What is this all about?

DRIVER
One of your… er… products, Mr Tyler. Is there a private office we could use?

TYLER
We don't believe in an office culture, Inspector.
We have a sterile laboratory through here.
(They walk)
Which of our products could possibly be of interest to you?

MOON
You make drugs, here, don't you sir?

TYLER
Yes, but not as you know them.

MOON *and* DRIVER *exchange looks.* MOON *mouths "They're drugs, Jim" silently as they go through a set of pneumatic doors.*

TYLER
We develop pharmaceuticals, very advanced ones. Nothing that would interest you people.

DRIVER
(Noticing security cameras)
You seem very security conscious, though.

TYLER
Industrial espionage can be a problem. That and the animal-rights loonies who think we test on animals. We don't, by the way. Well, only on rats, if we have to. And nobody minds about that much.

MOON
Because their tails are naked.

TYLER
I beg your pardon?

MOON
If rats had furry tails, there'd be a campaign to protect them. *(Beat)* They'd look more cuddly.

TYLER
(Checks his watch)
Quite. Is there anything *relevant* you want to
say to me?

DRIVER
It's about Coletoxore.

TYLER
(Slowly)
Very... well. In here.

They enter a sterile lab, stacked with computers, centrifuges, robot arms, etc. A young Asian woman in a white coat, ROMA, is working at a mass spectrometer. Through a glass screen can be seen the automated production line, producing vials of a clear liquid.

TYLER
This is where we do the final analysis on
Coletoxore and this is Dr Roma Patel, one of
our senior chemists. Dr Patel? These are policemen. You may have to look after them for me. I
have a conference call booked. They have some
questions, I believe.

ROMA
If I can help... .

DRIVER
We need to know something about Coletoxore.
In layman's terms, though.

TYLER
Don't worry, Dr Patel's been specially trained to
talk down to... *(Falters)*... laymen.

ROMA
What do you need to know… Mr… ?

DRIVER
Inspector Driver, Jim Driver. This is DS Moon.
We need a crash course in Coletoxore. What it
is, how much it's worth and what would be the
black market in it?

TYLER
Now, wait a minute, Inspector. There is no black
market in Coletoxore. This isn't something you
buy from the black kids on the street corner.

ROMA glares at the back of TYLER's head.

TYLER
Coletoxore is a high-value pharmaceutical at
the cutting edge of cancer research.

ROMA
Experimental. It's an experimental treatment.

DRIVER
So it's a cure for cancer?

ROMA
(Cutting in on TYLER)
It helps. It's a treatment, not a cure.

DRIVER
A treatment that works?

TYLER
We're getting excellent clinical reports
from all over the world.

DRIVER
So there is an international market for it?

ROMA
Yes, but it's a specialised one. Hospitals, clinics,
hospices. You won't get it on prescription from
a family doctor, nor would you drop it at a rave
(Looking at TYLER) or buy it from a black kid
in the playground. It doesn't give you a high.

MOON
Not even if you mix it with anything?

ROMA
(With distaste)
I'm afraid not. It's of no interest to street dealers.

DRIVER
So who would buy it?

TYLER
Any reputable medical institution.

ROMA
With four million pounds to spare.

TYLER
(Glaring at her)
Dr Patel, here, thinks we should give it away,
without realising that we would also be giving
away her salary.

DRIVER
So what do you get for your four million quid?

ROMA
Ten thousand vials of 10 milligram doses is the
usual batch size.

MOON
And that's what? A barrel-full? A tanker load?

ROMA
Actually it's an insulated cube, specially
strengthened, about this big – *(She describes a
cube with her hands)* – weighing about three
hundred pounds. *(Puzzled)* Why?

TYLER
Yes, why, inspector? Why the interest?

DRIVER
Because we believe there will be an attempt
made to steal a consignment of Coletoxore.

ROMA
When?

DRIVER
We're not sure, but very soon.

TYLER
How?

DRIVER
We don't exactly know.

ROMA
Where?

DRIVER
We don't know that either.

TYLER
(Sarcastic)
I don't suppose you know *who's* going to steal
it?

DRIVER
(CLOSE UP)
Oh, yes. We know that.

FADE.

CUT TO the shop where BLIND HUGH works. He is carrying crates of fruit and vegetables to put on display. He stops to examine one crate, dips into the okras or peppers and pulls out a mobile phone, wrapped in plastic. There is a note stuck to the plastic saying: BIG BENNY – 12 O'CLOCK.

CUT TO Indian restaurant, where BLIND HUGH is facing BIG BENNY, ASH and RAFIK.

BIG BENNY
(Examining the phone)
Whoever this guy is, he must buy his mobiles
wholesale. What's this, number three?

BLIND HUGH glances away furtively but the others do not notice.

ASH
You've no idea where this came from, I
suppose?

BLIND HUGH
(Innocent)
It came in the peppers with this morning's delivery from the market.

RAFIK
(Tapping his forehead, looking at Hugh)
Budhu.
("He's slow")

BIG BENNY
Don't slag the man, he's doing a spanking job
for us. Give him his bus fare home.
(RAFIK reluctantly peels off some notes)
Now you take that, Hugh, and you keep your
eyes open for us. Keep checking the peppers for
more little presents, hey?

BLIND HUGH
The last one came in the tomatoes.

(Silence. RAFIK shakes his head.)

BIG BENNY
Check *all* your fruit and veg, then, eh?

HUGH picks up his money and backs out of the restaurant.

ASH
Why is he called *Blind* Hugh?

BIG BENNY
Because he never sees anything worth seeing.
*(The mobile rings with the tune "Goodness
Gracious Me".)*

BIG BENNY
(Picking it up)
Oh, very droll. But right on time. *(Into phone)*
Hello, there, Man of Mystery…

FADE

*CUT TO car, interior with MOON and DRIVER threading
through west London traffic.*

MOON
You know where this place is, Guv?

DRIVER
(Map reading)
It's somewhere between Heston and Southall,
on an industrial estate. There are loads of them
round here, all feeding into Cargo Village.

MOON
What's that, then?

DRIVER
I forgot. You're not from around here, are you?

MOON
What, jungle-land? Give me a break.

DRIVER
Hey, watch your attitude. Cargo Village is the
freight terminal at Heathrow. If you're sending
anything abroad by air, that's where it goes
from.

*[CUT AWAY to line of jets on the approach to Heathrow or
reflected in car windscreen]*

DRIVER
There's a plane every ninety seconds or so. They
come in from everywhere, they go out everywhere.

MOON
Sounds like thief heaven. Must be lots of temptation to go on the rob.

DRIVER
There is. But most of the security is geared to
stop things coming in. Nasty people, nasty
things, naughty substances. Take a left here.
We've got us a situation where someone's going
to nick stuff going out. This is it.

CUT TO *car driving into small industrial estate and pulling
up beside a warehouse complex. There is a sign saying:
ANGEL'S WINGS – INTERNATIONAL TRANSIT.*

CUT TO *office of the boss of Angel's Wings, a smart, young
Pakistani – NASEEM. There is a framed photograph of
Margaret Thatcher on the wall, and copies of the Directory of
Asian Businessmen on the bookshelf. He is talking to
DRIVER and MOON.*

NASEEM
Yes, we ship Coletoxore for Tyler
Pharmaceuticals, and I've already had Mr Tyler
on the phone telling me to co-operate with the
police. Though I cannot think why the police
should be interested.

DRIVER
They are high-value drugs, Mr Naseem...

NASEEM
But not as you know them, Inspector.

(MOON *stifles a giggle*)

DRIVER
Pharmaceuticals, then, worth £4 million per
consignment.

MOON
And they can't be insured, so we're told.

NASEEM
That's true, which is why we take extra care of
them. But the point is, the drugs aren't much use
to anyone other than a doctor in a hospital. Do
you really think a reputable hospital would buy
drugs off the street from someone like… a… a…
second-hand car dealer?

MOON
What about abroad?

NASEEM
You mean in places like Pakistan or India, where
everyone is corrupt?

DRIVER
(Jumping in)
My Sergeant didn't mean anything by that, Mr
Naseem. It's just that your company transports
Coletoxore abroad. You don't distribute it in
this country.

NASEEM
But somebody is going to steal a consignment
here, in this country?

DRIVER
That is our information.

NASEEM
So you are suggesting it must be someone here
at Angel's Wings. Then arrest me.

(He holds out his hands for handcuffs)
We're not a big company and I'm involved in
everything that goes on, so I must be the guilty
one.

DRIVER
We're not suggesting anything, sir.

MOON
Nothing's been nicked yet.

NASEEM
But you have information that something will
be?

DRIVER
Coletoxore, quite specifically, and from this part
of West London. The only distributors are you.
You do the freighting for Tyler Pharmaceuticals.

NASEEM
So you're saying we're the target, not the criminals.

DRIVER
That's what our information suggests, and that's
why we'd like to go through your procedures
and security.

NASEEM
I have been told to offer every assistance, but the
best person to talk to is my freight manager.
He's also responsible for any security precautions we have to take. I've already asked him to
join us and… .Here he is.

*McEVOY enters carrying a tray with four mugs of coffee and
sets it on the desk, only then noticing the policemen.*

McEVOY

I remembered the sugar this time, Mr Naseem. I
hope you chaps… .Hello, Jim.

DRIVER

Frank? I didn't know you worked here.

McEVOY

About nine months now, since the… you
know… retirement.

DRIVER

I thought you'd moved out of the area.

McEVOY

No. The wife did, but I stayed on to sell the
house and things, then sort of fell into…
(He sees Naseem's look) … saw the opportunity
to work here.

NASEEM

Former Inspector McEvoy has made lots of suggestions about our security arrangements. We
have state-of-the-art, closed-circuit TV and
alarms, and we are contracted to a 24-hour
security firm. I'm not sure about our safety
rating but it has certainly increased our over-
heads.

DRIVER

And you're in charge of shipping things abroad,
as well?

McEVOY

Middle and Far East, India, occasionally Japan.
Those are our main destinations.

MOON
For Coletoxore?
McEVOY eyes up MOON and checks first with
NASEEM, then DRIVER.

NASEEM
It's all right, Frank. Tyler Pharmaceuticals had
asked us to co-operate two hundred percent.

DRIVER
This is DS Moon, Frank. Just started working
out of Norwood Green. You used to call it the
posh part of Southall, remember?

McEVOY
Yeah. There's nothing wrong with my memory.

DRIVER
Didn't imply there was, Frank, didn't imply
there was. In fact, it might be useful to us.

McEVOY
(Suspicious)
So what's going on?

NASEEM
I would like to know, too, if I am allowed at this
reunion.

DRIVER
(Looks at MOON, then:)
I must ask you keep this to yourself, but we have
received certain information that certain individuals are planning a robbery, and the target is
the next shipment of Coletoxore you'll be handling for Tyler Pharmaceuticals.

McEVOY
(Sharp)
Which individuals?

DRIVER
Big Benny for one…
DRIVER remains in Voice Over.

CUT AWAY to BLIND HUGH finding another mobile phone, this time in a bunch of bananas, say, and delivering it to BIG BENNY and his gang. BIG BENNY listens to his instructions. We see him giving orders, meeting with a selection of hard-type criminals, perhaps auditioning them. We see gang members stealing a parked car and driving it to a disused warehouse, where BENNY, ASH, RAFIK and anonymous hardmen rehearse a hijacking with a police "stinger" – a roll-out spiked mat, which rips the tyres as the car is driven over them. The hijackers then spray paint over the windscreen of the car as it slows down, and they pull the driver out.

DRIVER (V/O)
Somebody is setting up Big Benny for a big job
and I don't mean setting him up to get pinched.
Big Benny's not that stupid, but he's not the
brains behind this one. He's organising the
muscle, putting a crew together and training
them. They're gearing up for a hijacking – a van
or a small truck. The target is one single container; a high value, one-off hit. The word is its
a new vaccine, worth four million a pop.

[In the 'silent' film, we see the hijackers using a trolley to remove a mocked-up container of Coletoxore. They even use a large (stolen) 'Speak Your Weight' machine to estimate the correct weight, and stopwatches to time themselves.]

DRIVER (V/O)
They know the size of the containers, that
they're insulated, and how much they weigh.
They know they can transfer the load into the
back of an estate car if they have to, and be
away on their toes sharpish. Everything we
know about the job they're planning points us
to something going through Cargo Village – and
fairly soon. We did some checking.

CUT BACK *to Naseem's office.*

DRIVER
Guess which vaccine-like product is packed in
insulated cubes, weighs three hundred pounds,
is worth four million quid and is exported
abroad from Southall through Cargo Village at
Heathrow?
It wasn't difficult to find it was Coletoxore.

NASEEM
So, we're going to be burgled but you don't
know when?

MOON
No, Mr Naseem – is that your surname, by the
way, or your Christian name?

NASEEM
It's my first name. *(Beat)* Constable. You were
saying?

DRIVER
(Cutting in)
Everything we know points to a hijacking.
Somewhere on the road between here and
Heathrow.

McEVOY
You sure? The security here's good but I
wouldn't say it was impregnable.

NASEEM
It had bloody better be after what you've made
me spend this year.

DRIVER
They're going after a moving target. We're sure
of that. We'll need to know your routes and procedures.

NASEEM
Do we have any choice in the matter?

MOON
(Smug)
Not really. *(Beat)* Sir.

NASEEM
Then McEvoy here will fill you in. Frank?

McEVOY
What do you need to know?

DRIVER
How exactly you ship something like
Coletoxore – how, when and who would know
about it.
*McEVOY moves to a large plan of 'Cargo
World' on the office wall.*

McEVOY

This is Cargo Village, handling all the freight in
and out of Heathrow, okay? It's basically in
three sections. First and biggest is British
Airways. They're a law unto themselves and we
don't use them. Smaller operators either use the
forwarding agents based here in this building,
called Southampton House, or they go direct to
the airlines, and most of them have their freight
offices here. *(CLOSE-UP on plan as he points)*
This is The Horseshoe, so-called because it's a
one-way system curving up and round a lorry
park. All the big names are here. Delta, Virgin,
Nippon Cargo, Air New Zealand, Air Jamaica,
Royal Jordanian...

CUT TO *car interior. MOON driving, McEVOY pointing
out the actual site to DRIVER.*

Planes fly over constantly.

McEVOY

Air France, Air Canada, Emirates... They're all
here, but these guys also carry passengers for a
living, so they have a limited amount of cargo
space, plus the fact that they might not fly on the
day you want them to, especially if you're
talking long haul to the Far East.

DRIVER
What happens then?

McEVOY
You go via The Hub.

MOON
And what's that when it's at home?

McEVOY

It's the mid-Eastern version of Cargo Village, in
Dubai. There are three planes a day from
London to Dubai, which gives you three times
the chance of getting something at least halfway
to India or Pakistan than trying to get on board a
long-haul, direct flight. You consign your delivery to the Hub in Dubai and from there it gets
freighted on the next local plane. The Hub is sort
of like a big left-luggage office for the East.

DRIVER

So this is where you'd bring a shipment of
Coletoxore?

McEVOY

Depends where we were shipping it.

DRIVER

You said you did mostly India.

McEVOY

Well, yeah, then we would. We'd fly it Emirates
Airline to The Hub and arrange transit onwards
from there.

DRIVER

And that's the only way?

McEVOY

No, you could go direct. Air India, say.

DRIVER

From here?

McEVOY

No. You'd go to their freight place, which is the other end of Cargo Village. It's called Peace and Harmony.

MOON

It's what?

McEVOY

Follow the Horseshoe round and turn back to the main road. You have to go out and come in again.
(To DRIVER)
You can't see anyone pulling a hijack here, can you? There's no room to manoeuvre; no place to go for a quick getaway.

DRIVER

Maybe they're not expecting to have to make a run for it.

McEVOY
(Shrugs. To MOON)
At the end here, left by the old police station and back out to the ring road.

CUT TO *exterior of car: DRIVER studying disused Police Station intently.*

FROM ABOVE, *car drives out of Cargo Village and doubles back on ring road, passing The Horseshoe.*

It turns right into a cul-de-sac of cargo offices with the names of airlines displayed: EL AL, AER LINGUS, AIR INDIA, PAKISTAN INTERNATIONAL AIRLINES, ALITALIA. It is deserted. No people around, just security cameras and electronic doors.

CUT TO *interior of car, slowing to a halt.*

MOON
I get it. This is called Peace and Harmony
because it's really a funeral home.

McEVOY
(Looking at his watch)
They'll mostly be at lunch – or prayer.

DRIVER
So what happens here?

McEVOY
This is where you come to see universal peace
and harmony. Look at it.

(Tracking shot of signs above door)
Alitalia, Aer Lingus, Air India, Pakistan
International, Middle Eastern, El Al. Catholics,
Hindus, Moslems and Jews, all living and
working together without fighting each other.
Doesn't happen anywhere else in the world.

DRIVER
So, it's a right little United Nations in the middle
of a cruel world. This is where you'd bring a
shipment if you wanted to send it direct, right?

McEVOY
If you didn't want to go via The Hub in Dubai,
sure. But the number of flights is less and space
is very limited. To get a consignment of
Coletoxore on a plane direct to Bombay, say,
you'd have to be related to the cargo manager,
the export agent, a couple of security guards
and maybe the pilot of the flight itself.

MOON
(Under his breath)
Bloody Indians…

McEVOY
You got a problem with Indians?

MOON
Not as much as you seem to have…

DRIVER
(Assertive)
Come on, let's take a look. Frank, walk me
through what would normally happen.

All three climb out of the car.

McEVOY
Normally, one of the contract drivers would
take the stuff, in our van, round to The
Horseshoe and book it on to a flight to Dubai.
As long as your paperwork's in order, it gets sent
on from The Hub to wherever it's going in a
couple of days.

DRIVER
Humour me, Frank. What if you were sending
direct?

McEVOY
Then I'd drive it round here myself and press
that bell there for the intake clerk.

MOON
Mr Naseem lets you drive the company van,
does he?

McEVOY ignores him and presses the bell by the Air India door. An elderly, distinguished Indian, KULI, appears and greets him. They exchange greetings in Hindi. Then:

McEVOY
This is Mr Kuli. Kuli, these are policemen.

KULI
(Quietly)
Suerkabacha!

McEVOY
(Pointing)
Sergeant Moon. And this is Inspector Driver. We used to work together.

KULI
How is your Superintendent these days, Inspector? I haven't seen him at the Rotary Club for several months now.

DRIVER
Er… pressure of work… .He's a busy man.

KULI
As are we all . What can I do for you?

McEVOY
The officers want to know what would happen if we were to ship something direct to Bombay.

KULI
(Shrugs)
How big?

McEVOY
One container, insulated. Just over a metre cubed.

KULI
How heavy?

McEVOY
Three hundred pounds plus.

KULI
Please, in kilos.

McEVOY
One hundred and forty or fifty.

KULI
(Whistles softly)
I am assuming this is legal?
(They all nod)
Export licence in order?
(They nod again)
It's nothing explosive or corrosive?
*(They shake their heads. KULI consults a clip-
board manifest)*
Then I could suggest the night flight on the
second Sunday in December.

DRIVER
What? Nothing sooner?

KULI
Not for something that size and weight, unless
someone on the airline made special arrangements.

MOON
You mean like slipping somebody...

DRIVER
Sergeant!

KULI
(Cool, ignoring them)
Why don't you ship to The Hub? You could
have it in Dubai tonight if you wanted to. If
everything was in order.
(He glares at MOON)
And legal. It could be onward shipped to
Bombay within two, three days.

McEVOY
I told you.

DRIVER
Thank you, Mr Kuli, but is there no way you
could get something on a direct, long-haul
flight?

KULI
Well, of course, if it was something smaller, one
could try, but I get the feeling that we are talking
smuggling here, Inspector, and that worries me.

DRIVER
Of course it would, Mr Kuli, no one is suggesting… .

KULI
No, you misunderstand, Inspector. Smuggling is
coming *in* to this country, not going *out*. Are
you sure *you* have the right end of the stick?

FADE

*CUT TO Driver and Moon getting in car. McEVOY shaking
hands with KULI in background. Planes going over, landing.*

MOON
What did he call me – a sewerkeybotch?

DRIVER answers but a plane landing drowns out the sound.

MOON
A what?

DRIVER
You don't want to know.

FADE

CUT TO Tyler Pharmaceuticals. TYLER meeting with Dr ROMA Patel in the laboratory. White-coated staff are packing vials, preparing a container.

TYLER
Dr Patel, we must talk.

ROMA
Certainly, Mr Tyler. Is there a problem?

TYLER
Yes, I think there is. That policeman who called
has been on the phone. He wants us to go ahead
with our shipment to Bombay next week.

ROMA
So?

TYLER
He wants us to go ahead, *knowing there's a
robbery being planned.*

ROMA
But if the police know, they can stop it.

TYLER

Pah! You trust them not to cock it up? You
know what happens if anything goes wrong and
that shipment doesn't get to Bombay when it's
supposed to?

ROMA

You don't get paid.

TYLER

None of us gets paid! Do you know how long
it's taken me to get the Indians to agree to the
right price?

ROMA

Right… … right for us?

TYLER

Of course right for us. We're ahead of the
Americans at the moment, but not for long.
Bombay always wants it cheaper – wants to
haggle. We've got to get a foothold in there.

ROMA

Get them hooked on it, you mean?

TYLER

You know it's not that sort of drug. It's poten-
tially a life-saver.

ROMA

But you sell it like a street dealer.

TYLER

You know what I mean. You know what those
people are like. We can't give them any excuse
to renege on the deal.

ROMA
So don't play ball with the police.

TYLER
I haven't got an option. The police made it quite
clear to me that they had a duty to inform our
insurance company if we don't co-operate. They
insist we go ahead with the Bombay shipment.
They're using us as bait.

ROMA
But if they *know* about the robbery, they'll stop
it, surely? And our consignment can go as
scheduled.

TYLER
If they stop the robbery. And what if they need
the Coletoxore for evidence or something? They
could tie us in knots and Bombay could claim
we didn't deliver on time.
Where are we on the paperwork, anyway?

ROMA
All done. We're ready to roll.

TYLER
(*Indicating the packing going on*)
So what are you doing here?

ROMA
This is Batch B, the reject consignment.

TYLER
What are you doing with it?

ROMA

What you told me to do. Pack it up, seal it and
get Angel's Wings to deliver it to the chemicals
disposal point. It seems such a waste…

TYLER

I know, I know. You want to try your refining
technique, don't you?

ROMA

It works in the lab, Mark. There's no reason it
can't work on a commercial scale. These
samples are rejected because they're only 99.9
per cent pure. I *know* I can wash out that 0.1
per cent and it's not a difficult process.

TYLER

For God's sake, don't ever say that out loud.
Our price is based on 100 per cent purity and
any statistical sampling must back that up. If
our competitors knew how easy it was to refine
reject Coletoxore, they'd set up their own plants
to produce it crude, and undercut us.

ROMA

I still think… .

TYLER

That we should provide free health care for
everybody on the planet, yes, I know you do.
But we have all our research costs to recoup.
This *is* a business.

ROMA
But it can't be good business to have to dump
this reject batch. With my secondary process,
you can ensure 100 per cent purity and still get a
good price.

TYLER
But we'll lose our quality premium, have to
explain to the government inspectors, and our
competitors will get wind of it.

ROMA
It seems such a shame when people are ill and
could benefit. Just to throw it away like this.
Such a waste, not to do *something* with it.

TYLER
(Slowly)
Yes… … .

CUT TO *staff labelling the consignment "REJECT" and
"FOR AUTHORISED DISPOSAL ONLY". FADE.*

CUT TO *interior, police briefing room: the same SENIOR
POLICE OFFICER (S.P.O.), and others, are being briefed by
MOON. They have a large-scale map of Southall/Heston and
Heathrow pinned up, with a road route highlighted in red.*

S.P.O.
Where *is* Inspector Driver?

MOON
He's been called away, sir, but he won't be long.
A possible development in the investigation, I
believe. He asked if it would be OK for me to
make a start?

S.P.O.
Yes, yes, get on with it.

MOON
Thank you, sir.
(He uses the map and a pointer)
Tyler Pharmaceuticals will deposit a consign-
ment of their drug, Coletoxore, with the Angel's
Wings transit company here in Southall, over
the weekend. Their job is to get it to here –
Cargo Village, four miles away – on Monday
morning.

S.P.O.
And what's to stop it being hijacked on the way
to Angel's Wings?

MOON
Because we'll be delivering it, sir. Only Mark
Tyler knows when it will leave his company and
only we know the route it will take. Angel's
Wings know a delivery is coming, but not when.

S.P.O.
And the airlines?

MOON
They know nothing at all. Given that our most
likely security leak is somewhere in Cargo
Village itself, we'll keep it that way. The consignment will leave the industrial estate as it
would normally, and we will have Observation
Posts set up along the route, especially *here*.

S.P.O.
(Staring at map)
Isn't that a mosque?

MOON

I believe it is, sir. We have permission from the…
er… the head man there, to use the entrance
hallway. It's an important site for us because we
know that Big Benny's gang use a pair of lock-
up garages dead opposite, just down this street,
off the High Road.

(Tracing route)

We have our rapid-response units at strategic
intervals but we are more and more convinced
that the robbery will be in Cargo Village itself,
here, on what is called The Horseshoe. We'll
have our main unit here, undercover in the lorry
park, with an Obs Point here.

S.P.O.

That's the old police station, isn't it?

MOON

Yes, sir. It will be operational HQ and we can
slip people in throughout the night before.

S.P.O.

Hoping nobody will notice… …

MOON

Cargo Village is a 24-hour-a-day place, sir,
people coming and going all the time. We
shouldn't… . Ah, here's Mr Driver.

DRIVER hurries into the room, nodding apologies.

DRIVER

Sorry, sir. There's been a development and I'm
afraid it's important.

S.P.O.
I hope it is, Inspector.

DRIVER
I took a call from my informant, sir, as I was on my way here. I had to go and see him just to confirm things.

S.P.O.
What things? Please don't keep us in suspense.

DRIVER
Whoever is planning this robbery delivers his messages by mobile phone.

S.P.O.
Are we any nearer to tracing him?

DRIVER
'Fraid not, sir. Every time he sends instructions, he sends a new phone with a new number. One trip, one call. If we knew *his* number, the cell-phone companies could pinpoint him for us within a minute or so. But at the moment, we can't.

S.P.O.
So what's your development?

DRIVER
Another phone arrived today.... .

CUT AWAY to BLIND HUGH in his shop, discovering another plastic-wrapped cellphone, examining a label tied to it. DRIVER's voice narrates in V/O.

DRIVER (V/O)
… but this one wasn't addressed to Big Benny
and his gang. This one had to be delivered to
someone else.

CUT AWAY to Blind Hugh grabbing his coat, leaving his
mother in charge of the shop, going out on to the street and
catching a bus.

DRIVER (V/O)
Someone we know very well, I'm afraid. And no
friend of Big Benny's.

BLIND HUGH jumps off a bus and looks for something,
then crosses the road into a seedy pub called The Waterman.
Fairly obviously, this is a villains' pub, with a mixed-race
crowd around a pool table. BLIND HUGH approaches one
of the players nervously and hands over the phone.

DRIVER (V/O)
If anything, Mortlake Eddy has a record longer
than Big Benny's, and his crew have a reputation for being unsubtle and a touch crude in
comparison.

Inside the pub, MORTLAKE EDDY (silently) gives orders
for BLIND HUGH to sit and be threatened with the thick
end of a pool cue.

DRIVER (V/O)
Mortlake Eddy's immediately suspicious, of
course, wanting to know who the phone comes
from. My source doesn't know. He's only following orders, but Eddy doesn't believe that and
rather fancies shooting the messenger if he
doesn't get an answer. Then the delivery boy is
saved by the bell.

In the pub, EDDY is surprised by the phone ringing, but answers it and eventually listens intently, his expression changing from suspicion to pleasure. Then he hangs up and says something to his gang.

DRIVER (V/O)
We don't know exactly what he heard, but suddenly he's is a really good mood. And he says to his gang...

CUT TO Waterside pub interior in sound:

MORTLAKE EDDY
Anybody know where we can pick up a JCB digger for Monday?

CUT TO police briefing room.

S.P.O.
(Horrified)
He said *what*?

CUT TO Waterside and repeat:

DRIVER
Anybody know where we can pick up a JCB digger for Monday?

CUT TO police briefing room.

S.P.O.
Oh my sainted bollocks! They're going to do it again, aren't they?

FADE.

TITLE CARD:

Cargo Village People

CUT TO exterior of Emirates Airlines office, on The Horseshoe, in Cargo Village. McEVOY and MOON are talking to HASAN SHARIF, the intake clerk at Emirates, watching a CCTV video playing.

HASAN
(Pointing at screen)
There. That's them. Fifth time in three days.

McEVOY
That's Big Benny in the back, for sure. Rafik
Jarman driving. What about the other one,
Hasan?

HASAN
That's on yesterday's tape.

(He changes video tapes)

MOON
Did they attempt to stop or get out, Mr Sherrif?

McEVOY
(Correcting him)
Sharif. Hasan Sharif.

HASAN
No, just drove around The Horseshoe a couple
of times. If we notice a car, we always keep an
eye on it. Most deliveries come here in trucks or
vans, so cars are a bit unusual. This was the
other one. It did two circuits on the trot and
then came back an hour later.

(They view screen)

> **McEVOY**
> That one there? *(To MOON)*
> Recognise anyone?

> **MOON**
> Guy driving is called Mortlake Eddy. Know
> him?

> **McEVOY**
> Name rings a bell. Small-time street hood, oper-
> ates over Isleworth way.

> **HASAN**
> What's he want with that digger?

> **MOON**
> What? What digger?

> **HASAN**
> *(Pointing at screen)*
> That one, there, following the car.

> **MOON**
> *(Unconvincing)*
> What makes you say they're connected?

> **HASAN**
> That digger's followed them round The
> Horseshoe. Twice.

McEVOY snaps a killer look at MOON. FADE.

*CUT TO exterior on The Horsehoe. McEVOY pushing
MOON (holding video tapes) up against his car.*

> **MOON**
> Don't you put your hands on me, old man.

McEVOY
Then you tell me what's going on. What's this
Mortlake Eddy geezer got to do with anything?

MOON
It's a new development. I'm not authorised to
brief you on it yet.

McEVOY
Then why don't you get authorised? *(Beat)* You
knew they had a digger, didn't you? When
Hasan called in about the cars, you knew it
would be this Mortlake Eddy guy. With a digger.
Just what the fuck's going on?

MOON
Look, I'd make allowances if I could, just
because you used to be in the Job. But I can't.
You're too close to them.

McEVOY
(Angry)
Close to who?

MOON
Them. The bloody Asians that run this place.

McEVOY
You're sick, you are. Sick and sad.

MOON
Least I haven't gone bleeding native.

McEVOY
What?

MOON
You heard. You know what they used to call
you down Dogberry Road? 'Kipling', that's
what, 'cos you didn't know there wasn't an
Empire left.

McEVOY
I'm Irish, for Christ's sake.

MOON
Yeah, well, more bloody immigrants.

McEVOY
(Quiet)
Correction. You're not sick, you just make me
sick. I'll get Hasan to call me a mini-cab.

MOON
Suits me. Didn't want the smell of curry stinking
out the car anyway.

*MOON unlocks his car. McEVOY starts to walk off, looking
up at the planes constantly arriving overhead. Suddenly he
stops, thinks and turns back on MOON.*

McEVOY
Dogberry Road. The JCB. You're setting up
another Dogberry Road stake-out, aren't you?

MOON
(Getting in his car)
If we are, we won't be using talcum powder this
time.

*MOON drives off, leaving McEVOY mouthing the word
'bastard'.*

CUT TO *Tyler Pharmaceuticals. TYLER and ROMA PATEL are handing over the Coletoxore to NASEEM, who has a van backed up to the laboratory (as the police did at the drugs-bust house). Two police cars wait to escort him back to London.*

TYLER
You know how much this consignment means
to me, Mr Naseem?

NASEEM
Of course. We will take every precaution.

TYLER
A robbery wouldn't do *your* business much
good either, would it?

NASEEM
They're not generally good for customer confidence.

TYLER
(Eying him suspiciously)
No, they're not. That's why *we* are not going to
let it happen.

A lab technician drives a small fork-lift truck towards the van. It carries a box crate and gently drops it in the back. Then turns back to pick up a second, identical crate and begins to load.

TYLER
You did what I asked?

NASEEM

To the letter. I have two sets of documents. As
far as the police are concerned, the Coletoxore
goes out at eight o'clock tomorrow night to the
Dubai Hub on the Emirates flight. Hasan Sharif
is expecting the paperwork for onward shipment.

TYLER

And our backup?

NASEEM

If anything happens on the way to Cargo
Village, I take the second load personally, direct
to Air India. The intake clerk there, Kuli Khan,
has promised me he can get it on the ten o'clock
long haul, direct to Bombay.

TYLER

And if nothing happens?

NASEEM

I wait until the last moment and I take the real
Coletoxore to The Horseshoe and tell Hasan
Sharif there's been a mix up and we swap loads.

TYLER

Will he have a problem with that?

NASEEM

Not if the paperwork is in order. Do you have
two export licences?

ROMA
(Handing them over)
It's all here. The real stuff is coded PQ on the
manifest, for Passed Quality. The second batch
has an R code, meaning Reject. You'll have to
make sure that your contact at Emirates has the
PQ paperwork. The R-code manifest isn't
cleared for onward shipment from Dubai, only
the PQ one.

NASEEM
I think I can manage that, Miss... ?

ROMA
Doctor.

TYLER
I'm sure Naseem can handle things. The only
thing to remember is that if the police want to
play silly buggers with my company's future,
they do it with the reject product.

NASEEM
I'd better get off. I don't want to keep my escort
waiting.

NASEEM begins to supervise the loading.

TYLER
He's a good man, that Naseem. Knows which
side his bread's buttered.

ROMA
I hope he doesn't have many women working
for him. Shouldn't think he has. Probably
prefers them at home – buttering his bread for
him.

TYLER
You don't have to like somebody to do business
with them, Roma.

ROMA
No, you don't. *(Beat)* But it can help.

FADE.

*CUT TO Southall High Street and BLIND HUGH's shop,
his mother behind the counter. HUGH enters from the back,
carrying a box of tomatoes. He is grabbed quickly and vio-
lently by McEVOY and pressed into a display of chillis and
peppers.*

McEVOY
Right, you little shagger, what's going on?

BLIND HUGH

(Panic)
Mr McEvoy... haven't seen you for ages... what
do you mean, what's going on? I don't know
what's going on.
*(C/U on HUGH's face as he focuses on the
chillis an inch from his nose.)*
Oh... no...

McEVOY
Come on, Hughie, don't go *baywakoof* on me.

BLIND HUGH
It's honest innit, Mr McEvoy. I don't know what
you're talking about.

McEVOY
You been doin' a bit of business lately? Police
business?

BLIND HUGH
Hey, I didn't know the force was still with you,
Mr McEvoy.

McEVOY
(Reaches for a chilli)
Don't get cheeky with me, you little…

McEVOY feels something among the chillis and pulls out a cellphone, wrapped in plastic. Then another.

McEVOY
Well, what have we here? A telephone among
the chillis. You could call that a hotline, couldn't
you? It says here it belongs to Big Benny. Now
there's a name I remember. And look, another
one! They must be breeding. This one's for
somebody called Mortlake Eddy. What
happens, Hughie? Do you have to ring them?

BLIND HUGH
No, Mr McEvoy, I have to deliver them, like
straight away.

McEVOY
(Relaxing)
Well, you'll be wanting a lift, won't you?

CUT TO police briefing room. S.P.O. being briefed by DRIVER, in front of Cargo Village map.

DRIVER
… We'll have one team here in the lorry park, on
The Horseshoe, which is positioned so that it's
no more than twenty yards from any part of the
actual road. And we'll have another team
camped overnight in the old station house, here,
at the base of The Horseshoe.

S.P.O.
You're *sure* that's where they'll hit?

DRIVER
It's the logical place if you want maximum con-
fusion to cover your getaway. Plus, Moon has
seen closed-circuit video of them cruising the
scene.

S.P.O.
But in theory, they could hit anywhere between
Angel's Wings in Southall and Cargo Village
itself?

DRIVER
True, and we'll be following the load with a
mobile unit, but there's too many things could
go wrong on the way. Traffic snarl-ups, road-
works, pedestrians. Too many witnesses
around. No, I reckon it will be The Horseshoe.

S.P.O.
You're not thinking that just because it fits your
theory of a double take?

DRIVER
It does all fit, sir. Big Benny's gang is rehearsing a
truck hijack. The stinger, the paint, it all points
to that.

S.P.O.
And where did they get a stinger?

DRIVER

We don't know. You can probably buy one on
the Internet these days. But everything Benny's
doing is geared to stopping a moving truck.
Whereas Mortlake Eddy's crew are going into
the smash-and-grab business.

S.P.O.

You assume.

DRIVER

It's like a re-run of the Dogberry Road hit. Big
Benny's being set up to get caught on The
Horseshoe. We collar his lot and while we cart
them off to be charged, Mortlake Eddy's lot
drives in and grabs the Coletoxore from the old
nick. It's in even poorer shape than Dogberry
Road was.

S.P.O.

Don't keep mentioning Dogberry Road. We
can't *afford* another Dogberry Road.

DRIVER

We're ready this time.

S.P.O.

We were ready and waiting last time. Are we
absolutely *sure* of the way this is going to go
down?

DRIVER

(Carefully)

Sergeant Moon has been evaluating all the intelligence we've had coming in. There are so many
pointers... .

S.P.O.
But our main source is this Blind Hugh chap?

DRIVER
Well, yes... but there's other gossip; word on the
street...

S.P.O.
That is a code name, isn't it?

DRIVER
He was one of the former Inspector McEvoy's
trusted sources, sir.

S.P.O.
And that in itself makes me nervous. This isn't
an elaborate scam to get back at McEvoy, is it?
He did make enemies.

DRIVER
The way I see it – and DS Moon agrees – this is
somebody setting up Big Benny.

S.P.O.
(Thoughtful)
And we've no idea who that might be?

DRIVER
No sir, we've drawn a complete blank.

S.P.O.
Well, somebody is pulling the strings. I mean,
who set this up in the first place? Why this
chemical – Coletoxore? What are they going to
do with it if they manage to steal it?

DRIVER
There's one possibility, sir. From what we can
gather, Tyler Pharmaceuticals isn't exactly cash
rich. It might be that Mr Tyler wants his
wonder-drug stolen and has the insurance claim
form already filled out.

S.P.O.
(Shaking head)
Unlikely. It's not insured.

DRIVER
What? Four million quid's worth…

S.P.O.
Unless he divulges the production process to
assess replacement costs, nobody will insure it.
That's why he's been on the phone to me. He
also pointed out that if anything goes wrong,
the headlines will say 'Police Lose Life-Saving
Mercy Mission Drugs'. I don't want that headline, Jim. That's why I'm giving you a deadline.
Assuming we pull the hijackers, we get everything sorted at the old police house.

DRIVER
That's the plan, sir.

S.P.O.
We ship the villains back to Southall for charg-
ing but the Coletoxore stays there, until
Mortlake Eddy makes his move. Right?

DRIVER
Yes, sir.

S.P.O.
If he doesn't make his move by seven o'clock
tomorrow night, then the Coletoxore gets
taken to the airline for transit to this Haj
place...

DRIVER
The Hub, sir, in Dubai.

S.P.O.
Wherever. If Mortlake Eddy hasn't made his
move by then, we scrub the operation. The
bottom line is that those drugs are on a plane
out of here tomorrow night.

DRIVER
Very well, sir. I think we can manage that.

FADE

*CUT TO Angel's Wings' warehouse, early morning.
Seemingly deserted but actually teeming with police, guarding the Coletoxore. McEVOY arrives, dressed in a boiler suit,
as a company driver. NASEEM is talking to the DETEC-
TIVE in charge.*

NASEEM
Frank? What are you...

McEVOY
(Like a waiter)
I'm your driver for the morning, sir. It wouldn't
be fair to use one of the contract boys.

NASEEM
Are you sure this is wise, Frank?

McEVOY
You up for the insurance if one of our regulars
gets bonked on the head?

NASEEM
That's a point. Well, if you feel up to it, go for it.
This is Detective...

DETECTIVE
DC Sugar. I'll be running things from here.
You're Inspector McEvoy, aren't you?

McEVOY
I used to be. You one of Jim Driver's boys?

DETECTIVE
That's right. I'm to stay here and keep a channel
open throughout the day. We've got Observation
Points along the route and we've got a tracker
device on your van. Don't stop anywhere unless
somebody makes you.

McEVOY
Do I get to wear a wire?

DETECTIVE
No, but we've got you an earpiece and neck
mike for a mobile phone, so you can use it
hands-free. Keep it on and just press Send when
you want to talk.

McEVOY
I've seen one before. Shall we get loaded?

NASEEM
(Quick)
I'll do that. *(Beat)* I can still drive a fork-lift. I
used to do it during the summer holidays.

McEVOY
(Suspicious)
I'll get the paperwork, then.

NASEEM *drives the Coletoxore container to load into the
back of his van while McEVOY goes into the office to collect
a sheaf of papers. He notices that NASEEM's desk drawer is
open, looks in and finds the second set of manifests. He
weighs them in each hand…* .

CUT TO *warehouse, where NASEEM is manoeuvring the
fork-lift. Behind a pile of boxes, hidden from the others, is the
second container of Coletoxore.*

CUT TO *police house at The Horseshoe. DRIVER on the
phone. Lots of hastily installed equipment, police men and
women. The S.P.O. supervising.*

DRIVER
We have a Go, sir. Van's moving off and the
tracking device is working.

S.P.O.
Warn all concerned we're in an active Green
condition.

CUT TO *entrance to Southall Mosque. MOON and three
policemen, looking totally out of place, on a mobile phone.
He gives the others the thumbs up.*

CUT TO *a police 'SWAT' team in body armour, crouched in
the back of something that could be a large truck, though it
isn't clear yet. The lead OFFICER listens to his radio and
gives his men the thumbs up.*

CUT TO Emirates Airlines. HASAN SHARIF on a phone. He nods, hangs up. Behind him we see another 'SWAT' team crouched down.

CUT TO the Air India office on 'Peace and Harmony'. KULI KHAN is also taking a phone call and nods wisely to himself. He is watching a CCTV monitor, which shows The Horseshoe: lorries parked; normal, everyday traffic.

CUT TO police command centre.

S.P.O.
Situation report on our suspects, Inspector?

DRIVER
Both gangs in place, sir. DS Moon has Big
Benny's lot under obs from the mosque. They'll
be the first to move.

S.P.O.
What about the second team?

DRIVER
They all turned up for work bright and early, sir.
We've got them pegged but no movement yet.

CUT TO large, anonymous warehouse. MORTLAKE EDDY and a gang of six or seven are sitting on parked cars surrounding a JCB digger; smoking, eating, playing cards, watching daytime TV on a small portable.

CUT TO command centre. DRIVER listening into an ear-piece.

DRIVER
Report coming in from the Mortlake Eddy
stakeout, sir. Seems to be something happening.

CUT BACK TO *warehouse entrance from the POV of a police observation team across the road. A pizza delivery boy arrives on a scooter. EDDY appears, takes a pile of pizzas, cuffs the delivery boy round the head and goes back inside.*

CUT TO *command centre.*

DRIVER
It's nothing, sir. Still no movement. Benny will
go first.

CUT TO *Big Benny's hideout. The gang are all pulling on gloves and manhandling a 'stinger' device into the back of a van. BIG BENNY is on a mobile. When the call finishes, he casually throws the phone away.*

BIG BENNY
That was the Mystery Man.
*(ASH, RAFIK and the rest stand up and put
sunglasses on, begin walking in a line to their
vehicles)*
Let's go…

RAFIK
Let's go to work?

BIG BENNY
(Genuinely bemused)
No. Let's go *now* – so we can be back in time for
lunch… (?)

CUT TO *the van driven by McEVOY, moving through the traffic, as he talks into his hands-free phone.*

McEVOY
You'd better get through to Sergeant Moon. Tell
him I'll be coming up on the mosque in about
two minutes… .

CUT TO inside Southall Mosque. MOON is holding a camera at the open door, having photographed Big Benny's gang moving out. Behind him, and the policemen, there are twenty to thirty Muslims, kneeling in prayer.

MOON
(To policeman)
Got 'em. Clear shots of Big Benny, Ash the
Cash, Rafik Jarman and at least two others…

MOON's mobile rings loudly. Behind him, all the men kneeling in prayer reach for their mobiles, unable to work out which one is ringing.

MOON
Yeah? Right. It's going down. We'll follow on…

CUT TO overhead shot of BIG BENNY's two vans being followed by McEVOY's van, being followed by MOON and unmarked police cars. The convoy enters Cargo Village and makes for The Horseshoe, turning into the one-way system by the disused police house.

CUT TO police command centre.

S.P.O.
Give the order to stand by, Inspector.

DRIVER
(Into radio)
All units. Stand by.

CUT TO police 'SWAT' team hiding in truck.

OFFICER
Standing by.

CUT TO Emirates office. HASAN SHARIF and a uniformed policemen watch the CCTV and nod to each other.

CUT TO *Air India office, where all is as normal. KULI KHAN is stamping a document for a messenger delivering a small package. He smiles, hands over the papers. The small TV on his desk is showing ZEE TV, the Asian satellite station. As soon as the messenger leaves, KULI switches channels back to CCTV and watches Big Benny's vans as they enter The Horseshoe.*

CUT TO *The Horseshoe. BIG BENNY's vans slow down until McEVOY, in the Angel's Wings van, gets into the one-way system. Benny's men jump out of their vans and throw the police 'stingers' across the road, in front of and behind McEvoy. He tries to avoid driving over them but fails. His front tyres blow. He rams the van into reverse and goes over the rear stinger. As his van skews to a halt, the gang spray his windscreen with paint and start trying to hammer the back doors open.*

CUT TO *command centre.*

DRIVER
(Shouting into microphone)
Go, go, go!

CUT TO *the lorry park in the middle of The Horseshoe, only yards from the action. There is a large lorry parked up. On the side it advertises "EAT BRITISH PORK". The doors burst open and 'SWAT' Team 1 pours out. From the Emirates office, 'SWAT' Team 2 joins in to subdue the gang. In the course of the melee, McEVOY is pulled from his van and, for a second, makes eye contact with BIG BENNY. Gradually, the gang is handcuffed.*

CUT TO *Air India office. KULI watches on his TV with interest, then pointedly looks at his watch.*

CUT TO *exterior of The Horseshoe. DRIVER directing operations by shouting and into a radio.*

DRIVER
Come on, calm down, let's be having you.
(He sees Big Benny being handcuffed)
Hello, Benny, nice of you to drop in. We'll have
a little chat later, me and you.

BIG BENNY
I want… .

DRIVER
Let me guess. You want your dodgy lawyer.

BIG BENNY
I want my lunch, actually. My lawyer's already
on the way.

*DRIVER, irritated, jerks a thumb towards the police vans,
which are arriving, and makes his way through the crowd to
where McEVOY is leaning against his van.*

DRIVER
Get them moving. I want them all over to
Southall for charging. You okay, Frank?

McEVOY
(Sly)
It's thief-taking, Jim, but not as we know it.

DRIVER
Eh? What's up? You get hit on the head or anything?

McEVOY
No, they never laid a glove on me. I just mean
it's not over, is it? This was just Phase 1.

DRIVER
Can't say I know what you mean, Frank. We're
very grateful for your part in this.

McEVOY
I've talked to Blind Hugh, Jim. I know about
Mortlake Eddy. I've seen him – yesterday –
having advanced driving lessons on a JCB
digger, in a warehouse over in Isleworth.

DRIVER
This isn't your business from now on, Frank.
You've done your bit. We've got Big Benny.
Walk away.

McEVOY
I'm supposed to be delivering this
(He points to the Coletoxore container)
to there.
*(He points to the Emirates Airline office, a few
feet away)*
I can get on with my job, can I?

DRIVER
Can't let you do that, Frank. Not yet, anyway.
It's evidence.

McEVOY
Which you are going to leave as bait for
Mortlake Eddy. You're going for the double,
aren't you Jim?

DRIVER
Well, you never managed it, Frank… .

FADE

CUT TO Angel's Wings offices. DETECTIVE SUGAR is manning the phones and radio. He takes a call then turns to NASEEM.

DETECTIVE
It's all happening down at Cargo Village.

NASEEM
The van?

DETECTIVE
The hijackers hit right on cue. It sounds like we got the lot.

NASEEM
And Mr McEvoy?

DETECTIVE
He must be okay. All reports saying nobody got hurt. Seems it went like clockwork. I guess we can relax now.

NASEEM
(Collecting some papers from his desk)
So you won't mind if I get back to work, then? I've got deliveries to make.

DETECTIVE
No, feel free.
(To the policemen there)
Okay, you lot, I'll start to pack up here. You get back down the station to help with all the new visitors we're expecting... .

In the background, we see NASEEM driving by in the warehouse on a fork-lift truck.

CUT TO *exterior police command centre as it starts to get
dark. From the side, through a set of old, iron gates, the consignment of Coletoxore sits just waiting to be stolen. Inside,
are S.P.O., DRIVER, MOON and McEVOY.*

S.P.O.
Where *are* they?

DRIVER
The Obs Post still has them in the warehouse,
sir. They haven't moved all day.

S.P.O.
Is there a back door? Something we've missed?

MOON
I checked the place myself, sir. There's only one
way in and one way out if you're driving that
digger.

S.P.O.
You sound very sure, Sergeant. I hope you are
right. Is *anything* happening?

DRIVER
Southall reports that Big Benny's lawyer is
raising the roof, demanding to see you.

S.P.O.
Me?

DRIVER
Seems so. It's that toad Tim Mawson – again.
The same as…
(He falters as he catches McEvoy's eye)

... last time. Apart from that, the only thing
we've logged is that Mr Tyler of Tyler
Pharmaceuticals keeps ringing Angel's Wings to
see if his delivery's been made. He insists on
talking to Naseem, Frank's boss.

McEVOY
Where is Naseem?

DRIVER
How should I know? DC Sugar's still out there,
wrapping this up. He says he went out with
some deliveries a couple of hours ago.

McEVOY
Where to?

DRIVER
I don't know, do I?

MOON
(Takes a call on his mobile)
It's Southall, sir. Big Benny's lawyer's really
kicking up a stink, demanding to see you.

S.P.O.
I'll have to go, I suppose. I want this done by the
book. Jim, you've done your best, but we'll have
to call it a day and stick with what we've got.
(Looks at watch)
If Tyler's consignment is to make its flight, we'll
have to release it to the airline soon, anyway.
You'd better start the stand-down procedure.
We've still got men in those trucks?
(He wrinkles his nose)

DRIVER
If you want to call it off, sir, then I suggest we
make sure that Mortlake Eddy's crew are still
where they're supposed to be. We could pay a
call.

S.P.O.
On what grounds?

DRIVER
They've almost certainly nicked that JCB digger.

S.P.O.
I suppose that's something…. .

Phone rings, MOON answers and listens.

DRIVER
Mortlake Eddy?

MOON
No, sir. It's a message from DC Sugar out at
Angel's Wings. He says he's had a call from a
Kuli Khan… ?…. of Air India. He wants to
know where Mr Naseem got to as he's missed
his flight.

*They look at each other. McEVOY grabs the operational map
showing Cargo Village.*

S.P.O.
What's this Air India connection?

McEVOY
I knew he was up to something. I bet he's
booked a direct flight as a back-up plan. I
spotted two sets of papers on his desk.

DRIVER
What the fuck are you saying?

McEVOY
He had a second consignment of Coletoxore.
This one's probably a ringer. He didn't want the
real one risked in a hijack.

DRIVER
But… .the consignment's safe. It's here… .

McEVOY
But he didn't know that; didn't know there'd be
all these coppers sitting on it. He just thought it
was too risky to use it as bait.

S.P.O.
But surely, it was explained … .

McEVOY
Naseem didn't know there was a second crew of
robbers waiting in the wings. Nobody did.

MOON
(Nervous)
Mr Driver thought it best to keep security tight,
sir.

S.P.O.
So this Naseem chap has taken it upon himself
to get the stuff through? The real stuff? What
are we guarding?

McEVOY
Look, Kuli Khan's office is here…
(Points to map)

… .just down the road. Get one of your
unmarked cars down there quick.

S.P.O.
Do it.

McEVOY
And see if Mortlake Eddy's still where he's supposed to be.

S.P.O.
(To an almost paralysed DRIVER)
Do that too. *Now!*

*CUT TO the warehouse previously seen under observation.
Two policemen break in to find MORTLAKE EDDY and his
entire gang (outnumbering them) still there, playing football,
reading the papers. The POLICEMAN from the Observation
Post challenges them.*

POLICEMAN
Everybody stay where you are!

(Nobody moves)
I mean it!

*(The gang don't move but look at each other as if agreeing not
to)*
You're under arrest!

MORTLAKE EDDY
What for?

POLICEMAN
(Frantic, pointing to the JCB)
Nicking that!

MORTLAKE EDDY
Nah, mate. We're looking after it for a friend,
innit?

CUT TO *The Horseshoe. Police stream out of hiding, into
cars, sirens going, light flashing in the dark. From above we
see the lights come out of Cargo Village and drive to Peace
and Harmony which is a ridiculously short journey. On the
road into the warehouses, the police vehicles surround (and
light up) a wrecked Angel's Wings van. There is a stinger
across the road where it ripped the tyres. The windscreen is
sprayed with paint. NASEEM lies in the road, unconscious,
his hands handcuffed behind his back. the back doors of the
van are open.*

*The S.P.O., DRIVER and MOON arrive and push through
the gathering throng as cars and ambulances arrive.*

S.P.O.
(Looking at the empty back of the van)
Oh, my sweet Lord...

DRIVER
(Under his breath)
Oh, fuck... .

MOON (V/O THINKS)
(Looking sideways at Driver)
This was your idea... .

CUT TO *The Horseshoe. Lots of sirens in the distance, but
few police about, mostly dashing into cars, talking into
radios. Rather sedately, HASAN SHARIF drives towards the
disused police station on a fork-lift truck. He heads directly
for the consignment of Coletoxore.*

CUT TO Southall police station, where the initial briefings took place. The S.P.O., DRIVER and MOON, with McEVOY in tow. Already there is MARK TYLER, pacing up and down, chain-smoking.

S.P.O.
Mr Tyler? I was told you were here but this will have to be brief. It's going to be a busy night.

TYLER
Where's my shipment, Superintendent? I can't get any sense out of anyone.

S.P.O.
The situation is still a bit confused, sir, but it appears that the consignment you entrusted to us has been dispatched, safe and sound, on schedule.

TYLER
What?

S.P.O.
We had it confirmed on our way here. Your shipment caught the scheduled flight to Dubai.

DRIVER and MOON exchange relieved looks.

TYLER
To *Dubai?*

S.P.O.
I believe that was the destination we were informed of.

TYLER
But the other shipment… to Bombay direct…

DRIVER
Of which we were not made aware, sir.

S.P.O.
I'm afraid that has been stolen. We have no idea
where it is.

CUT TO *night shot of an Air India jet in flight.*

CUT TO *inside cargo hold and container of Coletoxore.*

PAN BACK *to see two containers side by side.*

CUT BACK *to police station set-up.*

TYLER
(Defeated)
At least it only went as far as Dubai.

DRIVER
I'm sorry, sir?

TYLER
The consignment you had. It was only mani-
fested as far as The Hub in Dubai. If it had got
through to Bombay there would be hell to pay.

DRIVER
What do you mean, sir?

TYLER
That consignment was reject serum. It was
labelled R on the manifest. My customers
would not have been pleased and wouldn't
have paid up.

McEVOY
Er… there might be a problem.

S.P.O./DRIVER/TYLER
(Together)
What?

McEVOY
I switched the paperwork.

DRIVER
So the real stuff went to Dubai?

McEVOY
No, I didn't switch the containers. I wasn't told
there was a second one. I just found two sets of
manifests. I told you I had.

MOON
(Quickly to S.P.O.)
Yes, he did, sir.

DRIVER
So?

McEVOY
So I took the paperwork that was for Bombay. It
was coded PQ. It'll be in The Hub in Dubai for a
day or so before it goes on to Bombay. I could
get the shipment stopped and sent back for you.

TYLER
If I pick up the bill?

McEVOY
It won't be cheap.

TYLER
Can you have it destroyed out there?

McEVOY
If you sign me a release, sure.

S.P.O.
If you gentlemen wouldn't mind, we have some
police business to conduct. Could you sort out
your personal business somewhere else?

McEVOY and TYLER shrug and leave.

S.P.O.
I've got to see Big Benny and his loathsome
solicitor now. *Nobody* lets it slip that what Big
Benny is going to be charged with is theft of a
reject consignment, okay? I'm not having a
repeat of Dogberry Road.

DRIVER
Will he do a deal?

S.P.O.
What for?

DRIVER
The man behind it. Mr Mobile Phone. He must
have set up a third team we knew nothing
about.

S.P.O.
Did we get anywhere with the phones angle?

MOON
No joy, sir. You can buy them anywhere these
days.

*CUT TO exterior of Angel's Wings warehouse, night.
BLIND HUGH and another Asian YOUTH are disabling a
CCTV camera.*

YOUTH
You sure about this, Hughie?

BLIND HUGH
Place is deserted. Cops here all day but they've
gone, putting their feet up. It'll be open house.
(He starts to climb over the wall)

*CUT TO police briefing room. BIG BENNY, handcuffed to a
uniformed officer, MAWSON his solicitor, S.P.O., DRIVER
and MOON.*

MAWSON
Thank you for seeing us – eventually,
Superintendant. My client is anxious to make
police bail if you have no objection.

S.P.O.
Only a few minor ones, Mr Mawson, such as
charges of robbery with violence… .

MAWSON
Attempted robbery. And there was no violence
on my client's part, except as part of a complete
over-reaction by the police.

S.P.O.
… Illegal possession and use of police property.

MAWSON
Those 'stinger' devices? Yes, well, as a gesture of
good faith, my client is willing to admit that he
did know those things were stolen. In fact,
stolen from Dogberry Road police station some
six months ago when, I believe, an *Acting*
Inspector Driver was station commander. My
client is, of course, quite happy to say this in
open court.

S.P.O.
(Gritting teeth.)
Conspiracy to... .

MAWSON
Ah yes, conspiracy. Now we're getting to it.
What you really want, Superintendent, is not
my client here, is it? You want the man who set
this up, don't you? The man with all the mobile
phones.

S.P.O.
And your client knows who it is?

MAWSON
No, he has no idea. But he has his phone
number. In case of emergencies. I think we could
call this an emergency, don't you?

*CUT TO Angel's Wings warehouse. BLIND HUGH and
YOUTH have broken in and are filling large shoulder bags
with anything worth stealing. The YOUTH breaks open a
large box on the warehouse floor.*

YOUTH
Fuck me, Hughie, look here.

BLIND HUGH
(In awe)
Spanking! Do they work?

*He kneels down and pulls the box over. Hundreds of mobile
phones fall out and cover the floor around him.*

*CUT TO police briefing room. A new POLICEMAN sits at a
phone unit connected to a tape recorder.*

POLICEMAN
I'm linked up to the phone company now, sir.
They're ready to trace the phone once he
answers and we'll tape it as well.

S.P.O.
Good. Mr Mawson?

MAWSON
(Shuffles a paper he's been reading)
I suppose this will do. I know it has no real legal
weight but every little helps with the Crown
Prosecution Service. My client is ready.

*MOON pushes a phone across the desk to BIG BENNY. He
picks it up and begins to dial.*

BIG BENNY
He did say emergencies only. Of course, he may
have left the country…

*He finishes dialling and listens. A mobile phone trills loudly
in the room. They all look around amazed. In a panic,
DRIVER rips his phone from his belt and automatically puts
it to his ear.*

DRIVER
Get off the…. .

BIG BENNY
Hello?

DRIVER
(Horrified)
Hello?

*They realise they are talking to each other. The POLICE-
MAN by the phone/tape recorder leans forward.*

POLICEMAN
Phone company's got it, sir. He's in Southall.
Must be really near.

CUT TO *street scene. BLIND HUGH and YOUTH are walking down Southall High Road, carrying bulging shoulder bags. They near a police car stopped at traffic lights and try and look innocent.*

Suddenly, all the phones in their bags start ringing at once. They do a double take at their bags and then at the police car, then they start running down the street.

FREEZE FRAME.

FADE

OPEN ON TITLE CARD:
Double Take
Two months later

CUT TO white-walled corridor in something like a Crown Court. DRIVER is in full police uniform, hat on his lap, sitting on a bench seat as if waiting to be called somewhere. Behind him, through a window, jets can be seen above London. DRIVER is heard thinking in V/O, reviewing the case and seen in CU, his face showing his doubts.

DRIVER (V/O)
It's just not possible. Not possible for one
person to arrange everything. It would be just
too much. How could they have arranged a
long-haul flight at short notice?

CUT TO the sequence at Air India, with KULI KHAN shaking his head and saying:

KULI
… unless someone on the airline made special
arrangements.

CUT TO new scene with KULI KHAN sitting in the cockpit of a jet, laughing and joking with the pilot. Above his seat, the pilot has a photograph of his graduation day. KULI is obviously his proud father.
CUT BACK to DRIVER in CU.

DRIVER (V/O)
And sending that consignment to Dubai after all
the mix-ups with the paperwork and all hell
breaking loose… ?

*CUT TO HASAN SHARIF driving the fork-lift towards The
Horseshoe police station. We see (for the first time) that he
uses a lock pick to open the gates and that he produces false
sets of papers from inside his jacket, exchanging them for the
real ones on the consignment.*
CUT BACK to DRIVER in CU.

DRIVER
And what would they do with it, anyway?
There's no market for the good stuff and they
can't use the reject stuff.

*CUT TO previous scene at Tyler Pharmaceuticals with Dr
ROMA PATEL.*

ROMA
With my secondary process you can ensure 100
per cent purity and still get a good price...

*CUT TO Dr ROMA PATEL in a laboratory we have not seen
before, holding up a vial, running tests. An Indian scientist in
a white coat is working with her. She points to the LCD
display on a spectrometer and gives a thumbs up. The scientist – and then we see others – all begin to applaud her. PAN
BACK to see the Coletoxore consignment, clearly marked
"R" for Reject. Then we see the "real" consignment, marked
PQ, as well.*

CUT BACK to DRIVER in CU.

DRIVER (V/O)
And how would anyone know about the real
consignment? We didn't know about that so
how could the third team hijack it? No one
knew about that.

*CUT TO scene at Angel's Wings, with NASEEM holding out
his hands as if for handcuffs.*

NASEEM
We're not a big company and I'm involved in
everything that goes on, so I must be the guilty
one.

*CUT TO the ring road to Peace and Harmony on the night of
the hijack. The Angel's Wings truck stops. NASEEM gets out
and throws down a stinger in front of his own wheels, then
begins to spray his own windscreen with paint.*

CUT BACK to DRIVER in CU, shaking his head.

DRIVER (V/O)
And who set up Big Benny? And Mortlake
Eddy? And the third team? *Was there a third
team?* It had to be someone with inside knowledge.

*CUT TO scene where McEVOY and DRIVER are at Peace
and Harmony.*

McEVOY
Maybe they're not expecting to have to make a
run for it… .

CUT BACK to DRIVER in CU.

DRIVER (V/O)
… And access to a lot of mobile phones.

*CUT TO the shop where BLIND HUGH works. McEVOY
is planting the cellophane-wrapped phones into the boxes of
chillis, as BLIND HUGH enters the shop from the back.*

*CUT BACK TO DRIVER in long-shot, sitting alone in the
corridor; he shakes his head again.*

DRIVER
(Shaking his head)

Naahh... They would have *all* had to have been
in on it.

SFX door opening. DRIVER looks up at the voice-off.

V.O.
Mr Driver? The Board's ready for you now.

*DRIVER stands and puts on his cap, straightening his
uniform.*

*CUT TO street scene as in opening shot, except this time it
really is India. Close in on a restaurant at the end of a street.
Sound of high-heel shoes on cobbles. Street noises, children
laughing, getting louder. Crowd of children around a man
doing magic tricks. The high heels come into focus, then a
woman's ankles and then the bottom edge of a white (lab)
coat. PAN UP to reveal two briefcases carried by the woman.*

*The man comes into focus. It is NASEEM, demonstrating to
the street kids how he can slip in and out of a pair of handcuffs. He smiles at the approaching woman. From his POV it
is ROMA, beaming a huge smile, holding up the cases. They
embrace. With his arm around her, he leads her into the
restaurant. Sitting around the table, toasting her, applauding,
raising glasses, are: KULI KHAN, HASAN SHARIF and
FRANK McEVOY.*

*CUT TO the empty white corridor where DRIVER had been
sitting. CU on big wooden doors. From behind them comes a
deep VOICE:*

VOICE
Mr Driver, that is *the* most ridiculous thing this
Board has ever heard....

END CREDITS

The Do-Not Press
Fiercely   Independent   Publishing

Keep in touch with what's happening at the cutting edge of independent British publishing.

Simply send your name and address to:
The Do-Not Press (Dept. DT)
16 The Woodlands, London SE13 6TY (UK)

or email us: dt@thedonotpress.co.uk

There is no obligation to purchase
(although we'd certainly like you to!)
and no salesman will call.

Visit our regularly-updated web site:

http://www.thedonotpress.co.uk

Mail Order

All our titles are available from good bookshops, or (in case of difficulty) direct from The Do-Not Press at the address above. There is no charge for post and packing for orders to the UK and EU.

(NB: A post-person may call.)